Ne

1

A.M. Myers

Never Let Me Go
Bayou Devils MC
Book Six

A.M. Myers

A.M. Myers

Never Let Me Go

For Linzi,
My PA and my bestie
We both know I'd be lost without you.

Cover Design by Jay Aheer
Proofreading by Julie Deaton
Copyright © 2019 by A.M. Myers
First Edition

A.M. Myers

Never Let Me Go
Chapter One
Juliette

"Baby," someone whispers through the fog, his
voice calling out to me through the haze of the endless
darkness swallowing me up. It claws at me, frantically
trying to pull me back into its debilitating embrace but
that voice... it commands me, urges me to fight the
faux warmth of the darkness. "I miss you. Open your
eyes... please."

The plea in his voice is so potent, so sorrowful, that
I ache to reach out and let him know that I can hear him
and everything will be okay. But... who is he? He
sounds kind of familiar but I just can't quite place it,
like I'm scratching at the memory but unable to
dislodge it. It's maddening.

"Juliette," he says, his voice cracking. Oh, God,
who is this man and why does he sound so heartbroken
as he calls my name? My heart twinges at the
desperation pouring off of him. Everything begins to hit

me at once as I drift further from the darkness trying to hold me captive. There's a steady beeping sound to my right that soothes me but from somewhere else, I can hear an alarm blaring. Hushed voices hit me next, too quiet to be understood, and the smell of disinfectant fills my nose.

"Good evening, sir," a woman says, her feet shuffling on the floor as she approaches us. Her hands are cold as she presses her fingers to the inside of my wrist, checking my pulse. "I'm Colleen, the night nurse. Is there anything you need right now?"

"No," my mystery man answers as he grabs my hand and cradles it between both of his. The farther I float from the darkness, the more the real world comes into focus. Every part of my body throbs with more pain than I've ever felt in my life and my throat is bone dry as I try to move my fingers to get someone's attention.

Mystery man gasps. "Juliette?"

"Is there a problem, Mr. Hale?"

"She just moved her finger a little bit."

"Hmm," the woman hums as she pulls her fingers from my wrist. "I don't see any change to her vitals. It's possible it was just a reflex."

He grips my hand a little tighter. "No. She moved. I'm sure of it. Get the doctor in here now."

"Mr. Hale," she sighs. "I know this is hard but as I said, I'm sure it was just a muscle spasm. It's quite common in coma patients and I see no change in her condition. She would be in quite a bit of pain from the accident. If she was waking up, I would expect to see her heart rate go up at least a little bit."

"She moved," he growls, gripping my hand even tighter and I whimper as pain shoots up my arm. The pressure disappears immediately as the woman gasps.

"Miss Shaw? Can you hear me, honey?" She presses her fingers to the inside of my wrist, checking my pulse again, and I try to move but stop when my body screams in protest.

Oh, shit, that hurts.

I focus on each breath being pulled into my lungs as the pain slowly fades back down to a more manageable level before attempting to open my eyes. It feels like they're glued shut and I want to cry and scream at my body to just do what I tell it to.

"Jules, baby?" the mystery man asks, his warm, minty breath hitting my face as he leans in close and cups my cheek in his hand. "Can you open your eyes and look at me?"

The excitement and hope in his voice urges me on, despite the pain, and I slowly suck in a breath as I peel my eyes open, blinking at the harsh florescent light above me as I resist the overwhelming urge to shut them again. I try to move once more and cry out. Pain shoots through me like an arrow and tears sting my eyes.

Oh, good god, what the hell happened to me?

"There she is," mystery man whispers as I lock onto his piercing blue eyes hovering above mine and suck in a breath. Those are the kind of eyes a girl could spend her whole life getting lost in and if that wasn't enough, they have that mischievous sparkle that can get a very smart girl to do very dumb things in the name of love. But it occurs to me, that as gorgeous as his eyes are, I don't recognize them.

"Welcome back to the land of the living, sweetie," the woman says and I turn away from mystery man to glance at her. She's older with big blonde hair that reminds me of every soccer mom ever but her smile is sweet. "I'm Colleen, your night nurse. How are you feeling?"

"Ow," I squeak, my throat dry and painful. Raising my hand, I grip my throat to reiterate my point and she nods before turning to grab a small cup of water from the bedside table. She holds the straw in front of my lips and I take a sip, closing my eyes as the cool water coats my throat. I take another drink and she pulls the cup away.

"Small sips."

I nod and when she presses the straw to my lips again, I take a couple small sips of the cool refreshing liquid before pulling back and nodding to her. She smiles in encouragement and pulls the cup away, setting it back on the table next to my bed.

"Can you tell me where it hurts?"

I nod and meet her gaze. "Everywhere."

"And on a scale of one to ten, can you rate your pain?"

"Seven, I guess."

She grabs a pen from her pocket and a little

notepad. "We'll get some more pain meds on board for you, okay? Can you tell me your name?"

I nod. "Juliette Shaw."

"Very good," she answers, her smile widening. "And what is your date of birth?"

"May third, nineteen-ninety."

She nods her approval as she jots down some notes, glancing between the paper in her hand and the monitor next to my bed. "And what year is it, Juliette?"

"Two thousand fourteen."

Her pen stalls and her gaze snaps up to mine as her mouth falls open. "Do you know what city you're in?"

"Baton Rouge," I answer with a nod. She scowls before nodding and pointing to the other side of the room.

"And what about that guy there? Can you tell me who he is?"

Rolling my head to the side, I scowl and study mystery man again as he grips my hand. He's ridiculously handsome in a classic sort of way that reminds me of expensive suits, caviar, and private planes. His medium length brown hair is slicked back, making him look completely put together, like he could throw on a suit and command a boardroom, but the stubble along his angular jaw and the dark circles under his blue eyes give away how exhausted he is. I feel like I should know him but no matter how hard I study his face or search my memories, I just can't place him. His gaze searches mine, full of fear and hope, silently begging, and as much as I would love to give him whatever he's so desperate for, I'm not sure what he wants from me. I glance down at his hands encasing mine before slowly shaking my head and turning back to Colleen.

"No. I don't know who he is."

"Oh, God," he whispers, pain filling his voice as he drops his forehead to our hands. Colleen scowls.

"Okay. Let me go tell the doctors you're awake."

"Juliette," mystery man says as soon as she leaves the room and I turn back to him, my gaze falling to our entwined hands again. I don't want to be rude but it's a little too much from someone I don't even know. Although he seems to know me very well which makes me wonder again, who the hell is he? I suck in a breath and drop my head back onto the pillow.

Okay, what do I know?

Clearly, I'm in a hospital and something horrible happened to me since I feel like I've gone ten rounds with a heavyweight. What's the last thing I remember? I got off work and called Mercedes to see if she wanted to go out for drinks and we went to that country bar downtown that we love so much. After a few drinks, we decided to go home and shared a cab and then... nothing.

"Juliette? You still with me?" mystery man asks and my eyes snap open. I meet his gaze and nod.

"Yeah." My throat aches and I point to the cup of water. "Could I have some more of that?"

He nods and releases my hand to grab the cup from the bedside table as I breathe a sigh of relief. As he brings the cup back to me and holds the straw in front of my lips, I tuck my hand under my leg and lean forward to take a sip as my muscles scream in protest. Studying him, I search my memories for his face. Maybe I met him at the bar… although I feel like I would definitely remember if I did and he doesn't really seem the type to hang out in a country bar no matter how much fun the mechanical bull is.

"Thank you," I whisper as I pull away and he nods as he sets the cup back down and reclaims his seat next to my bed. He reaches for my hand, frowning when he realizes that I've hidden it. As he meets my gaze, he sighs and folds his hands on the bed.

"Who are you?" I ask before he can say anything else. Maybe it's rude of me to be so forward but I need answers and I have no qualms about starting here. He opens his mouth but before he can say anything, a tall man in a white coat walks into the room.

"Good Morning, Miss Shaw. I'm Dr. Wilson. How are you feeling?"

I open my mouth to reply before looking back at mystery man. I have no clue how to answer that question. It's like I'm hovering over my body, watching this all go down as they both stare at me, waiting for my answer. I'm quick enough to realize that I'm missing something here but I can't, for the life of me, figure out what it is. Mystery man sighs.

"I think she's a little confused."

"So I heard," he replies, frowning as he glances down at my chart. "Are you in any pain?"

13

"Only when I breathe," I quip and a smile tugs at his lips, his brown eyes sparkling as he meets my gaze.

"Well, it's good to see you still have a sense of humor. Can you rate the pain for me?"

I nod. "Probably a five until I move; then, it's a seven."

"That's to be expected," he answers, flipping through a few pages and scanning them before looking up at me again. "Colleen tells me you're having some trouble with your memory. Can you tell me the last thing you do remember?"

"Uh... I was having drinks with my best friend, Mercedes, to celebrate me moving to Miami... and then I woke up here. What happened to me?"

He sighs as he folds his hands in front of his body. "You were in a very serious car accident, Miss Shaw, and you've been in a coma for the past week."

"What?" I gasp, my eyes growing wide as I stare up at him. My mind drifts to Mercedes. We took a cab back to my place after the club. "What about my friend, Mercedes? Is she okay?"

The doctor glances at mystery man before turning back to me. "Can you tell me what year it is, Miss Shaw?"

"Two thousand fourteen," I answer, my patience quickly slipping away. Why the hell is he avoiding my questions about Mercedes? Did something happen to her? "Is Mercedes okay? She was in the car with me after the bar. We were going back to our apartment."

Dr. Wilson sighs, compassion flashing across his

face. "Miss Shaw, your friend, Mercedes, wasn't with you."

"Yes, she was," I insist, interrupting him. I don't know what kind of game he's playing but I want to know where Mercedes is. That girl is like the sister I never had and if something happened to her, I'll never forgive myself for forcing her to go out for drinks with me.

"Juliette," he says, his voice soft but commanding. "She wasn't with you when you came in because it's two thousand nineteen, not two thousand fourteen. You're in Miami and the man sitting beside you is your fiancé."

"What?" I ask, my mind reeling as my gaze flicks back and forth between the two of them. Mystery man offers me a hopeful smile. "No. That can't be right."

"It is right, baby," the man... my fiancé... says, grabbing my hand again and I stare at him with wide eyes. "I'm Gavin, your fiancé."

I slowly shake my head, my heart thundering in my chest as my head aches. No, this isn't right. "I don't have a boyfriend... or a fiancé. I only broke up with Rick a few weeks ago. He... didn't want to make the move with me so we ended things."

"That was five years ago, sweetheart," Gavin says, his voice soft and I continue shaking my head. No, it wasn't. It was just three weeks ago. None of this makes any sense. Tears sting my eyes as I look back and forth between the two of them again, trying to organize my thoughts and make sense of everything they're saying

15

but after a few moments, it's still a jumbled mess. I turn to Gavin.

"You're my…"

"Fiancé," he supplies with a nod and I suck in a breath as I mirror him. How is this possible? How can I be engaged to a man that I don't even know?

"And how long have we been together?"

He smiles as he reaches up toward my face. I jerk back on instinct and his expression falls as well as his hand. Guilt fills me.

"I'm sorry."

"Nine months," he answers, his voice low and full of pain. "We've been together for nine months."

"I…" I start before snapping my mouth shut. The sorrow in his eyes makes me ache for him but I have no clue what to say. Even as I stare at him, knowing that he's my fiancé and searching my memory for just a glimpse of his face, I don't recognize him. He's a complete stranger to me.

"So, they didn't have any Sprite…" a woman says as she walks into the room. Her voice trails off as she stops and turns to look at me, her eyes popping open before she grins. "You're awake!"

She sets a can of Mountain Dew down on the table and runs over to me, knocking the doctor out of the way and he grunts.

"Oh my God, Jules. I was beginning to think we lost you," she says as she wraps her arms around me and I wince as pain washes over me. She pulls back with an apologetic expression. "Sorry, babe. How are you

16

feeling?"

I study her as she stares back at me, trying desperately to place her but she's just as much of a mystery to me as the man to my left. She's adorable with her purple streaked dark hair and combat boots and something about her makes me feel at ease but I have no clue who she is or how I'm supposed to know her. I frown.

"I'm sorry. Who are you?"

Her gaze snaps up to Gavin before returning to me. "I'm Nico... your personal assistant and like best friend. You don't remember me?"

"She doesn't remember me either," Gavin adds and I didn't think it was possible but Nico's eyes widen even more before she turns to the doctor.

"What the hell is going on here?" she demands, getting in his face with a ferociousness that surprises me. "Why doesn't she remember us?"

"Miss Shaw," Dr. Wilson prompts as he turns to me, completely unbothered by Nico's outburst. "Are you okay with me discussing your medical condition in front of Mr. Hale and Miss Harris?"

I shrug. "Yeah, I guess."

"Okay," he answers, stepping forward and placing a comforting hand on my shoulder. "One week ago, you were in a very serious car accident with your father. You sustained a serious head injury in that accident as well as a few cracked ribs. All in all, I'd say you are incredibly lucky. Your injuries should have been much worse."

I take in everything he's saying but it's like I'm in a fog. "Okay…"

"Why can't she remember us?" Nico asks, her voice growing impatient and Dr. Wilson sighs.

"I can't be certain until we run some more tests but based on everything I've seen so far, it seems she's suffering from retrograde amnesia." He turns his attention to me. "As I mentioned before, it is two thousand nineteen and you seem to be missing the last five years of your life."

"I can't believe this," I whisper, laying my head back against the pillow as I stare up at the tiles of the ceiling. How can I just not remember the last five years of my life?

Years where I apparently moved to Miami to be closer to my father and met someone I loved enough to get engaged?

How is all of that just gone?

My mind drifts over everything he just told me when I realize that he said my father was in the accident with me. I turn to him.

"You said my dad was in the accident, too?"

He nods.

"Is he okay? Can we call him and get him here?"

I may not recognize the man sitting next to me or the woman standing at the end of the bed, staring at me expectantly but there is no way I won't recognize my own father. It has been just the two of us since my mother died when I was nine and I am a total daddy's girl. He is my whole world and the reason I'm moving

18

from Baton Rouge to Miami. No, wait… the reason I did move. Sucking in a breath, I remind myself that it's five years later than I think it is. Dr. Wilson sighs, shaking his head.

"I'm so sorry, Miss Shaw. Your father was brought into the ER after the accident and he had already lost a significant amount of blood. We worked tirelessly on him but we were unable to save him."

I blink and tears sting my eyes. "He's… dead?"

"Yes." He nods. "Again, I'm so sorry."

Sucking in a stuttered breath, I drop my gaze to my lap and twist my fingers together as a sob tears through me. Tears spill down my cheeks and I clamp my lips together to fight back another sob but it overpowers me anyway. My body aches for someone to wrap their arms around me, provide me even a molecule of comfort, but the one man I need the most right now, the one man I've always had in my corner, I'll never see again.

A.M. Myers

Never Let Me Go
Chapter Two
Juliette

Every summer when I was a little girl, this little carnival set up shop a few towns over for two weeks and my mom always made sure we went at least a couple times before they packed up and moved on. When they started showing commercials on TV for the carnival the year after she died, I would get so upset that I would turn it off and spend the rest of the day in my room. My father worked a ridiculous amount of hours but somehow he found out about my daily meltdowns and he took two weeks off work to make sure we went to that carnival every single day. One of Mom's favorite rides was The Zipper. It took us up in the air and our basket flipped over and over as the entire ride did its own loop, plunging toward the earth so quickly that it stole the breath from your lungs before flinging up into the air again. We rode that thing more times than I could count and each time we stepped off, I would stumble but Daddy never let me hit the ground. Even though he'd just been put through the same whirlwind I had, he was steady, strong, and there to catch me before my knees could hit the dirt. With him there, I felt safe and happy for the first time since my momma had died. My head spins the same way it did all those times I stepped off that ride now as I stare at the man I am supposed to marry in three short weeks. Only this time, Daddy's not here to catch me and make sure I'm safe and I've never felt more lost.

"Listen," Gavin whispers, reaching over the bed rail to reach for my hand but I pull it back and he sighs. "I have no idea what you're going through right now and I know it has to be terrifying but I'm here and I love you."

"But I don't know you."

He nods. "I know but ask me anything, okay? Maybe if you hear about us, some things will start to come back to you."

I study him for a moment before shrugging my shoulders. Okay, fine. What the hell could it hurt, right? Nothing makes me more uncomfortable than feeling like I'm living someone else's life right now so I need answers.

"How did we meet?" I ask, picking at a loose string on the blanket draped over my legs as I glance up at him. He smiles and a dimple pops out in his cheek as I drop my gaze back to the blanket. God, he is handsome, I'll give him that and by all accounts, he seems perfectly nice but he's still a stranger to me.

"We met at a bar downtown. You and Nico were having a night out after you landed some big contract and the moment I saw you, I was hooked."

"So you walked right up to me and asked me out?"

He laughs and shakes his head. "No, actually. Usually that would have been my go-to move but I got nervous and you left before I could work up the nerve."

"And we ran into each other again?"

"Yeah, at a charity thing a couple weeks later. I'd been kicking myself for not talking to you and I couldn't stop thinking about you so when I saw you again, I didn't waste any time."

His words don't bring any memories rushing back but I enjoy hearing him talk about the way he felt when we first met. And it's cute to see the slight blush in his cheeks as he details seeing me for the first time.

"Where did we go for our first date?" I ask as I slowly lean forward and grip the cup of water before bringing it to my lips. The pain medicine they've been giving me works pretty dang well but I'm still sore as hell.

"Fiji."

I choke on my water and he jumps up, taking the cup from my hand as I try not to die. "I'm sorry, say that again."

"We went to Fiji on our first date," he answers with a knowing smile. My eyes widen as I study him and I lie back on the bed with a huff.

"Well, that seems a little... extra."

"Maybe," he agrees as he sits back down. "But after

spending most of the evening with you the night of the event, I knew that I was already falling and I wanted to impress you more than I ever wanted anything in my life."

I fight back a smile. "And was I impressed?"

"No."

A laugh bubbles out of me and he joins me, shaking his head.

"In fact, you told me I looked like an asshole and you weren't that kind of girl."

I nod in agreement. "Damn right, I'm not... but surely I came around, right?"

"Only after you insisted on paying for half of the suite and informing me that there was absolutely no way we were having sex on that trip."

"Good," I answer, smiling as I nod in approval. I may not remember that girl right now but I'm damn proud of her. "Remind me how long we've been together."

"Nine months." He reaches over the bed rail and this time, I let him grab my hand. His touch is comforting and still a little strange but I stopped jerking away from his touch after the first few hours of being awake. I'm still not entirely comfortable with him just grabbing my hand anytime he pleases. The eagerness on his face and the desperate look in his eyes as he tries to force me into remembering something is frustrating, but then I remind myself how hard this has to be for him. The woman he loves doesn't know who he is and jerks away from his touch. Even for the most secure man in the world, that has to sting. I can feel his pain, filling up this hospital room like fog.

"Do we live together?"

He smiles. "Yes, baby. We do."

I nod, lifting my gaze to the window behind him. The sun shines brightly over the city of Miami and I sigh, wondering where I fit in all this. When the doctor came to check on me this morning, he mentioned possibly sending me home in the next day or two but I have no idea where my home is. I don't know where to go. I don't know which key to use. Hell, I wouldn't even know if I was in the right apartment once I got in. Not to mention, that home feels like Baton Rouge right now, not Miami, but it does bring me a little bit of comfort to know that Gavin can get me home safely at least. I just don't know how I'll feel about being there with him.

"Miss Shaw?" someone calls from the doorway and I turn as an older man with salt and pepper hair in a sharp blue suit walks into the room. He flashes me a kind smile that instantly puts me at ease despite the fact that I am confronted with yet another person I don't recognize. "I'm Daniel Robash, your father's attorney."

I sigh. "I'm sorry. I don't remember you."

"Oh, no. You wouldn't, Miss Shaw. We've never met."

Relief washes through me.

Thank God.

"Could we speak in private for a moment?"

"Of course." I glance over at Gavin and he sighs,

defeat flashing across his face before he's able to hide it. Turning to me, he smiles and releases my hand before standing from his chair next to the bed.

"I'll run home and grab a shower before coming back for the night, okay?" He leans over me and presses his lips to the top of my head as I resist the urge to shudder. God, I wish he would stop doing that. The hand holding I'm getting used to but kissing is still too much for me.

"You don't have to do that. I'm sure you probably want to sleep in your own bed," I reply, glancing down at the chair he's been stationed in for Lord knows how long and he shakes his head.

"I'll sleep at home when you do." He kisses me again and my shoulders jerk up before I can stop them. His heavy sigh greets me and I'm overwhelmed with guilt. "Be back soon. I love you."

I nod and bite my lip as he steps away from the bed with pain etched into his face. Does he expect me to say it back to him? Does he hope that if he says it enough times, miraculously my memory will return and everything will be right in his world again? I'm trying so hard to be understanding of his feelings in this messed up situation but I can't pretend to feel something I don't. I mean, Jesus… I woke up yesterday and my whole world is flipped upside down. I don't recognize a single person in my life and my father, the one person I could always count on, is gone.

On top of all that, I have a man claiming to be my fiancé and telling me how much he loves me. And it doesn't really matter how attractive I think he is or how much all the nurses keep telling me of his devotion to me because when I look at him, I feel absolutely nothing.

Sighing, I watch Gavin walk out of the room before turning back to my father's attorney. "What can I do for you, Mr. Robash?"

"I'm sorry for the intrusion, Miss Shaw," he says, offering me a sympathetic smile and I shake my head. Truthfully, I'm thankful for his interruption. I needed a break from the suffocating feeling of Gavin hovering over me. I needed just a moment to myself where I didn't have to be a stranger's fiancée or best friend. "And I'm so sorry for the loss of your father. I've known him for many years and he was a great man."

Pain pierces through me as I stare down at my hands resting in my lap and nod. "Thank you."

"I'm here about his will, actually." He motions to the chair next to my bed and I nod. "Your father had very specific instructions for me in the event of his death."

Arching a brow, I watch him cross the room and sink into the seat. "Which were?"

"Your father and his business partner, Silas Owens, had an agreement that upon his death, Silas would purchase your father's half of the label at two-thirds of its value and that money as well as your father's personal wealth would all be signed over to you."

I blink. "Oh."

When my father was eighteen, he and his best

friend, Silas, started their own music label, O'Shaw
Records, in my grandparents' garage. From the way
they used to tell it, it was slow going at first and they
spent a couple years wondering if they'd made a
mistake before they found Calliope, my mother. She
sounded like an angel, lit up a room with her smile, and
people fell in love with her as soon as they heard her
voice. Combine that with a couple of really talented
songwriters and she became their cash cow as well as
the love of my dad's life. They were inseparable and by
the time I was born, she was so big that she only went
by one name like Cher or Beyonce but to me, she was
always the woman that made up silly songs to sing me
to sleep or wake me up in the morning, the woman who
baked chocolate chip cookies with me, and encouraged
me to dance like no one was watching. She was wild,
free, but full of so much love for her family and when I
was nine, she was ripped away from us when an
obsessed fan killed her.

Her death devastated my father and me as well as
everyone at O'Shaw records, who we had always
considered family, but Dad never stopped building the
label and taking in new artists. He always said that she
wouldn't want him to fall apart and he was building a
legacy for me so it's weird now to think that it's just
gone.

"Is everything okay, Miss Shaw?" Mr. Robash asks
and I blink, snapping out of my thoughts as I turn to
look at him again.

"Yes, I'm sorry. I was just a little lost in thought."

He nods. "I understand that all of this is a lot to take in. I actually have a letter for you from your father that might help you process everything."

My eyes widen as he holds an envelope out in front of him and my hands shake as I reach up to grab it. I can't believe this is the last thing I'm ever going to read from my father but then again, at least I'll be able to remember it.

With my heart pounding in my chest, I pop open the seal on the envelope and pull the crisp paper out before unfolding it and sucking in a breath.

"How about I go grab some coffee and give you a minute to read that?" he asks and I nod, grateful for his suggestion. I never would have kicked him out on my own but now that he brought it up, I feel like I need to read this in private. Flashing me a sympathetic smile, he pats my hand and stands before walking out of the room. I stare at the empty doorway for a second before glancing down at the letter on my lap and picking it up.

To my baby girl,

If you're reading this, then I suppose it means I'm no longer there with you. I can't tell you how much it hurts to even write this letter or think of the pain you're going through right now but I don't want you to be too sad, sweet girl. You are strong enough to get through this and I have faith that I'm finally with your mama again and we're watching over you from Heaven.

A.M. Myers

A sob bubbles out of me and I drop the letter into my lap as I slap my hand over my mouth, unable to go on. Hot tears spill down my cheeks and my chest aches, wishing he were here to wrap his arms around me right now and tell me that everything will be okay. It always used to make me feel so safe and I don't know how I'm supposed to go on without it. How do I move on without the only man I've ever been able to count on? Through my tears, I pick the letter back up and keep reading.

You, my darling girl, are more than I could have ever dreamed of and I was so incredibly proud to call you mine each and every day I spent on this earth. You brought more joy to my life than I could ever find the words to explain and my hope for you is that one day you find the kind of love and happiness I found with you and your mom.

Now, on to business...If Mr. Robash has given you this letter, I can only assume that he's told you the details of my will. I've spent most of your life telling you that I'm building the label as a legacy for you but it's become quite clear to me in the past couple years that you are following your passion and I couldn't imagine keeping you from that. Silas and I have come to an agreement that in the event of my death, he will buy my shares in the label from you for two-thirds of their value. I offered them to him at half their value and

30

he offered to buy them at their full value. Silas has thought of you as his daughter, too, since the day you were born and he didn't feel right taking your half of the company at half the price and I didn't feel right making him buy half of the company we built together at full price so we had to compromise. If you have any questions or concerns, bring them to Mr. Robash. He's a good man and someone that I've asked to look out for you after I'm gone.

Before I go, I have to leave you with a word of warning. I'm leaving you a great deal of money and I know there are people out there who will try to extort that. They will see you as an easy target and it will be hard, at times, to know who you can trust. That said, I know you can handle yourself, sweetheart. Just trust your instincts and remember who you are.

All my love,
Dad

Sucking in a stuttered breath, I let the letter fall to my lap again as I wipe the tears from my face. The loss of my father is so deep, so profound, that I can feel it molding me into a new person as I lie in my hospital bed, truly alone. Squeezing my eyes shut, I picture him in my mind and search my memory for the last time I saw him but it's still blank, a darkness fogging over the last five years of my life that seems deeper than a moonless night. With a sigh, I relax back into the bed and stare up at the ceiling, letting the tears drip down my face and into the pillow.

"Miss Shaw?" a voice calls from the doorway and I lift my head, forcing a weak smile to my face as Mr. Robash walks into the room. "Are you ready to continue?"

I nod. "Yes."

He walks in with his coffee cup in hand and sits next to my bed again before pulling some paperwork out of his briefcase. Clearing his throat, he flashes me a sympathetic expression.

"In his will, your father left everything else to you, including his house currently valued at three point two million, the three vehicles in his name, and the remainder of his net worth."

"Okay…" I breathe. Even if I still had my memory, I wouldn't be able to tell you how much my father was worth. It was never something that I was concerned with especially after I turned eighteen and I was given access to my two million dollar trust fund. "How much is that?"

"After everything was paid off, the amount left to you is…" He glances down at the forms in his hand. "Three hundred and fifty-six million dollars."

My eyes widen and I drop my head back to the bed as I stare up at the ceiling. I knew my father and Silas had done well for themselves but the label was never something I was interested in and it didn't really matter to me how much money he made but, Jesus… The words from his letter come rushing back to me and I suck in a nervous breath. He was right. This is the kind of money that will bring people out of the woodwork and right now it feels so overwhelming that I can't even begin to wrap my mind around it.

One thing I know for sure is that for the second time in two days, my life has changed completely.

A.M. Myers

Never Let Me Go
Chapter Three
Juliette

"Bed one-oh-six, Juliette Shaw," Lisa, the nurse during the day shift, says as she walks into my room with Colleen at her side. Both women have tablets in their hands, taking notes as Lisa goes over my last vitals check to turn over to Colleen for the night. After Lisa is finished speaking, Colleen smiles and walks up to the side of my bed, pressing her fingers to the inside of my wrist.

"Good evening, Miss Shaw."

I smile. "Hi, Colleen."

"How are you feeling?"

"Pretty good," I answer with a nod. Sure, my body is still sore from the accident but even that has dulled significantly in the past three days and the only real pain comes when I try to move too quickly. For the most part, I feel like myself again... or myself five years ago, I suppose, since my memory still has a giant blank spot in it.

"You're looking great," she says, pulling away to type some notes into her tablet. "Doc might even let you go home tomorrow."

I force a smile to my face as I clasp my shaking hands together. Each time someone mentions going home, it's the same reaction from me and I know it may not be fair to Gavin, but going home with him when I barely know him terrifies me. Not to mention, that I won't recognize anything in my world. Laying my head back against my pillow, I sigh. I know it's not fair to Gavin that I don't remember him and I wish more than anything, I could go back and stop all this from happening. I would if I could and not just for myself. He's showed me over the past few days that he's a good man and completely devoted to me but it's just hard to be who he wants me to be when I don't even remember who she was. As far as I'm concerned, I'm Juliette from five years ago and it's becoming quite clear to me that she's a different person than the woman Gavin knows. So as much as being cooped up in this hospital bed is driving me crazy, it seems better and safer than the alternative.

Gavin's stomach growls and I turn my head to look at him.

"You should go grab some food from the cafeteria."

He shakes his head and crosses his arms over his chest without looking away from the game show rerun on TV. "No, I'm good."

I watch him for a moment before sighing and

36

turning back to Colleen. She smiles and pats my hand before quietly excusing herself from the room. Turning back to Gavin, I study his face and sigh again. He looks exhausted with the circles under his eyes even darker than they were when I woke up three days ago and I know he's not sleeping well on the little couch in the corner of the room. Not to mention, that he refuses to leave me long enough to do anything and he hasn't eaten since coming back to the hospital last night. He's a stubborn man, especially when it comes to taking care of me but as much as I appreciate that, I don't see how neglecting himself helps me.

"I'll be okay for a little while on my own," I assure him but he just shakes his head and I sigh again. "Gavin, you need to eat."

He meets my gaze, his blue eyes blazing. "I'm not going to leave you by yourself."

"Knock, knock."

We both turn to the door as it swings open and Nico stomps in, a perfect contradiction in her floral knee length dress that hugs her curves and black combat boots. Her purple streaked hair is pulled back into two poofy buns on either side of her head and her makeup is dramatic with a cat eye and a bold lip. I'm slowly realizing her signature style is taking things no one else would ever think of putting together and making it work. She's effortlessly cool; she doesn't give a damn what anyone thinks about her.

Her eyes land on me and she flashes me a smile as she struts into the room. "How you feeling, babe?"

"I'm good," I answer with a smile. "Just trying to convince Gavin to feed himself."

She turns to him and nods. "Go eat. I'll keep her company for a while."

He peeks over at me and I can tell he's almost convinced so I offer him a smile. I suppose it really is sweet the way he looks after me and I know I haven't been exactly warm and welcoming to him in the past few days but I just hope he understands how weird this is for me. Finally, he sighs and nods.

"How long can you hang out?" he asks Nico. "I'd love to run home and grab a shower, too."

"Take all the time you need. She's stuck with me all night," she quips, flashing me a grin as she winks and I stifle a laugh. There's something so infectious about Nico's personality that doesn't make me feel weird and out of place like I have since I woke up and realized I was missing a huge chunk of information. Being around her is just easy and it doesn't matter that I don't remember her because it feels like I've known her for years.

Gavin lets out a sigh of relief and I fight back a grimace. I knew staying by my side was wearing on him but what I am supposed to do if he refuses to leave me alone? At least he's taking care of himself now, I guess. He stands and throws his arms over his head in a stretch. His dark t-shirt rides up, revealing taunt muscles and a line of dark hair leading into his jeans.

Damn.

God, the man is too hot for my own good. All this

time, I've been picturing him in a suit and that image alone is enough to intrigue a girl but to see what he's working with under his clothes, I don't stand a freaking chance. A blush creeps up my cheeks and I bite my lip as I turn away from him. Nico meets my eye and flashes me a little grin as she nods as if to say, "I know, right?" My blush deepens and she laughs.

"All right," Gavin says, drawing my gaze back to him as he leans over the bed and presses a kiss to the top of my head. Thankfully, the jerking away from his touch has calmed down some because I know it was taking a toll on him and it made me feel terrible each time it happened. When he pulls back, he grabs my hand and gives it a squeeze. "I'll try to hurry back."

"Take whatever time you need. I'll be okay."

Nico nods. "Yeah, get out of here. We need some girl time."

"Yes, ma'am," he answers with a hint of a grin on his face and I suck in a breath.

Jesus.

The man is too handsome for my own good.

"Love you, baby," he calls to me as he heads for the door and I nod, watching him until he closes the door behind him. When Nico and I are finally alone, I release a breath.

"Okay, so how is it really going?" she asks after a second and I shrug.

"As well as can be expected, I think."

Rolling her eyes, she grabs my hand and gives it a squeeze. "I know you don't remember this but we're like best friends and I know when you're bullshitting me so how about you be real with me, chick."

"I don't know. It's all so weird. He seems very sweet and devoted to me since he hasn't left my side since I woke up except to shower but I don't know him. I can't remember how we met, our first kiss, or our first date. I have no idea how he likes his coffee or which side of the bed he sleeps on and it's just a lot to take it all at once."

She nods as she grabs her bag off the floor. "I get that. Which is why I brought pictures for you and I happen to know all the answers to your questions because when you met Gavin, you could not stop talking about him."

"Really?"

"Oh, absolutely," she says as she sets a folder down on my lap. "I spent hours last night putting together as much of the last five years as I could get my hands on to maybe help you remember."

Tears sting my eyes as I glance up from the folder and meet her eyes. "You did that for me?"

"Of course." She points to herself before pointing to me. "Best friends, remember?"

"How did we meet?"

She grins. "We met in a coffee shop, actually. It was about two years after you started your company and you were getting a little overwhelmed with the business side of things because you just wanted to design and make jewelry."

"Why do I feel like there's more to that story?"

"Because there is," she answers with a laugh. "You walked in to get a drink and I was right in the middle of chewing out the barista for screwing up my order for a second time that day. By the time I got around to instructing him on how to better organize his workspace and make himself more efficient, you said you knew I was perfect for the job."

I drop my head back on the pillow as I laugh. "I have no trouble at all seeing that."

"What can I say? I see a problem and I just have to fix it."

"How is the company doing now?"

She beams. "Phenomenal."

"Really?" I ask, my heart feeling lighter than it has in days. She nods.

"Absolutely." Leaning forward, she opens the folder and points to a stack of papers on the left side. "Articles, features, designs, and photos about the company are all on this side."

I pull out a stack of papers and start leafing through them. There are a few articles that mention the start of my company and a few more that talk about its growth before I find one that names me on a hot businesses on the rise list. After the articles, I find a few of my designs and tears well up in my eyes as I study them. When I was in college, I always dreamed of starting a jewelry line and I would spend hours drawing up designs and dreaming about the day that I could walk down the street and see someone wearing one of my pieces. It's just a shame I can't remember any of that now. The first tear drips down my cheek followed by a few more and I set the papers down before clamping my hand over my mouth. I've cried so much in the past few days, over my situation and missing my father which led to thoughts of my mother and that always leads to more tears.

"Whoa, what's wrong?" Nico asks, her brows knitted together in concern and I shake my head.

"I'm so sorry, Nico. I really appreciate all this but it's just... a lot. This business was my dream for so long and I just wish I could remember it."

She shakes her head as she stands up and wraps me up in her arms. "Hey, don't apologize to me. I can't even imagine what you're going through right now and I just want to help however I can. We'll just go as slow as you want and we'll have you remembering in no time."

"Thank you," I whisper as she pulls away. "I can tell what a great friend you are even if I don't remember you."

Shaking her head, she sinks back into her chair. "Aw, babe. Honestly, I always think about how lucky I am that you found me and decided to take a chance on me. I absolutely love working with you and I'm even happier to have you as a friend."

"Oh, God!" I shriek, wiping the tears from my face as I shake my head. "Enough with the sappy stuff."

Nico laughs. "You may not remember her but you're still the same girl you were before the accident."

"You don't know how much it means to hear you

42

say that. I feel so out of place, all the time. It's like I want to just go home and feel safe and comfortable but it doesn't exist anymore."

"Sure, it does. It would just be home from five years ago."

I study her as I remember my apartment in Baton Rouge and my chest aches so fiercely that I almost cry out again. Oh, God, what I wouldn't give to be back there… Nico is absolutely right. Nothing feels right here because Miami isn't home but just the thought of Baton Rouge is enough to put me at ease.

"Well, should we get back to this?" I ask as I swallow back my desire to go home and pick up the folder again. "Tell me about Gavin."

She smiles. "What do you want to know?"

"Did he really take me to Fiji on our first date?" I ask, remembering my conversation with him. Nico laughs.

"Oh, yeah, he did. The day after the charity event, you were floating in the dang clouds and so happy after spending the entire evening with him but when you got back from that trip, I could tell that you were pissed."

"So how did he win me over?"

Shaking her head, she crosses her arms over her chest and rolls her eyes. "Showed up at the office every day with a new bouquet of flowers for you until you agreed to one more date."

I resist the urge to purse my lips. From the outside, it doesn't seem like something that would win me over but who knows how I really felt back then when I was

43

really living it.

"Tell me I put up a good fight, at least?"

"Two weeks," she answers with a laugh and I smile as I give myself a little nod of approval. "And even then, you only agreed to a lunch date. When you got back, everything was back on track between the two of you."

I pick up the first paper on the right side of the folder, a newspaper clipping of our engagement announcement. It's dated two months ago with a gorgeous picture of Gavin and me featured front and center.

"How did he propose?"

"Oh, he took you to one of the fanciest restaurants in town and dropped down on his knee in front of a dining room full of people."

I fight the urge to scrunch my nose up. When I was a little girl, I always imagined I'd find a boy I loved and he'd take me somewhere romantic with just the two of us before asking me to marry him. It would have been private and intimate, not in a crowded restaurant with a room full of people looking on but that's just one more thing that I can't judge since I don't remember a second of it. Before I can ask her anything else, someone knocks on the door and my head jerks up as two men in suits walk into the room.

"Miss Shaw?" the shorter one asks and I nod as they both stop at the end of my bed and flash shiny gold badges at me.

"I'm Detective Bennett," the tall one says before

motioning to the other man. "And this is my partner, Detective Mason. We're here to ask you a few questions about the accident."

I glance over at Nico before meeting Detective Bennett's gaze. "I'm not sure I can help. I don't remember anything."

"A lot of folks think that, Ma'am," Detective Mason answers. "But you might have seen something you didn't even realize at the time."

"No, you don't understand…"

"Don't you want to find the person responsible for killing your father?" Detective Bennett asks, cutting me off and I arch a brow as I cross my arms over my chest. "Think of all the other people he could hurt if you don't tell us what you know."

"Am I allowed to speak now?"

They both nod.

"As I was trying to say, I cannot help you because I don't remember anything from the last five goddamn years of my life so yes, maybe I saw something but I can't remember what it is."

"You have amnesia? Seriously?"

"Yes, she has amnesia," Nico snaps, standing up from her chair. "She woke up three days ago and didn't recognize me or her fiancé but hey, here's an idea, why don't you two do your damn jobs and tell us what *you* know about the accident?"

They share a look before Detective Mason steps forward. "Please forgive us, Ma'am. We didn't get a chance to speak to the doctor before we came in here and we didn't realize that your memory is gone."

"It's fine," I answer with a nod as Nico flashes me a look that I ignore. "Can you tell me what you know?"

"Honestly, Ma'am… not much. We were really counting on your account of what happened. We did find white paint on the driver's side door but there were no witnesses and no surveillance cameras caught the accident."

I nod, my mind racing with new information. "Where did it happen?"

"About a mile and a half from your father's estate. The other driver ran a stop sign and t-boned your father's car. He was behind the wheel and took the brunt of the impact."

"Are you thinking it was a drunk driver?" I ask and Detective Bennett shakes his head.

"It's possible but there is just no way to be sure at the moment."

"This is my card," Detective Mason says, stepping forward and handing me a business card. "We'll leave you be but if you think of anything or your memory returns, please give me a call."

I nod. "I will. Thank you."

We watch them leave before Nico turns back to me and plucks the card from my hand before setting it on the table.

"Don't worry, Jules. I'm sure they'll find him."

Not feeling as confident as her, I give her a half-hearted nod and lie back into the pillows with a sigh. Someone knocks on the door and I turn as Dr. Wilson walks into the room. He flashes me a kind smile and I force myself to return it.

"Good news, Miss Shaw. You just might get to go home tomorrow."

My cheeks ache as I force an even bigger smile to my face and my heart thunders in my chest, fear creeping up my spine. Here in the hospital, it's so easy to pretend like everything is okay, like my life isn't completely falling apart but what happens when I leave here? What happens when I have to go back to being a Juliette that I'm not sure exists anymore?

A.M. Myers

Never Let Me Go
Chapter Four
Juliette

Sunlight beams down on me through the car
window as we race down the interstate toward an
apartment that everyone keeps telling me will help me
get pieces of my life back but my stomach is in knots.
Closing my eyes, I take a deep breath and feel the heat
seeping into my skin. There was a park in Baton Rouge
that was about a block from the apartment I shared with
Mercedes all through college. I loved to go there and
just sit by the river while I soaked up some sun. It
always made me feel so peaceful and grounded,
something I'm desperate for right now. When Dr.
Wilson walked into my room right after breakfast this
morning and told me that I was going home today like
it was the greatest news I'd hear all week, I had to force
a smile to my face and pretend like the thought of going
home excited me but that couldn't be further from the

truth. I wish I was truly going home right now but the more I think about it, the more home feels like that amazing apartment in the heart of downtown Baton Rouge.

Mercedes and I first met when we were paired up as roommates freshman year and with our similar backgrounds, we hit it off right away. She quickly became the sister I'd never had and I was the same for her so when she went through a really bad breakup right before our sophomore year, we made the decision to live together again. I guess it's no surprise that I can still see our place so clearly in my mind. For me, it was just the other day that I was living there and I miss its exposed brick walls, dark wood floors, and high ceilings. Living with Mercedes was the very best years of my life and I'm almost certain that I'm not just saying that because I can't remember anything else.

"Here we are," Gavin says, pulling me out of my thoughts and I open my eyes as he slows down and pulls into an underground parking garage.

Oh, fuck.

My belly does a little flip as my heart thunders so loudly in my chest that I'm surprised Gavin can't hear it in the confined space of the car. We drive past a line of very nice cars, each one with a number painted on the concrete wall in front of it, before he slows again and pulls the car into a spot marked "penthouse".

"Wait for me to come help you out," he instructs as he turns off the car and I nod, remembering how wobbly I felt just from the walk between the wheelchair and the car when they released me from the hospital. The accident and lying in a bed for the last week and a half have really taken it out of me.

I watch him as he climbs out of the car and rounds the back before opening my door and holding his hand out to me. Sucking in a breath, I take it and swing my legs around before letting him gently pull me up out of the car. My body aches with each little movement but I push through it as I suck in a breath through clenched teeth. A bout of dizziness sets in and I wobble for a second before righting myself and forcing a smile to my face. Gavin beams at me and as he wraps a firm arm around my waist and pulls me into his side, I can feel his body vibrating with his excitement.

"I'll come back down after I get you settled upstairs and get your things."

I nod. "Okay."

He closes the door with his free hand and we begin our trek from the car to what I assume is our private elevator twenty feet away. It's slow going but Gavin is patient as he holds me up safely in his arms and guides me to the elevator. It opens right away when he pushes the button and he ushers me inside before hitting the only button on the panel. It prompts him for a code and I watch him as he punches it in.

0503 - my birthday.

I commit the code to memory as the door closes and the elevator starts going up. The closer we get to the penthouse, the faster my heart races and the more my belly flips. As I suck in a quiet breath, I squeeze my eyes shut and count to ten in an effort to calm my erratic nerves.

It's going to be okay.

No matter how many times I silently repeat the mantra to myself, it doesn't seem to do any good. I have no idea what is waiting for me once those elevator doors open and I barely know the man at my side but what other option did I have? I could have gone to my father's house but just the thought of walking in there and knowing that I'd never hear his voice again or see his smile was too much to bear. So that left me with only one option since the place I truly want to be is damn near one thousand miles away.

"Welcome home, baby," Gavin says with a smile as the elevator glides to a stop and I suck in a breath as I open my eyes. The elevator doors open to a wide, round foyer with white marble floors and a large wooden table in the center. A vase of roses sits in the middle and I resist the urge to wrinkle my nose. I've never really been a fan of roses and I can't imagine why I would have them in my house. Gavin leads me through the foyer as it opens up to a large open floor plan. To my left is the kitchen which is also all decked out in white marble and to my right is the living room. There's a cream colored sectional positioned in front of a gas fireplace and large windows along the back wall allow the entire space to be flooded with light. It's gorgeous but a little sterile and not my taste at all.

Where's the color?

Where's the comfort and homey feeling I crave?

It's hard to imagine that I ever lived in this space and once again, I'm reminded of the many differences between whoever I used to be and the woman I am now.

Or the woman I was…

Oh, hell, this is so confusing.

"Let's get you to the couch," Gavin says as he begins guiding me toward the living room. "You can rest and I'll get your stuff up here. I gave the staff the day off but we can order something. Just let me know what you're in the mood for."

I nod as I sink into the couch and he makes sure I'm comfortable before flashing me a smile and going back to the elevator. As soon as he's gone, I stand up and gingerly make my way over to the bookshelf in the corner. There's a photo of Gavin and me all dressed up and grinning at the camera. I pick it up and stare at the woman smiling back at me before running my finger across her face and shaking my head.

"Who are you?"

I catch my reflection in the glass and even though we look identical, she's a stranger to me and the more I get to know about her, the more I wonder if I'd rather keep it that way. Nothing about this life makes sense to me or feels true to who I am and I can't help but wonder what happened over five years to make me change so much.

After setting the picture back on the shelf, I wander back over to the couch and sit down, gazing out at the view of the ocean below. A luxury penthouse right on the water… How in the hell did I even afford this place? Even if I still had all of my two million dollar trust fund, I highly doubt it would be enough to cover the price of this place. The elevator dings and I turn as Gavin walks back into the room with my bag.

"Did you decide what you want for dinner?"

I scowl up at him. "How did we afford this place?"

"It was a gift from your father when your company became successful. He said a CEO deserved a home worthy of the title."

Turning back to the window, I watch the waves crash against the shore as I nod. That does sound like something my father would do. He was always sneaking cash into my purse when I wasn't looking even though I had the trust fund. Anytime I complained and told him I had more than enough, he would give me a look and tell me that he worked his ass off to make sure I never had to go without and that was usually the end of the conversation.

"So… dinner?" Gavin asks again, interrupting my thoughts and I turn to him as my stomach growls. I've been eating gross hospital food for days now and I'm looking forward to something with flavor.

"A burger sounds good."

Gavin stops and turns to me with an arched brow. "Really? You were on a diet for the…"

"The what?"

"Uh… the wedding but I guess that's on hold now."

"Oh," I whisper, looking down at the massive rock on my hand. "I'm sorry."

He shakes his head, the surprise melting away as he smiles at me. "No. Don't even worry about it. I just hadn't thought of it yet because I was so worried about you."

"Okay," I whisper, turning back to the windows. There's something about the water that puts me at ease even though I'm in a strange home with a man I don't know.

"Food will be here in thirty minutes," he says and I turn back to him as he glances up from his phone and offers me another smile. I know he's probably trying to make me feel more comfortable but it's actually doing the opposite. The pressure to be the woman he remembers, the woman he's engaged to, is unreal and a huge part of me wishes I could go somewhere and be alone until I get my memory back. Then again, what happens if I get my memory back but I'm still not the person he's desperately waiting for?

God, this whole situation is a mess and the last thing I want to do is hurt anyone but it's just so much... so much weight bearing down on me and I feel like at any moment, my arms are going to give out and that weight is going to crush me.

"You mind if I take a quick shower before the food gets here?"

I glance up at Gavin and shake my head. "No, of course not. Just do what you would normally do."

"Well, normally I'd ask you to join me," he replies and I suck in a breath as images of him wet and naked play out in my mind. I pull my knees to my chest and hug them. He sighs. "Shit. I'm sorry. I shouldn't have said that."

"It's okay."

He sighs again and sits down next to me on the couch. "No, it's not okay. It's just so hard to always be on guard with you because two weeks ago, you were *my* Juliette." He takes my hand in his. "But I know you don't know me and I really am trying to make you as comfortable as I can."

"I know," I whisper with a nod.

"I have faith that we'll get back there though." He peeks up at me, his eyes shining with vulnerability and I nod as my chest tightens. Is it truly lying to him if my doubt is based on the fact that my whole life is up in the air right now and nothing feels hopeful?

I don't know if we'll get back there.

I don't know if I'll ever get my memory back.

I don't even know *who* I am.

"Okay," he says, releasing my hand and standing up. "I'm going to hop in the shower. Be right back."

I nod and watch him walk out of the room before turning back to the windows. A little girl runs along the water, giggling as her father chases after her and tears sting my eyes as I smile. Daddy hated to go to the beach. He said it was too crowded, too sandy, and stressed him out more than ten emergencies at work but every once in a while Mom was able to convince him to go with us and we'd spend hours building a sand castle or burying him up to his neck. After Mom passed away, getting him to the beach was even more difficult since it held so many happy memories with her but that didn't mean he missed out on special time with me. Instead, he had an amazing pool built in our backyard. It had gorgeous natural rock waterfalls, a hidden slide, and a huge spa. We spent so many weekends out there even as I grew into a teenager and I always thought of Daddy as my best friend. I could tell him absolutely anything and he never lectured me. He'd just listen and offer me helpful advice that I usually took.

A soft sob slips past my lips and I bury my face in my knees as the tears fall hard and fast. I can't believe how much I miss him and knowing that I'll never see him again, never hear his warm, booming laugh feels like a hot poker in my chest. There is still so much I need my father for in my life and I can't fathom how I'm supposed to move on without him. Without my parents, I'm truly alone. My mind drifts back to Mercedes and I look up, wiping the tears from my face as I stare out at the water. I wish I could talk to her. She's one of those people that has always been there for me but I have no clue what our relationship is like right now. Are we still friends? Did we lose touch after I moved to Miami?

"Food's on the way up," Gavin says behind me. My body jerks in surprise and I let out a little yelp before peeking over my shoulder at him. He arches a brow. "You okay?"

I nod. "Yeah, just scared me a little."

"Sorry."

I nod again, watching him as he walks into the

living room in a pair of mesh shorts and a gray t-shirt. His wet hair falls in his face and it gives him this whole "bad boy" vibe that teenage me would have eaten up with a damn spoon. But that was before I found myself a boyfriend who rode a motorcycle and did drugs. One month with him was enough to scare me straight.

"Do you want to eat in the living room or at the island?" he asks, pointing to the gorgeous white marble island with a waterfall edge and three chairs in front of it. I shrug. It really makes no difference to me where we eat dinner… unless that's usually something I get uptight about but I can't see that. Then again, there are a lot of things about my new life that don't make sense to me.

"Where do we usually eat dinner?"

He points to the island. "There. We save the dining table for special events."

"Okay," I answer with a nod as the elevator dings and a tall man in a suit steps out.

"Your dinner, Sir," the man says to Gavin before handing him a couple of paper bags.

"Thanks, Carl."

Carl turns to me and his face lights up. "Miss Shaw! So happy to see you back at home. How are you feeling?"

"Sore," I answer as I plaster a smile on my face, thankful Gavin supplied me with his name so I wasn't forced to have another awkward conversation with someone I don't know. "But good. Thank you, Carl."

"Excellent. Well, if you need anything at all, you

58

just let me know."

I nod. "I will."

He beams, pride shining through his eyes and from just a glance, I can tell how much Carl loves his job - taking care of the residents of this building and it immediately endears him to me. Gavin hands Carl a little bit of money and he slips it in his pocket before wishing us a good night and disappearing back into the elevator. Gavin turns to me with a perplexed expression.

"Do you remember Carl?"

I shake my head. "No. I just didn't want to explain that I can't remember anything again."

A look of understanding flashes across his face.

"Shall we?" he asks, holding his hand out to me and I take it as I stand up from the couch. He leads me over to the island and only releases my hand to pull a chair out for me. I smile up at him in thanks as I sit down.

"You want something to drink? We have water, wine, apple juice, or sweet tea."

I eye the bag of food before meeting his gaze again. "Tea, please."

"You sure? The wine might help you relax a little."

"No," I answer, shaking my head. "Better not with the pain meds."

He nods as he pulls a pitcher of sweet tea out of the fridge. "Right."

After grabbing a glass out of one of the upper cabinets, he fills it and sets it down in front of me. I watch him as he carries the pitcher back to the fridge and grabs a beer for himself before sitting down next to me. The past two weeks is starting to catch up to him and I'll be surprised if he stays awake long enough to finish his dinner. He passes out our food and I groan loudly as I take my first bite. The burger is juicy and so full of flavor, a stark contrast from the bland, beige hospital food I've been eating for the past four days.

"Good?"

I nod and wipe my mouth with the napkin. "Oh my God, yes."

"Good," he answers with a grin. "I was starting to worry about you. You've barely been eating anything since you woke up."

"Um, because it was terrible."

He laughs and nods as he grabs his beer and takes a sip. "Yeah, I suppose you're right."

As we eat our dinner, I ask him about where he grew up and he tells me about his hometown in California. When he shares with me that both of his parents have passed away, my chest aches but I also feel a connection with him that wasn't there before because I know exactly how he feels. He tells me more about the night of the charity event where we met and I can't help but smile as he admits how hard his heart was beating in his chest when he approached me and hearing him describe the two of us dancing the night away sounds like something out of a dream. By the time we finish, I'm more relaxed than I've been since waking up in the hospital and his eyes are drooping more and more with each minute that passes.

"Can you point me in the direction of the shower? I want to wash the smell of the hospital off me."

He nods and stands up from the island. "Of course. I'll show you where everything is."

Taking my hand in his, he leads me past the kitchen to a long hallway that opens up into a gorgeous master bedroom. Another wall of windows gives the space an ocean view and I suck in a breath as colors splash across the sky with the setting sun.

"Oh, that's incredible."

He smiles. "Isn't it? I can't wait for you to see how gorgeous it is in the morning."

I nod, gazing out at the water for a moment before letting him lead me into a massive en-suite bathroom. It's all white marble again but there are little pops of blue that remind me of the water below and it feels more like me than the living room or kitchen. I eye the giant tub in the corner before turning to the walk-in shower along the back wall. Gavin releases my hand and walks across the room to a cabinet. He pulls two towels out and hands them to me.

"Okay, I guess I'll leave you to it. Just yell if you need anything."

I nod, wishing I could usher him out of here without being rude. That shower looks too damn inviting and I didn't realize how badly I needed one until he led me into the room. Finally, he turns and leaves me alone. I make sure the door is locked before stripping out of my clothes, my body aching but I fight through it. Once I'm naked, I walk across the room and set my towels on the bench next to the shower before changing my mind and turning toward the tub. With my aching muscles, a nice long hot bath sounds perfect. Besides, how in the hell could I pass up this amazing tub?

Turning the water on, I set it to the perfect temperature before grabbing a jar of what looks like bath salts. After prying the lid off, I bring it to my nose and moan as the scent surrounds me. It's vanilla mixed with something fruity and I can't resist the urge to dump a scoop or two into my bath. When the bath is halfway full, I step inside and sink into the water, letting out a loud sigh. The warm water washes over my muscles, relaxing me and if I laid my head back, I think I could fall asleep right here. Leaning forward, I turn off the water and lie back, closing my eyes.

As tension seeps out of my body, my mind begins working overtime, thinking about the past four days, about how much I miss Baton Rouge and Mercedes and how weird I feel living in a house with a man I don't know. How is any of this supposed to help me? I just can't understand. The doctors kept saying how being in my own home with my things would help me and relax me but the pressure to be who Gavin needs and wants me to be is immense and I don't think I can handle it. Maybe I should just book a flight to an island and go relax in the sun until my memory returns… if it ever does. Even that doesn't sound as appealing as it should, though. The only place I want to be, the only place that's given me any kind of comfort in the last four days, is Baton Rouge.

Never Let Me Go

Sighing, I pull the plug and stand up. My head spins and I grip the edge of the tub for a second, taking deep even breaths until it passes. When I'm feeling steady again, I grab my towel and wrap it around my body as I step out of the tub. The house is quiet as I unlock the bathroom door and peek out into the bedroom so I tiptoe over to the closet I saw on the way in before realizing how stupid that is. It's my damn house. Why the hell am I tiptoeing like I'm a guest?

In the closet, I find a satin tank and short set that looks comfy and slip it on before venturing out into the living room in search of Gavin. As I step into the living room, I stop and smile. Gavin is splayed out on the couch, one hand thrown over his head and the other pressing against his chest as he snores quietly. Based on how hard he has been pushing himself these past four days, I'm surprised he didn't pass out sooner. I know how badly he needs the sleep so I grab a blanket off the back of the couch and lay it over him before returning to the bedroom.

The sun is down now and the stars are starting to peek out over the water, shimmering off the surface as lazy waves roll toward the shore. It's a peaceful night and a part of me wishes I could just go sit down there and let the water lap over my toes. With my luck, though, I'd probably get lost and not be able to get back home.

Sighing, I sit on the bed. I wish there were more personal touches in the apartment, something to help me piece together my life but it's like all of it is hidden

63

away. My teeth sink into my bottom lip as I look around the room. It's got to be hiding around here, somewhere, right? I glance around the room again before landing on the closet. That's the first logical place to look for clues, isn't it? With a nod, I stand up and walk over to the closet as I listen for sounds of Gavin stirring in the living room. Once inside, I stand in the middle of the large room and look around at the various racks of clothes before turning to what is clearly my side. Half of the wall is divided into shelving for shoes, bags, and accessories and the other half has two bars for hangers. I drop my head back and smile when I see boxes up on a shelf above the clothes.

Bingo.

There is a step stool tucked into the corner and I grab it before positioning it under the shelves and climbing up. A fine layer of dust covers the top of the old shoe box and I blow it off as I climb off the stool and sit down on a bench in the middle of the room. Sucking in a breath, I pull the lid off and smile at the photo of Mercedes and me from the day we met sitting on top of a stack of other photos. I pull out a chunk of them and start going through them. They are all from my college days and most of them contain Mercedes and me doing something crazy. The longer I stare at our smiling faces, the more my heart aches. God, I miss her which doesn't make any sense to me. As far as I can remember, I saw her just a few days ago even if I know that's not true but it doesn't matter because all I want is to hang out with my girl and tell her about the craziness that is my life right now. A tear streaks down my cheek and I flick it away before shoving the photos back into the box and slamming the lid down on top. Looking at old photos and reminiscing about all the good times we had isn't going to help me move on with my life now. No matter how hard it is, I have to try to move forward.

A.M. Myers

Never Let Me Go
Chapter Five
Sawyer

The truck rumbles through the parking lot of the apartment complex and my gaze sweeps over each car, checking for a threat hidden from view despite the fact that there is no reason to be on the lookout for danger today. We are just here to help Sammy move into her new place but after seven and a half years with the Bayou Devils, I've trained myself to always be hyper-vigilant. I can't help looking for trouble behind every tree or in every parked car. The guys like to give me hell for it but I can't stop either. I'm always alert, always watching even after the threat is eliminated because the one thing I hate more than surprises is failing one of these girls, something that hasn't happened often but each time it does, it's like a punch to the gut. To be honest, it's kind of exhausting to always be "on" but it's also necessary to keep everyone safe and nothing is more important to me than that.

Fuzz pulls up in front of one of the buildings and whips the truck around so he can back into the space in front of Sammy's door, allowing us to move boxes into her new apartment easily. I scan the second floor of the building adjacent to hers before turning to inspect the parking lot again. There is a fit older woman in pink spandex walking her yappy little dog along one of the walking trails between two other buildings and a man at the end of the building in front of us carrying his groceries up the stairs, his face contorted into a grimace as he struggles to cart a mountain of bags up in one trip. Scoffing, I watch him, mentally betting myself that he drops a gallon of milk before he makes it to his door.

"Twenty bucks says that milk ends up all over the stairs," Fuzz says, his gaze locked on the man stumbling up the stairs with a smirk on his face. I scoff.

"Pretty sure that's a bet you're going to win."

The man stumbles a few times before finally managing to make it to his apartment door without losing any of his food. I sigh and scan the parking lot again. Despite the fact that it seems like a large complex, it's fairly quiet which will be good for a girl like Sammy after the hell she's been through.

"Moose, give it a rest," Fuzz says, sighing as he runs a hand through his dark hair and checks his phone. "Sammy is safe now."

I nod, his words not quite sating my suspicion but I ignore it. "Nice place."

"Yeah, Streak hooked her up and made sure it was safe. Plus, it's close to the clubhouse so she can make it into the shop easily for work."

After we got Sammy out of a shitty situation with her ex-boyfriend, she had nowhere to go and it had been years since she had been allowed to have a job so her prospects weren't great. Thankfully, the club owns a couple of businesses and we so happened to be looking for a new receptionist at the auto shop where I work as a mechanic.

"Has she even agreed to work at the shop yet?"

Fuzz shakes his head. "Not yet but Blaze seems to think she'll be on board."

I nod as I stare out at the parking lot again. One of the first things that drew me into joining the Devils was the sense of brotherhood everyone always talked about but after being a prospect for only three months, I could see that wasn't what I had gotten myself into. I was just about ready to call it quits when everything changed. We were all selling guns and drugs back then and in a twisted turn of events, Henn got himself arrested and sent to jail which led to Blaze getting shot. Before that, we were a real outlaw club but I guess his near death experience made him rethink things. A few days after he was released from the hospital, the first girl this club ever helped literally fell into his arms and Blaze took it as a sign from above. He became passionate about helping people who couldn't protect themselves from all the bad in the world and when he brought it to the club, the ones who shared his vision stayed while the ones who liked the way things were, left. And we've been doing it ever since which is how we met Sammy.

Our first attempt to save Sammy was a while back. Her sister contacted us because Sammy was in big trouble and her crazy boyfriend rarely let her leave his sight. He kept her from her family and friends and didn't even let her have a phone. We came up with a plan but just before we put it into motion, Sammy disappeared. We searched for months but couldn't find her anywhere so we were surprised as hell when she contacted us a month ago to ask for our help again. This time, we didn't waste any time and rushed to free her and we were successful. Now, we're here to help her reclaim her life, starting with an apartment and a job.

"Come on," Fuzz says, pulling me out of my thoughts as he nudges me. "Let's get this shit done. I'm looking forward to an ice cold beer and my goddamn bed."

"That's right," I call to him as we climb out of the truck. "You were playing bodyguard last night, weren't you?"

His lip curls back in a snarl. "Don't even get me started, man. Spoiled little brat snuck past me and I spent half the night combing the city for her and her dumbass friends."

"You gotta tell Blaze we can't be taking jobs watching over spoiled rich girls anymore. What we do is bigger than that," I tell him as we meet at the back of the truck and he nods. One of the other businesses we run is a P.I. business and recently, our President, Blaze, has been thinking about adding security to that but the clientele we've gotten so far has been less than desirable.

"Yeah, but as Blaze reminded me when he heard me bitching about it this morning, the spoiled rich girls pay the way for the girls who really need our help."

I sigh. "Well, shit..."

"Exactly."

Never Let Me Go

Fuzz drops the tailgate and I reach for the first box when my phone starts ringing. I offer him an apologetic look but he brushes it off as I step back and dig the phone out of my pocket. My gaze drops to the screen and I sigh.

Tawny.

Just the sight of her name has me feeling exhausted and irritable. Shaking my head, I silence it and grab a box out of the truck as Fuzz shoots me a look.

"You going to get that?"

I shake my head. "Absolutely not."

"Everything okay?" he asks, his brow arching in question. I don't even get a chance to answer before my phone starts ringing again and I grit my teeth as I roll my eyes.

Goddamn it.

"Dude, just answer your damn phone if you need to."

"No," I tell him as he grabs a box out of the back of the truck. "It's just Tawny."

He throws his head back and barks out a laugh as he turns away from the truck. "Pretty sure we all told you not to go there, brother."

"Yeah, well, surprise surprise, I didn't listen."

"We got another Crazy Courtney situation on our hands with this one?" he asks as he knocks on Sammy's door and I shudder at the memory that name invokes before shaking my head.

"Naw. I don't think so."

The door swings open and Sammy offers us a timid

smile as she scans the parking lot before stepping back and allowing us to pass her. Good. It's smart of her to not let her guard down. That is how she will stay safe. "Thanks for your help today, guys, and I'm sorry for the inconvenience. You can just set stuff down wherever you find room."

"Don't mention it, Darlin'," Fuzz says as he sets his box down on top of two other boxes. "We're happy to help. You decided about the job at the shop yet?"

She forces a smile to her face and grips the back of her neck as she shifts from one foot to the other. "Um… no, not yet. Do you need an answer right now?"

I shake my head. "No. Take all the time you need."

"I… I want you to know how much I appreciate everything y'all have done for me and I don't want you to think I'm ungrateful. I just don't know…"

"Hey," I say, cutting her off and taking a tentative step toward her. "Don't worry about us, okay? Our only goal here is help you get back on your feet in whatever way we can."

She nods, her teeth sinking into her bottom lip as tears well up in her eyes. "I'll never be able to thank y'all enough. You saved my life and I promise I'll let you know as soon as I can."

I offer her a reassuring smile before glancing over at Fuzz as he claps his hands together to break up the subtle tension in the room.

"All right. Let's get the rest of your stuff in here so we can get out of your hair."

He heads toward the door and I nod in her direction

as I follow behind him. She retreats further back into the apartment as we walk out and when we reach the truck, my phone starts ringing again. I brace my hands on the tailgate and let out a heavy sigh as Fuzz chuckles.

"Might as well just answer it, brother. Doesn't seem like she's going to stop."

With another heavy sigh, I pull my phone out of my pocket and stare at the screen for a second before silencing it and shoving it back in my pocket. Whatever she wants, I don't have the energy to deal with it right now. Fuzz laughs as he grabs a box out of the back of the truck.

"Oh, you're going to pay for that one, Moose."

Before I can even respond, my phone starts ringing again and Fuzz's laughter disappears into the apartment.

"For the love of God," I growl as I dig the phone out of my pocket and think about how satisfying it would be to chuck it across the lot. If it was in a thousand damn pieces she wouldn't be able to call me incessantly anymore. Sighing, I press the green button and press the phone to my ear.

"Hello?"

"Hey there, stranger," she purrs, trying her best to sound alluring and all it does is make the fantasy of smashing my phone even more appealing. "I've been trying to get ahold of you."

I nod as Fuzz walks up to the truck and grabs another box. "Yeah, I noticed."

"Why didn't you answer my calls?"

"I'm kind of busy right now, Tawny," I growl as I plop down on the back of the truck, trying not to sound like an asshole. From the time I learned to talk, my mama ingrained good manners into me but there's no way in hell I'm apologizing to Tawny for ignoring her calls. Because one, I'm not really sorry and two, the last thing I need is Tawny getting any big ideas about the two of us. Before she and I started hooking up a few months ago, she tried her hand with most of the other guys in the club because Tawny's number one goal in life, at least at the moment, is for one of us to make her our old lady. My brothers warned me to stay away, that she was more trouble than the easy lay was worth, but like an idiot, I didn't listen and now I'm in a mess. She's getting more attached each time I call her up for a late night booty call and as nice as she is, I'm bored to fucking tears every time I'm with her.

Fuck.

That makes me sound like a real asshole but it's the God's honest truth.

"Oh. Well, do you have any plans tonight? Maybe I could come over and we could get some dinner?"

I pinch the bridge of my nose as I take a deep breath and think it over. Do I really want to spend another night listening to her go on and on about whatever drama she and her friends have gotten into since I've seen her last? Absolutely not but it seems better than spending the night alone on my couch while I think about how fed up I am with almost every damn aspect of my life these days. Then again, it is time to end this thing between us and even the thought of getting her under me isn't doing much for me anymore. In the beginning this was fun but now it's more like a damn chore. "I already have plans tonight."

"With who?" she asks and I don't miss the note of jealousy in her voice.

Shit.

This has gone too far already.

"The club."

"What about this weekend? There's this new Thai place I really wanted to try."

"I'll be in Miami for the club." Thank fuck, Blaze decided to assign this run to me. It's the perfect excuse to get out of a weekend of torture.

"Oh, that sounds fun. I haven't been to Florida in ages. Maybe I could go with you?"

I shake my head, relieved that I actually have a valid excuse for why she can't go no matter how tempting she might look in a bikini. "Sorry. It's club business."

"What the hell? I really need to talk to you, Moose."

I grit my teeth. I've asked her more times than I can count to use my real name but she continues to call me by my road name despite the fact that we've been sleeping together for months. "About what?"

"Well, I was hoping to talk to you in person..."

"Then, it's going to have to wait until after I get back," I tell her as Fuzz comes to retrieve the last two boxes. God dammit. Now I feel like an asshole for not helping him like I should have been.

"I don't want to do that either. Maybe you could get out of your thing tonight and meet up with me?" she whines and my phone smashing fantasy resumes. "Please. It's really important."

"Jesus Christ, woman. Just tell me now."

She sighs. "Okay... It's about us..."

"Tawny," I growl, the last band on my patience threatening to snap.

"No, just listen. I know when we started sleeping together, it was just fun but I've developed feelings for you and I think you and I could be really good together. I want you to give us a chance."

Fuzz walks back out to the truck with a questioning look on his face and I let him know it'll be another minute. He nods and slips behind the wheel to give me a little privacy.

"I'm sorry, Tawny, but I'm not on the same page as you."

"Oh," she whispers. "Well, maybe just take the weekend to think about it and then we can talk when you get back."

Fuck.

Am I really about to break up with this girl over the damn phone? My ma would skin my damn hide if she ever found out but then again, what choice do I have? I either do it now, over the phone, or I string her along for a few more days and do it in person which sucks just as much. I go back and forth in my mind, trying to decide which option is less cruel before sighing.

"No, I think it's best if we just call it quits now. My mind isn't gonna change in three days. You're a nice girl but we've run our course."

Silence greets me on the other end of the line, stretching on for so long that I pull the phone away from my ear to make sure she didn't hang up on me.

"Tawny?"

"Fuck you, Sawyer Michelson," she snaps and I can hear the tears in her voice. "You're going to fucking regret this."

The line goes dead and I sigh as I stand up and slip my phone back in my pocket before closing the tailgate and rounding the back of the truck.

"That sounded like it went well," Fuzz says, a grin on his face, as I climb in the truck and I shoot him a glare.

"Yeah, it was great. Her parting words were "You're going to fucking regret this" so I'm really looking forward to finding out what the fuck that means."

He barks out a laugh as he starts the truck. "Jesus, dude. You have the worst luck with women but don't worry, I'll keep an eye out for psycho blondes and tranquilizer darts."

"Fuck you, dude," I growl, remembering the disaster of a relationship that gave me my road name.

Shit.

Now that I think about it, I really do have an awful track record when it comes to women. For whatever reason, the ones I pick always turn out to be fucking

77

A.M. Myers

crazy and they fuck up my life time and time again but I never seem to learn. As we pull out of the parking lot, I shake my head and promise myself that I'm done with girls all together until I can get my shit together and pick one that isn't absolutely insane.

Never Let Me Go
Chapter Six
Juliette

Leaning back against the headboard, I stare out at the water as the sun begins creeping over the horizon, casting pastel shades of blue and pink across the sky. Gavin was right. The view from these windows in the morning is reason enough to buy the place. It's magical - even if I don't recognize a single thing in the expansive three thousand square feet of the apartment. My eyelids start to droop and I yawn as I wipe the sleep from them. After tucking my box of memories under the bed last night, I tossed and turned for hours before falling into a restless sleep. Confusing dreams of faceless people and vague places haunted me all night long and I feel like I barely slept. Yawning again, I throw the covers off my legs and swing them over to the side of the bed with a sigh. As much as I want to get some more sleep, I'm afraid it would just be more of the same.

My gaze flicks back to the water for a moment before I push myself off the bed and grab the blue satin robe hanging on the foot of the bed. It feels luxurious as I slip it onto my skin and I can't help thinking about how much my life has changed in the five years I've lost. When I was living with Mercedes, I liked the finer things but I was still in college and I was concerned with making my trust fund last as long as I could so they were occasional splurges but as I look around this apartment, luxury and money is all I see. A dull throbbing pierces the back of my head and I sigh as I cinch the belt as I wander out of the bedroom and into the hallway.

"Morning," Gavin says, looking up from his tablet as I stumble into the kitchen, yawning. He's all dressed up in a dark blue suit that makes his eyes pop like crazy and his hair is combed back again, that reckless bad boy look giving way to a devastating man. He commands all my attention and I stop short next to the island, unable to take my eyes off of him. Even with no knowledge of him or our relationship, I have to admit there's something about him that intrigues me.

"Morning." I turn away to hide my blush and scan the countertop for a pot of coffee. The clean, minimalistic look carries into the kitchen and I can't spot a single appliance in this place except for the refrigerator. "Is there coffee?"

I glance over my shoulder. Smirking, he points to a second cup sitting on the island next to him, steam rising from the rim and I sigh in relief before flashing him a thankful smile. He turns back to his tablet as I round the island and sit next to him. Warmth seeps into my skin as I wrap my hands around it and bring it to my lips, breathing in its rich aroma with a hum.

"How did you sleep?" I ask, glancing over at the couch and he laughs as I turn back to him and our eyes meet. He seems well rested and more carefree this morning.

"It's surprisingly comfortable." Reaching out, his eyes soften as he brushes a lock of dark hair out of my face and heat rises to my cheeks. "How did you sleep?"

I shrug. "Okay, I guess."

"So what you mean is, you slept like shit."

"I would ask you how you know that but you already seem to know everything about me," I muse as I bring my cup to my lips and take a sip of my coffee. It's exactly as I like it, reminding me again how unbalanced this relationship and my life is right now.

"That's what happens when you live together, sweetheart."

I nod, taking another sip of coffee. "I just wish I knew anything about you."

"Baby," he whispers, setting his cup down to turn to me and cup my cheek in his large hand. "You do know things about me and you're going to start remembering more. Just be patient."

"I don't like being patient," I mumble and he throws his head back with a laugh. Peeking up at him, I fight back a smile as the sound of his laughter washes over me. Maybe I don't remember him and maybe I don't remember anything about our life together but I can't deny that there is something here.

"See, I learned that little tidbit on the very first night we met. I asked for your number, you gave it to me and told me that you had no patience. You said if I tried doing that stupid thing where I made you wait three days before I called you, you'd block my number and never speak to me again."

I hide my face behind my coffee cup as I fight back a smile. "God, I sound like a terror."

"No, baby. It was incredibly sexy. So sexy, in fact, that I could barely wait until the next morning to call," he answers, his eyes sparkling as he turns toward me on his barstool and pulls me closer. "I think I started falling in love with you that first night."

"I wish I could remember."

He brushes his thumb over my cheek. "You will. Oh, and before I forget, I got you something."

"You did?" I ask. He nods as he turns back toward the counter and grabs a phone.

"It's not anything big but your phone was destroyed in the crash and I thought you'd like to be in touch with the real world again."

He hands it to me and I stare down at it for a second, searching for a way to turn it on but nothing happens. I glance up at Gavin as he grins.

"Swipe up on the screen."

I do as he says and a lock screen pops up on the phone, prompting me for my password. I look to him again.

Never Let Me Go

"Your birthday."

Nodding, I enter the code and smile when the phone unlocks, revealing a gorgeous photo of the view out of my bedroom windows at night. Scanning the home screen, I notice the eighteen unread texts and fifty missed calls before my gaze lands on the one hundred and fifty-three unread emails.

"Oi," I whisper as I set it down on the counter. Gavin chuckles as he stands up from his barstool.

"I guess that's what happens when the boss bails out on work for three weeks."

I nod, eyeing my phone. "Guess so. Maybe I should get back to work."

"Absolutely not," he growls, stepping up next to me and wrapping his arms around me. "You need to rest and recover. Nico is handling business while you're away so I don't want you worrying about a thing."

"Yes, sir," I mumble, feeling relieved that I don't need to focus on running a business I don't know anything about. He leans down and presses his lips to the top of my head before taking a step back.

"I have to run into work for a little over half the day but then I'll be back here with you."

"Okay... um, what exactly do you do?"

He grins as he slips his phone into his pocket. "Investment banking. It's very exciting."

"Sounds like it." I lean back on the barstool and take a sip of my coffee. His gaze drops to my lips for a second before he checks his watch and sighs.

"I've got to get going. You want me to bring

anything home for dinner?"

Meeting his gaze, I shake my head. "Whatever you want is fine with me."

"Okay." He leans in and plants another kiss on my head. "I'll see you later, baby. I love you."

I watch him leave before turning back to the counter and sighing as I set my coffee cup down. My phone stares back at me for a second before I scoop it up and unlock it. I have no idea what I'm looking for but there has to be something that can help me remember on here. A couple dozen apps litter the screen and I scan over them before choosing the easiest option.

Facebook.

My hand shakes as I tap the button and the newsfeed loads on the screen in front of me. I suck in a breath as I begin scrolling through the statuses, my heart pounding in my chest. After everything, I need something familiar, something that brings me a little piece of comfort because I don't know how much longer I can go feeling like I'm alone, living in a foreign country where I don't speak the language. Fish out of water doesn't even begin to describe this turmoil rolling through me each moment I spend in this apartment, trying desperately to grasp a memory from my past. There are a few people that I recognize from high school and college but for the most part, it's just another sea of endless faces and my heart sinks.

Shaking my head, I pull up my own profile and begin scrolling through it. At the very least, I have to find something of myself that I recognize, right? My page is filled with photos of Gavin and me, dressed to the nines and out on the town. I look really happy in the photos so there is that but I don't see very many photos with girlfriends or any of just me. I'm always with him. Do I not have friends here in Miami? No, that can't be right. There were so many people in my newsfeed that I didn't recognize. Surely some of them are friends of mine. Right? I go back to the newsfeed and scroll down, discovering name after name of people I've never met but none of them seem to really *know* me. Are they business acquaintances? I guess it's possible... Nico did say the company is doing very well but it's still overwhelming to see how much of my life has been wiped away. It's only been five years since I moved to Miami but it feels like my life is in the process of being ripped in half. Which side do I belong on, though?

I toss the phone across the countertop with a sigh, watching as it skids to the edge before standing up and grabbing my empty coffee cup. Rounding the island, I grab my phone and slip the cup into the sink before walking back to my room. The sun is out in full force now, shining through the glass and heating my skin as I pass the windows and sit down on the edge of the bed. What do I do now? I could spend some time going through the house again, looking for anything that might help me reclaim my memories but if what I saw last night is any indication, I won't find much. I've never been big on watching TV, not that I've even seen one since I've been here but like the rest of everything else, it's probably hidden in plain sight.

Sighing, I scan the bedroom again before standing up and pulling my box of photos out from under the bed. After I find a comfy spot in the middle of the bed, I open the box and toss the lid next to me. The first photo is one of Mercedes and me on our first Halloween in our apartment. She was determined to throw the most kickass party ever and we went all out. She even hired professional costume designers to turn us into authentic flapper girls. Running my finger over the photo, I remember how much fun we had that night and smile. The next photo is our second Thanksgiving together. Mercedes tried to cook a big dinner for all our friends and ended up burning the turkey. Her pouty, tear stained face in the photo makes me laugh as I set it down on the bed and pick up the next one. It's a photo I don't recognize of the two of us in our apartment, surrounded by boxes. I study it for a second and gasp. This must have been the day I moved or the night before so it was right after I went to that little country bar with Mercedes but I don't remember it at all.

Tears sting my eyes as I stare down at the photo, the magnitude of my confusion and loneliness crashing down on me. I feel like I can't breathe. I'm drowning in everyone's expectations of me, fear and this overwhelming feeling that I don't belong here. I look down at the photo again and a sob bubbles out of me. I have never felt more confused or lost in my entire life and I don't even have my best friend to talk to or guide me through this. But... why don't I? I eye the phone

Gavin gave me this morning and wonder if Mercedes' number is still in there. I could call her, couldn't I? Old me wouldn't have given it a second thought but I have no clue what's waiting for me on the other end of the line.

What if she and I don't talk anymore?

Did my move put too much pressure on our friendship?

Just the thought breaks my heart and I chew on my bottom lip as I continue studying the phone. Should I really do this? Before I can talk myself out of it, I scoop up the phone and unlock it. So what if it's been years since we last spoke and I make a total ass of myself? It's worth a shot. I need something to tether me because right now, it feels like I'm floating through someone else's life and I can't do it anymore. I need a little piece of me back. My heart thunders in my chest and butterflies flap around in my belly as I open my contacts and scroll down to M. When I find her name, I release a breath and press call. The phone rings in my ear and my heart hammers out of control.

God, what am I doing?

What if it's been years since we talked?

What if this whole thing is horribly awkward and I'm truly all alone in this strange world? What will I do then?

My hand trembles at my side and I consider hanging up.

Shit.

"Hello?"

A.M. Myers

My heart jumps into my throat. "Mercedes?"

"Hey, Jett," she answers, using my old nickname from college and it settles a piece of my soul. I sag back against the headboard as relief rushes through me. "What's up?"

I open my mouth to answer her but I don't even know where to begin.

"Is everything okay?"

"No," I answer, releasing a breath. "Not really… I need to ask you a weird question."

"Shoot, babe. You know you can ask me anything."

I nod, taking another deep breath as my pulse slowly returns to normal. "When was the last time we spoke?"

"Like two weeks ago, remember? You told me all about the wedding plans. God, I'm so excited to come down to Miami and see you again," she practically squeals. "It's been way too long."

"How long has it been?"

"What?"

I grab a pillow and hug it as I stare out at the ocean. "How long has it been since we've seen each other?"

There's a pause on the other end of the line and I hug my pillow tighter as I wait for her reply.

"What's going on, Juliette?"

I want to answer her but I need to know how much she's still involved in my life and if she can help me. "Just answer the question first. When was the last time we saw each other?"

"I came down there right after Christmas to

celebrate your engagement. Why don't you remember that?"

Closing my eyes, I let out a breath I didn't realize I was holding and nod. Okay, three months ago so that means we're still close.

"What the hell is going on, Juliette? And you better answer me because I'm one more awkward silence away from calling my pilot."

"I missed you," I say, fighting back a smile at her "take no shit" attitude. I may not remember this house or the man I'm engaged to but the woman on the other end of the phone is exactly the same as she was five years ago.

"Juliette," she warns and I open my eyes as I gather the courage to tell her everything that has happened over the past two weeks.

"I was in a car accident…"

She gasps and something crashes in the background. "When?"

"Two weeks ago."

"And you're just now telling me? What the hell, woman? What happened?"

Tears well up in my eyes again as I stare out at the ocean. "Apparently, my dad and I were driving by his house and someone ran a stop sign and t-boned us."

"Oh my God, are you guys okay?"

"No," I answer, my lip wobbling as tears begin dripping down my face. All my defenses crumble, brick by brick. "He's gone. My dad didn't make it."

"Oh, honey," she whispers, her voice thick and it

amplifies my own heartbreak. When we lived together, Mercedes kind of adopted my dad as a second father and they always had a special relationship. A soft sob hits my ear and her tears trigger my own as I think about my dad and the fact that I'll never see him again. "You're okay though, right?"

I shake my head. "Not really. I was in a coma for a week and when I woke up, I couldn't remember the last five years."

"What?" she gasps and I drop my head back as the tears fall faster, a barrage of pain slamming into me like waves crashing against the shore. Hearing the words out loud, saying them to someone else, makes them even more real. In this apartment, with just Gavin and me, it's easy to get swept up and forget that my life is falling apart around me. Or maybe I'm just compartmentalizing so I don't completely lose my mind. I don't know. But I guess that is kind of the point - I don't know anything. "What's the last thing you remember?"

"I clearly remember going out to that country bar to celebrate my big move and then the next thing I remember is waking up in the hospital four days ago."

"Jett," she breathes. "That was five years ago."

I nod. "I know."

"Jesus... I don't know what to say, honey."

"There is nothing to say," I whisper as I look out at the ocean again and wipe the tears from my face. "It is what it is."

"Wait... are you living in the apartment with

Gavin?"

I nod. "Yes."

"And you don't remember him?"

"Nope," I answer, sucking in a stuttered breath as my tears begin to slow. Closing my eyes, I remember waking up in the hospital four days ago and being told I had a fiancé. It still doesn't feel real despite the fact that I have this massive rock on my finger and I'm living in the same apartment with the man.

"Shit. Are you okay? How is Gavin handling all of this?"

My eyes snap open. "Why would you ask me that? Do you have any reason to believe that he wouldn't be anything other than a gentleman?"

"No, of course not, Jett. I'm just worried sick about you. What can I do to help?"

"I don't know."

She sighs. "I think I could move a few things around and fly down there in a day or two."

"You don't have to do that, Mer," I answer, fighting back the urge to beg her to hop on a plane right now. As much as I want that, I'm sure she has a life back in Baton Rouge. I can't just expect her to drop everything and run to my side.

"No, you need me. Especially if you can't remember anyone in your life there. You need to be around people that love you and can actually help you."

The thought of her coming here makes my heart drop and as I stare out at the water, the apartment we shared pops into my mind again.

"No, wait."

"What?"

I sigh and massage my temple. "I don't want to be here in Miami."

"So what are you going to do? Run away?"

"As you just mentioned, I don't recognize any part of my life and I'm living with a man I don't even know with no family or friends that I remember."

"Okay…"

"I want to come home, Mer." As soon as the words are out of my mouth, a kind of peace settles over me and I know it's exactly what I need to do. The doctor told me I can't drive for a while but I can pack a bag and head to the airport. My thoughts drift to Gavin and my chest aches. It really isn't fair of me to run out on him but I can't stay here anymore. Mercedes is right. I need to be in a place I recognize with people that love me and the longer I stay in this apartment, the more out of place I feel. "I don't know if I'll be able to catch a flight today but I'll look into it and call you back."

"Wait! Don't go buying anything just yet."

I scowl as I stare out at the water. "Why not?"

"Because I'm not too crazy on the idea of you hopping on a plane all by yourself when you don't remember anything from the last five years."

"Okay, so what's your plan?"

"Shit," she hisses. "I have something I can't get out of or I would just fly down there today and pick you up."

I roll my eyes as I lean back against the headboard

again. "I think I can manage to take a flight all on my own, Mer. I'm a big girl."

"Absolutely not. I need to make a few calls but go pack anything you want to take with you and I'll call you back as soon as I know something."

She hangs up without another word. I pull the phone away from my ear and stare at it for a second before tossing it next to me and glancing back out at the water. The thought of seeing Mercedes and being back in Baton Rouge makes my belly flip. A smile stretches across my face and I jump out of bed, more than ready to be home.

A.M. Myers

Never Let Me Go
Chapter Seven
Sawyer

Palm trees line the perimeter of the gas station and I
resist the urge to roll my eyes as I pull my truck into the
lot. Shaking my head, I pull the truck up to one of the
gas pumps and throw it in park before turning it off and
glancing back at the offending trees. I swear, ever since
we crossed the border into Florida, all I see are damn
palm trees. It's like the people here don't even realize
other kinds of trees exist. Sure, Baton Rouge has a palm
tree here or there but nothing like this. I suppose I
shouldn't take my frustrations out on the trees but it
seems like the safer alternative.

"I'm going to run inside but I'll be quick," Cora
says as she grabs the door handle and I nod as I pull my
wallet out of my back pocket. After pulling out a
twenty dollar bill, I hand it to her.

"Would you mind grabbing me a coffee and a candy
bar?"

"Cream or sugar?"

I shake my head. "Black."

"And the candy bar? Any preference?"

"Anything with chocolate will do."

Nodding, she hops out of the truck and I watch her walk into the gas station before climbing out and prying open the gas cap. As the truck is filling up, I lean back against the side and sigh, rubbing a hand over my face. We started our thirteen-hour trip in Baton Rouge at three this morning and I swear I'm ready to crash out before driving back tomorrow. Normally, we wouldn't leave so early but in this case, it was necessary. Cora first contacted the club three months ago when a man on the cleaning staff at the company she worked for started stalking her. At first, it was harmless enough - flowers sent to her apartment and gifts left at her door but he soon made it clear that he was always watching her and she panicked. When we stepped in, we put a guard on her for a little while - just to let him know that he couldn't get to her so easily - and Rodriguez confronted him about his behavior but without much evidence, our hands were tied so Cora made the decision to leave everything behind and start over in Miami with her sister. Freddie, her stalker, works the night shift so leaving so early in the morning gave us the biggest head start before he realizes that she is gone and I'm hoping the thousand miles I have put between them today will be enough to keep Cora safe.

My phone starts ringing and I sigh as I dig it out of my pocket and check the screen. This damn thing is the other reason I'm so damn irritable today. Tawny's name flashes on the screen and I decline her call before slipping the phone back in my pocket. The day after her infamous "you're going to fucking regret this" speech, Tawny started calling me again, apologizing for her crazy behavior and begging me for another chance but there is no way in hell I'm falling down that rabbit hole again. Before she and I hooked up, I thought I wanted something real but if this is what I have to look forward to, maybe I was wrong. Then again, my brothers make it look so damn appealing.

My phone rings again and I growl as I dig the phone out of my pocket and hit the decline button. She's fucking delusional if she thinks any of this is going to work but of course, just telling her that has gotten me nowhere so I have to just keep ignoring her calls for now. It's not the best solution in the world but it is all I've got until I can get back to Baton Rouge and make things clear to her. When my phone starts ringing for a third time, I shove myself off of the truck and barely resist the urge to punch something before digging it out of my pocket. Just as I'm about to throw it across the lot, I notice Blaze's name on the screen and my body sags as I release a breath and answer it.

"Hey, boss."

"Moose," he replies. His voice is all business but I can hear the guys in the background, laughing and having a good time.

"Y'all decide to throw a party without me?"

"Naw, we're just lettin' off some steam. How are

things going?"

I nod as I watch the number tick by on the gas pump. "Good. We're about an hour outside of Miami."

"No trouble?"

"Nope. It's been a quiet trip so far, knock on wood. We got eyes on Freddie?"

He sighs. "Yeah. He just woke up and realized she's gone."

"Is he losing it?"

"Like you wouldn't fucking believe but don't worry about a thing. If he makes any moves, we'll know about it."

I nod. "Sounds good."

"Listen, I just got a call from Ali. Apparently, her boss, Mercedes, has a friend out in Miami that needs a lift back to Baton Rouge. You mind hanging out tonight and driving back with her tomorrow?"

I check my watch and shrug. "Yeah, I was planning on grabbing a hotel room anyway so it's not a big deal. Is she in trouble?"

"Not that I know of but Ali didn't know much more than I told you."

I nod, all the different scenarios running through my mind. This could turn out to be dangerous if she is in some kind of trouble and I'm out here on my own but Storm's old lady, Ali, is family and we would all do anything for her. Or any of the girls, really. In the last couple of years, most of the guys have found "the one" and put a ring on her finger before she wised up. Fuzz, Streak, and I are the only single guys left in the club and it certainly has changed the dynamic but I can't say that I mind. We are a family now in a way that we never were when it was just the guys.

"Moose? You still there?"

I nod, pushing off the truck. "Yeah, sorry. Where am I picking her up?"

"Mercedes sent me the address of a restaurant. She said she'll meet you there at midnight."

"Midnight, huh?" Certainly doesn't sound like someone who just needs a ride. "What's her name?"

"Juliette."

Cora walks out of the gas station with her hands full and I nod. "Yeah, all right. I'll pick her up and call you before we take off tomorrow."

"Sounds good. Make sure you call if you run into any trouble."

I nod as Cora stops at the hood of the truck. "Will do. Talk to you tomorrow."

We say good-bye and Cora steps closer with a smile as she holds out my cup of coffee to me. She has a plastic bag in her other hand and my stomach growls as I spot a couple different candy bars.

"Can you put the coffee in the cup holder for me?" I ask as the numbers on the pump slow. She nods and carries my drink and her bag of goodies around to the passenger side before climbing in. When the tank is full, I pull the nozzle out of the truck and grab my receipt on my way back to my door.

"How much longer?" Cora asks as I slip behind the wheel and drop my phone in the holder before bringing up the GPS.

"About an hour."

She nods and begins typing out a text to her sister on the burner phone I gave her at the start of this trip. I barely make it out of the parking lot when she sighs and shakes her head. "Gah, I hate this thing."

"As soon as you're settled, you can get a new phone but we couldn't risk him following you."

"I know," she whispers, peeking up from the phone. "He has to know I'm gone by now."

I nod. "He does."

"Is he freaking out?" she asks, her voice shaking and it sends me into a rage. Nothing in this world makes me angrier than a woman with terror in her voice and tears in her eyes. I've seen way too much of it for my liking and I wish there was more I could do.

"You don't need to worry about him anymore. We're keeping a close eye on him and you are safe."

She sighs. "Thank you again for this. I'm sure you have better things to do with your weekend than babysit me."

"Don't worry about it. We just want you to be safe."

My phone starts ringing before she can reply and I growl when Tawny's name pops up on the screen again. Leaning forward, I silence it as her gaze bores into the side of my head.

"Girl trouble?" she asks as the cab falls silent again. I scoff, my grip tightening on the wheel.

"Yeah, something like that." I glance over and find her studying me with a curious expression.

"Wanna talk about it?"

I bark out a laugh. "No."

"Oh, come on. We have to pass the time somehow and it'll be nice to think about someone else's mess for a little while… please?"

"Fine," I grumble, rolling my eyes and she claps her hands before turning to face me on the bench seat.

"Okay, start at the beginning. How did you meet her?"

Reluctantly, I start telling her all about Tawny - how we met at a clubhouse party after she'd tried her hand with a few other guys and how it was only supposed to be casual but then she started getting attached.

"You know what I think?" she asks, interrupting me and I shake my head.

"No, but I'm sure you're going to tell me."

She nods. "Yes, I am."

"Go on, then. Tell me why I can't pick a good woman."

"Oh, you're perfectly capable of picking a good woman. You just choose not to."

Turning to her, I blink in confusion as I try to process her words but she doesn't give me any time to respond.

"See, I think you want something real. I think you want the same thing your brothers have found but there's something holding you back. You're scared which is why you chose someone that you *knew* it would never work with. You sabotage yourself."

I suck in a breath and turn back to the road in front of us. "I'm not afraid of a relationship."

"Mmhmm," she hums, turning to the front of the truck. "You can deny it all you want but you know I'm right. If you truly want something real and something that will last, you have to push yourself past whatever it is that scares the shit out of you."

"How the hell did you get that I want something real from what I told you? I was only looking for something casual."

"Then why the hell did you pick a woman that made it very clear she wanted a relationship?"

I open my mouth to reply but nothing comes out. Shit. Why *did* I choose to hook up with Tawny knowing she wanted more than just sex? It was a disaster from the start and I knew it. There was always that little voice in my head telling me what a bad idea it was but the loneliness forced that voice to shut the hell up real quick.

"Now, you just need to figure out what scares you so badly about being in a relationship."

I grunt and shake my head. "It doesn't matter. I'm swearing off women until I get my shit together."

"Yeah." She laughs. "Good luck with that. I can't tell you how many people I know who have said the same thing and the next thing you know, they've met their soul mate."

"Yeah, right. I think I'd have better luck with the lottery."

She points to my face. "And you just proved my

point."

"Which point would that be?"

"That you want a relationship," she answers, looking smug. "But you're also scared to open up your heart to someone."

"What is it you do for work again?" I ask, glancing over at her. I'm certain she's not a therapist but I feel like I just got thoroughly shrinked and now I'm questioning everything I thought I knew. She laughs.

"I'm an accountant."

I scoff, shaking my head. "Maybe you should think about a career change because you have a talent."

"Naw. Girls are just better at this kind of thing. Besides, I did a whole lot of work on myself in the last year but I'm glad to see my self-help book addiction helped someone."

She starts telling me all about her massive shelf of self-help books and how each one helped her and the closer we get to Miami, the more animated she becomes. It's like watching her being released from a cage and one of my favorite things about the work we do. Each woman we help does things at her own pace but at some point, she realizes she is safe and she is free. She starts living again and I love watching the life spark in their eyes again. For some, it takes years of therapy and work but for Cora, all it took was getting away from Freddie and her life in Baton Rouge where the memories of his torment haunted her everyday of her life.

"So what is it?" she asks. Her whole body is twisted

103

in the seat so she can study me as I drive and I glance over at her with an arched brow.

"What is what?"

"The reason you're scared."

My gaze flicks between her and the road a couple times before I let out a sigh. "Let's just say past heartbreak and not take it any further."

"And now you're terrified to open up to someone again."

"Something like that," I grumble, refusing to look in her direction. The things in my past are not something I want to talk about… now or ever. "Looks like we're getting close to your sister's place."

She nods and launches into telling me about some other book she thinks might really help me but I keep my gaze focused on the road in front of me, fighting back painful memories. By the time we pull into her sister's neighborhood, she has run out of things to talk about but her leg bounces like crazy and she squirms in her seat, the excitement almost too much to bear.

"When was the last time you saw your sister?" I ask as we pull up in front of a cute little coral colored cottage near the beach.

"Almost two years ago. It'll be so nice to reconnect with her."

I nod as I put the truck in park and open my door. The front door of the cottage swings open and a woman who looks identical to Cora steps outside and runs down the sidewalk as Cora jumps out of the truck. They crash together, wrapping each other up in a tight hug as

Never Let Me Go

I round the back of the truck and pull Cora's bags out of the bed. As I set them on the sidewalk, Cora's sister glances up at me with tears in her eyes and beams.

"You must be Moose. Thank you so much for taking such good care of my baby sister," she says, releasing Cora to shake my hand and I nod.

"Just call me Sawyer, Ma'am, and it was my pleasure."

"It's nice to meet you, Sawyer. I'm Lana and thank you again. I've been so worried about her with that psycho running around," Lana says, wrapping her arm around Cora's shoulders.

"Like I said, it was my pleasure."

"Excuse me if this is rude but are you sure he didn't follow you? Does he even know she's gone yet?"

I nod. "We stopped for gas about an hour ago and I spoke to my president. Freddie knows she's gone but y'all don't need to worry about a thing. If he starts heading your way, we'll know about it and beat him here."

"Okay," she whispers, uncertainty lighting up her eyes for a moment before she blows out a breath and shakes it off. She turns to the bags before gasping and spinning around to face me again. "You should stay for dinner."

"Oh." I shake my head. "Thank you but I really should get going."

"I insist," she urges, grabbing onto my arm and I glance at Cora, who shrugs. As nice as a home cooked meal sounds, I'm afraid if I get too comfortable, I'll just

105

pass out wherever I land. I gently pull my arm from her grasp and shake my head.

"No, that's all right. I don't want to intrude and I'm sure y'all have a lot of catching up to do."

"Besides, I'm sure he'll want to get some sleep. He's been up since three this morning," Cora adds and I nod, wondering if it would be possible for me to catch a nap in my truck before I have to go pick up Juliette. Lana frowns.

"Well, okay. If you're sure…"

I nod. "I am but thank you for the offer. It was very kind."

Lana nods before turning to grab the bags and I glance at Cora.

"Stay safe and remember, if you ever need anything, just give any of us a call. We'll keep an eye on Freddie until we're sure that he's not a threat anymore."

She nods, tears welling up in her eyes. "I know Lana already said this several times but truly, thank you. I was beginning to think I'd never feel safe again but you guys changed that for me."

"Of course." She launches herself at me and I give her a quick hug before I take a step back and hold up a hand to wave good-bye. They both inch closer to the front door of the cottage before turning back to wave.

"Drive safe!" Cora yells as I round the hood of the truck and I nod, waving to them again before climbing behind the wheel and starting the truck. When I'm on the next street over, I pull over to the side of the road and grab my phone. I'll need to get a hotel room for the night but there's no way I'll be able to wake up in a couple hours if I get into a bed. Opening the internet, I search for a secluded beach and program it into the GPS before pulling away from the curb again. It's not ideal but at least I'll be able to grab a couple hours of sleep before I need to pick up Juliette. Hopefully, Blaze was right and she just needs a ride back to Baton Rouge but, as usual, I've got a bad feeling about the whole thing.

A.M. Myers

Never Let Me Go
Chapter Eight
Juliette

My stomach churns and my throat feels tight as I wring my hands together and trek across the bedroom. The moonlight casts an eerie, blue hue over the room as it shines down on me through the wall of windows and I suck in a breath as I turn and walk back along the same path. I've been like this for an hour, at least, pacing through my room and struggling to breathe as I wait to make my move. I swear, if a pin dropped across the apartment, I'd be able to hear it and there's a fairly good chance it would make me jump out of my skin. Grabbing my phone, I pull up the text Mercedes sent me a couple of hours after I got off the phone with her this morning.

Mercedes:
His name is Sawyer and
he'll meet you at the diner down
the street from your place at midnight.

Sucking in a breath, I read the text two more times before checking the clock again. Eleven fifteen. Time to go. As I tuck the phone into my back pocket, I walk over to the little desk in the corner of the room and sink into the chair in front of it. A stack of letterhead with my company's logo greets me as I open the first drawer and I pull out a piece before grabbing a pen. My pen hovers above the page for a second before I sigh. This whole situation… it's just so fucked and me running out on Gavin in the middle of the night isn't fair but neither is expecting me to hang around here when nothing feels right anymore. I know I need to go find my memories in my own way, in my own time but it doesn't make it any easier.

After hanging up with Mercedes this morning, I spent hours going through the massive closet and packing everything I wanted to take with me before wasting the rest of the day thinking about all the things I want to do when I get back to Baton Rouge. It's weird that even though I don't remember being away, I somehow miss my city and the longer I spend in Miami, I'm wondering what it was that kept me here. Was it Dad? My company? None of it makes any sense which is all the more reason why I need to go even if I do feel guilty for what I'm about to do to a perfectly nice man. It also doesn't help that he came from work this afternoon with flowers in hand and cooked me a delicious meal that I could barely eat due to my tumultuous stomach. I got away with telling him that I didn't feel well, which wasn't as much of a lie as I thought it would be, and disappearing into the bedroom right afterward. Sighing, I stare down at the paper and shake my head as I start writing.

Gavin,
I'm sorry.

Tossing the pen down, I sink back into the chair and cross my arms over my chest. Shit. I can't just leave him that, can I? But I don't know what else to say. I am sorry that this is what I need and I'm sorry that everything worked out this way. Mostly, I am sorry that this is going to hurt him. That's not what I want to do but I don't see any other option in front of me. My stomach aches as I lean forward and grab the pen again.

Gavin,
I'm sorry... for a lot of things but most of all is that this is going to hurt you. In the time we've spent together, you seem like a good man but the trouble is, I don't know who I am anymore. I look around this apartment we shared and I don't recognize any piece of myself. I need to go figure things out on my own but to ask that you wait for me when I can't promise you a single thing isn't fair so I hope you find a way to move on with your life and be happy again. And please, don't come after me. If this is real, if you and I are meant to be together, I have faith that the universe will bring us together again.
Xoxo,
Juliette

I stare down at my words for a few seconds before setting the pen down and grabbing the note as I stand up from the chair. With my note in hand, I grab my bags and inch toward the door, listening for movement on the other side but it's been quiet for a while now. At dinner, Gavin informed me that he would be crashing in the spare bedroom at the top of the stairs until my memories came back and I was so relieved that he wasn't trying to force anything on me. I imagine it's incredibly painful for him to be in this house with me but unable to touch me like he's used to and unwelcome in his own bedroom but he never puts any pressure on me and never *tries* to make me feel bad for the way things are. Just one more reason to feel guilty about what I'm about to do.

The door creaks as I slowly pull it open and I wince, my ears straining as I stare into the darkness. It certainly looks like he's gone to bed for the night. I creep forward, trying to be as quiet as possible as I roll my suitcase behind me and clutch the note in my hand. The apartment is dark and the only sound is the soft tick of the large clock mounted on the wall in the living room. I stop in the kitchen, next to the island and set the note down before pulling my engagement ring off and laying it on top as tears sting my eyes.

I'm so sorry.

I stare at the ring for another second before turning away and grabbing my suitcase handle again. My gaze flicks to the closed door at the top of the stairs as I walk to the elevator and I silently ask him for forgiveness and understanding. But even through the guilt I feel over the hurt this is going to cause him, there isn't a single part of me that feels like leaving is a mistake. In fact, it feels like the best thing I've done since waking up in the hospital a week ago. With newfound resolve, I close the distance between me and the elevator and press the button. The doors immediately slide open and I step inside, pressing the button for the lobby. As the car begins its descent, I release a breath and lean back against the back wall. Just a little bit farther and I'll finally be on my way home again. My heart jumps as the doors open again in the lobby, revealing Carl. He glances up and his look of surprise melts away as he smiles at me.

"Can I help you, Miss Shaw?"

I smile and shake my head. "No, thank you, Carl. I'm all good."

"Going on a trip?" he asks, eyeing my bags and I glance back at the suitcase I'm pulling behind me. Should I tell him where I'm going? In my note, I asked Gavin not to try and find me but do I really expect him to do that? From the little I know about him, I don't know that I can see him as the type of man to sit idly by and just wait for the woman he loves to come back. Turning back to Carl, I force another smile.

"Just a little mental health vacation."

He arches a brow. "Somewhere tropical, I hope."

"Fiji."

"Excellent." He flashes me a smile for a second before it falls. "I meant to tell you how sorry I was to hear about your father's passing. He was a great man."

I nod, tears stinging my eyes. "Thank you, Carl."

"Of course. Will Mr. Hale be joining you on your trip?"

"No," I answer, shaking my head. "He won't be able to make it this time."

He nods and glances to the door. "Would you like me to call you a cab to the airport?"

"Thank you, Carl, but no. I have an errand or two to run before my flight."

His brows knit together as he studies me. "Miss Shaw…"

"Have a good night, Carl," I say, interrupting him as I step around him and head for the door. When I glance back over my shoulder, he is still studying me and I flash him another smile as I wave, hoping it will convince him to let it go. Finally, he shakes his head and sighs.

"You, too, Miss Shaw."

Once I'm outside, I glance back again and release a breath when I see Carl leaning over the counter as he thumbs through a magazine. Thank God. I thought he was going to blow up my plan before I even made it out of the building. When I'm out of his sightline, I pull my phone from my pocket and program the address Mercedes sent me earlier into the GPS and study the map. It's only a couple blocks down the street. Turning toward the diner, I start off down the street, hoping that I find an ATM along the way. I need to grab as much cash as I can before we leave the city so that I have a little bit of a head start before Gavin starts looking for me.

As soon as the thought hits me, my steps falter and I stop as I suck in a breath. Of course he's going to chase after me. What man in his right mind, who loves his woman, would just sit by when she breaks off their engagement via a note and runs away in the middle of the night? Especially a man like Gavin who has the means to do so. No matter how hard he tries to honor my wishes, it's only a matter of time before he searches me out and if I'm being honest with myself, I always knew that but it doesn't mean I am going to make it easy for him. I need whatever space I can get and I need to find myself, whether that is some version of the me he fell in love with or if it is this girl I see in the mirror, a weird mix of who I was five years ago and pieces of the woman I started to discover when I woke up in the hospital a week ago and it would be harder to do around him. The tension leaves my body as I release the breath I'd been holding and begin walking down the street again, feeling more confident. There's only about a thousand miles between Miami and Baton Rouge but I'll do whatever I can to buy myself the time I need to work this all out.

An ATM sign catches my attention and I rush over to it as I pull my wallet out of my purse. I slip my card into the machine and my eyes widen when it prompts me for my pin. Shit. What the hell is my pin? God, this is what I get for throwing this plan together so fast. My foot taps against the pavement as I run through important dates in my head and I whisper a curse as I key my birthday into the machine.

"Please work," I whisper. My heart drops when an error message pops up on the screen before asking for my pin again.

Shit.

Running a hand through my hair, I shake my head and key in the only other sequence of numbers bouncing around in my head - my parents' anniversary. This time the menu pops up and I smile as I press the withdrawal button and key in a thousand dollars. The machine begins to make a whirling noise and spits my money out below as a receipt prints from a slot next to the screen. I grab the cash and shove it in my wallet. I'm about to ball up the receipt and throw it away when the words from my dad's letter come back to me. Staring down at the astronomical number under account balance, I suck in a breath before quickly shoving it in my bag.

"Okay," I breathe as I pull my phone from my pocket and check the GPS again. I'm only a block from the diner and it's almost midnight so I need to get moving. Electricity zips through my body as I continue down the street, thinking about being back in Baton Rouge and seeing Mercedes again. Once I'm there, I can figure out my next move but right now, I'm just too excited to care about the small details of this plan that I didn't have time to flesh out.

The sign of the diner comes into view, boasting the best pancakes in Miami-Dade county, and I can't fight back my smile. This is it. I made it and I'm actually going home. I scan the parking lot and notice a man sitting in a parked truck with the engine running, the windows rolled down and Louisiana license plates. That has to be Sawyer. His light brown hair is falling into his face and he brushes it back with a hand covered in bright, colorful ink. The tattoos snake up his arm and into the sleeve of his black flannel shirt. He lays his head back on the seat before bringing a steaming styrofoam cup to his lips and takes a sip. A flash of metal catches my attention and I cock my head to the side. Is that a nose ring? Usually I can't stand it when men have their noses pierced but just from the side profile, it works for him... really well. Almost as if he can sense me, he turns and the bluest eyes I've ever seen slam into mine. I suck in a breath and stumble back as my heart kicks in my chest.

His gaze narrows and he studies me for a second before his gaze drops to the bags behind me and he sets his coffee cup down as the door opens. When he steps out of the truck, I begin walking again, putting one foot in front of the other without any instruction from my brain, almost as if he's pulling me into him, drawing me in with a look alone. I close the distance between us and stop in front of him, dropping my head back to meet his eyes again.

"Sawyer?" I ask and he nods as he glances down my body.

"Juliette?"

I nod and lick my lips as my heart thunders in my chest. "That's me."

Jesus Christ.

Could I possibly get anymore awkward? You would think I'd never spoken to a man in my life or maybe it's just been so long that my brain, even without my memories, has no idea what to do. Lord, what is happening to me right now? Our eyes meet again and warmth rushes through me.

"Here," he says, breaking the spell as he reaches for my suitcase. "Let me get that loaded up in the back of the truck."

I nod, mesmerized into silence as he takes my things and lifts them into the bed of the truck before turning to face me again. He shoves his hands in the pockets of his jeans, looking almost shy, as he glances up at me and I swear, my heart skips a beat. This man checks off every single "bad boy" box I could think of and even some that never occurred to me and damn if my traitorous body isn't responding like I'm still an overzealous teenager instead of a grown woman who runs her own damn company. He's not just "bad boy" though, that much is clear from our brief interaction and I tilt my head to the side as I study him, frustrated that I can't figure him out.

"Are you ready to go?"

I blink. "Uh... actually, I need to run to the bathroom first. I'll be right back."

I leave him standing by the truck without waiting for a response as I book it into the diner and find the bathroom at the back of the dining room. As soon as I'm locked in the stall, I dial Mercedes' number.

"Jett? Everything okay?"

"Um..."

She sucks in a breath. "What is it? Did you make it to the diner okay?"

"Yeah, I'm here."

"And is Sawyer there?"

I close my eyes as I picture him standing next to his truck and nod. "Yep."

"Then what is wrong?"

"Nothing," I answer, pinching the bridge of my nose as I picture the man outside. My heart thumps and I press my trembling hand to my chest. Oh, this is ridiculous. "It's just... how well do you know this guy?"

"Sawyer?"

I nod. "Yes, Sawyer."

"Well, I've never actually talked to him…"

"Mercedes," I hiss, rolling my eyes as my shoulders fall back against the wall. "You sent a stranger to drive me back to Louisiana?"

She laughs. "I mean, kind of, but you just have to trust me. All those boys in the club are top notch. You can trust him with your life."

"The club?"

"Yeah, he's in the Bayou Devils."

An image of that sexy man out there straddling a bike pops into my mind and I suck in a breath. "Jesus Christ."

"Just go with it, Jett." She laughs. "Would I steer you wrong?"

"No, I guess not," I grumble. When I was little, my mother used to say that the universe gets bored sometimes and likes to have a little fun at our expense which is why things happen to us when we're least expecting it. She liked to say that in the end, things usually worked out the way they were supposed to but that didn't mean it wasn't a huge mess in the middle so it makes complete sense that I'm wildly attracted to a man I just met only moments after breaking off my engagement to a man I can't remember. On second thought, maybe that's all this is. My life has been upside down for the past week and it's making me a little crazy. Of course.

"Is there something else?" Mercedes asks and I shake my head.

"No, I trust you."

"Good."

"All right, I'm turning my phone off for the

night but I'll text you with updates."

"You'd better," she replies. "I love you."

"Love you, too. See you soon."

We hang up and I suck in a breath before making my way back out to the truck. Sawyer glances up from behind the wheel as I step out and the butterflies in my belly take flight as I blow out a breath and slowly shake my head.

Get a grip, girl.

As I turn my phone off, I walk to the passenger side and slide my phone into my pocket before climbing inside. He arches a brow as he studies me.

"You good?"

I nod. "Yeah. I just had to call Mercedes and let her know I got here safe before we take off."

"Actually, I was going to find a hotel room for the night. I started driving at three this morning and only got a quick nap in the truck before I came to get you."

"Oh," I reply, nodding. "Of course."

"Do you have any preference?"

I stare at him for a second, my mind blank, before shaking my head. Even if I did have a preference, I have absolutely no clue what it would be. He nods.

"Okay, then."

He pulls his phone out of his pocket and spends a few minutes on it before clipping it into the holder attached to the air vent.

"Looks like there's a decent place on the way out of town and it's next to another one of these." He points to the diner and flashes me a wry grin. "I'm dying to try the best pancakes in Miami-Dade county

120

after staring at this sign for the past hour."

I nod, breathless. "It would be damn near criminal to leave Miami without putting their claim to the test."

"Or you could just tell me if they live up to the hype," he says as he backs the truck out of the parking space and pulls out onto the road.

"And rob you of the experience? I think not." Truthfully, I have no idea how good or not the pancakes are because I can't recall if I've ever even seen one of these diners but that's not something I want him to know. I'll admit that I briefly considered filling him in on my situation, especially after Mercedes' "you can trust him with your life" comment but it's nice that he doesn't know. I can be around him and not put on an act or wonder who he expects me to be. It's a breath of fresh air after a week of living someone else's life.

He scoffs and peeks over at me. "Figures."

Fighting back a smile, I sink into my seat and turn to stare out of the window as we drive through the streets of Miami. A little piece of me hopes the city will bring a memory back but as we ride to the hotel in silence, my mind is still as blank as the day I woke up in the hospital. When we reach the hotel, Sawyer parks in front of the office and leaves the truck running to run inside and get us a couple rooms while I power on my phone and send Mercedes a quick text to let her know we're spending the night in a motel. As soon as I know the message was delivered, I turn my phone off again without waiting for her reply. Earlier today, before Gavin even got home from work, I turned off my location and spent hours online figuring out how to turn off the "Find my iPhone" app but I still don't want to take any chances of Gavin finding me before I have a chance to figure some things out.

The door to the office swings open and Sawyer stalks out with a scowl on his face before stomping over to his door and yanking it open. I arch a brow and study him as he climbs behind the wheel and lets out a heavy sigh. He mentioned that he has been up and driving for almost twenty-four hours now and I can see that catching up to him pretty quickly.

"So apparently," he growls. "There's some big convention thing in town and they only have one king bed left."

"Okay…" What exactly is he suggesting? That we share a bed? Heat creeps up my neck as I think about lying next to him in bed.

"We can try somewhere else if you want?"

I shake my head to clear my thoughts and sigh. "No. If there's something going on in town, I don't think we'll have much luck anywhere else. Besides, it's getting really late."

"True," he answers, nodding his head. He runs his hand over his face as he sighs. "Okay, I'll be right back."

He leaves me in the truck as he runs back inside and after a few moments, he walks back out with a key in his hand before driving us to our room around the back of the U-shaped building. Once we're parked, he hands me the key before rounding the back of the truck to grab our bags. I unlock the door and step inside as I look around. As far as motel rooms go, it is average with a large king-sized bed in the middle of the room, a couch against the adjacent wall, and a round table with two chairs in front of the window next to the door. My gaze falls on the couch again and I scoff. Sawyer is a big guy and there is no way in hell he is going to fit on that tiny little couch.

"How is it looking in here?" he asks and I glance over my shoulder as he walks into the room and sets the bags down. He is so close that the scent of his cologne envelops me and I turn back to the room as I close my eyes and take a deep breath. God, he smells good. It is subtle but an incredibly masculine scent that makes me think of things I should not be thinking right now when my life is such a damn mess.

"Not great."

"I'll take the couch." He steps up next to me and his arm brushes my shoulder. Sucking in a breath, I peek over at him as my belly does a little flip.

"It's way too small for you."

Meeting my gaze, he smiles - this cocky but still kind smile that does all sorts of crazy things to my insides.

"I'll make it work."

I nod, unable to break eye contact with him. My heart thunders in my ear and my skin tingles as I turn toward him, once again my body moving without permission. His brows knit together and his lips part as he faces me, his gaze dropping to my lips before falling further to the curve of my neck.

"We…uh," he says, his voice deeper and full of gravel. "We should get some sleep. I was planning on getting an early start tomorrow."

Releasing a breath, I nod. "Right."

He takes a step back and looks at the floor, killing the moment and I suck in a breath as a blush creeps up my cheeks. I turn to my suitcase and grab the handle before turning back to him and pointing to the bathroom.

"I'm just going to go change."

"Yeah, okay… me, too."

We stare at each other for a second before I force myself to walk away from him and roll my suitcase into the room. As soon as the door is closed and locked, I brace my hands on the edge of the sink and glance up at my reflection. For a week, the girl looking back at me has been a stranger and even though that's still true, she looks lighter. There's no confusion in her eyes or stress on her face because away from Gavin, I have the freedom to take my time figuring out who I am now - memories or not. I flash myself a smile as I push off the counter and open my suitcase. My pajamas are sitting on top - a pair of soft cotton shorts I've had since college and a white tank top. Biting my lip, I peek over my shoulder at the door and consider finding something else to sleep in. When I packed this morning, I had intended on being alone or with Mercedes when I wore this and the shorts are, admittedly, on the little side but before I can overthink it too much, I strip off my clothes and slip into my pjs before throwing my dark hair up into a messy bun.

Turning back to the mirror, I press my hands to my belly and rise up on my tiptoes to check the length of the shorts. They hit me at the top of the thigh but as I spin to check the back, I'm happy to see that none of my ass is hanging out. I turn back to face the mirror with a shrug and ruffle the bun on top of my head until it looks cute. As I'm inspecting myself again, I stop and shake my head. Crap. Why do I even care if I look cute for this guy? I'm certain that my attraction for him is nothing more than a week full of confusion and heartache urging me to seek out something uncomplicated because that is what I need right now. Sighing, I close up my suitcase and turn toward the door.

"Are you decent?" I call out and his light, husky laugh sends a rush of warmth sweeping through my body.

"Yeah, darlin'. I'm decent."

I step out of the bathroom and he looks up from where he's sprawled out on the couch in a pair of mesh shorts and a wife beater. More tattoos decorate his tan skin and his large muscles bunch and flex as he moves. His gaze immediately drops to the bronzed skin of my thigh and his lips part as one brow shoots toward his hairline. I can feel his eyes as he slowly drags them back up to my face and when we connect, the look he flashes me makes me feel like I'm on fire. I've never felt sexier than I do right now in some of the oldest, rattiest clothing I found in my closet.

Okay…

So, maybe there is something more to this than I thought.

"Uh… so I was, uh, thinking we should try to get out of here around seven and that should get us back to Baton Rouge around eight or nine."

I nod. "Sure."

"'kay." He nods and our eyes meet across the room. My heart is pounding so damn hard that I'm certain he can hear it on his side of the room and when his gaze falls to my chest, I suck in a breath. God, I can't even imagine how good it would feel to kiss him but I sure as hell want to find out. No. What am I

125

thinking? This is the last thing I need right now.

"Goodnight, I guess," he says, cutting off my thoughts and my head jerks in agreement as I turn toward the bed and pull back the covers. When I was in middle school, I had this huge crush on this boy named Johnny but every time I tried to talk to him, I ended up tripping or mumbling or stuttering. Basically, I was a mess and there is something about Sawyer that makes me feel the exact same way. Maybe it is just because of everything I've been through recently or maybe it's more. Honestly, I don't know but I'm not going to figure it out tonight, that's for damn sure.

As I climb under the covers, I peek across the room. His back is facing me now and I wince at the position Sawyer is curled up in as he tries to fit his large frame on the miniature couch. Sighing, I glance to the other side of the bed before turning back to him.

"Sawyer?"

He glances over his shoulder at me.

"You look miserable over there."

Scoffing, he turns to face me. "You saying that just to rub it in how much this is going to suck for me."

"No." I giggle, shaking my head and he cracks a hint of a smile. "Come sleep on the other side of the bed."

"Are you sure?"

I nod. "You stay on your side and I'll stay on mine. We're both adults. I think we can handle it."

"Only if you're sure…"

"I am," I answer and he releases a breath as he tries to roll off the couch but ends up falling to the floor with a loud thunk and a grunt.

"Thank fucking God."

Never Let Me Go

I laugh as I watch him lumber to his feet and round the bed. As he climbs under the covers, I turn away from him and curl up on my side. He flips the lights by the bed off and when he's settled, I look up at the ceiling and mentally try to tell the butterflies in my stomach to shut the hell up.

"Goodnight, Juliette," he whispers and my heart skips a beat.

"Goodnight, Sawyer."

A.M. Myers

Never Let Me Go
Chapter Nine
Juliette

A horn blares through the room, piercing the morning stillness and jerking me from the first night of restful sleep I've had since waking up in the hospital a week ago. My mind screams in protest, trying desperately to pull me back into peaceful dreams and I'm just so damn warm and cozy that I might give in. Humming at the comfort surrounding me, I snuggle into my pillow and throw my arm over my ear to block out the noise but it's persistent, demanding I heed its call.

"No," I moan, trying to fall so far into the bed that I disappear. "Make it stop."

Something between a groan and a hum greets me in return and my pillow, or what I thought was my pillow, moves underneath me. I jerk up in bed, blinking to clear the sleep from my eyes as I glance down at the bed. Sawyer cracks his eyes open and our gazes meet. My lips part as I suck in a breath, the situation crashing down on me as a blush creeps up my cheeks.

Oh my God…

"So much for you staying on your side of the bed, darlin'," he quips as a sly grin stretches across his face and he reaches over to the nightstand to grab his phone and turn off his alarm. Silence descends on the room and I groan again as I drop my face into my hands. I'm going to die of embarrassment. His soft chuckle pierces through my imminent demise and I move my fingers to peek out at him. My cheek is still warm from where it was pressed against his chest and my fingertip traces over the indentations left from his shirt.

"I'm sorry," I squeak and he laughs again. The sound is rich and warm. It's the kind of laugh that immediately puts you at ease and makes you yearn for more, the kind of laugh that will have me doing all sorts of stupid things just to hear it again. With a sigh, I drop my hands into my lap and stare at him, unable to look away as he throws one hand behind his head and lays the other over his taut stomach. Even through his wife beater, I can see the definition of his muscles and my mouth waters.

"Hell, I'm not," he replies, looking up at me with a shit eating grin. "Been a long time since I woke up with a gorgeous woman in my arms so I'm certainly not going to complain."

My lips part as I suck in a breath. "You think I'm gorgeous?"

"I do have two functioning eyes and twenty-twenty vision so…yeah."

"Oh," I whisper as I drop my gaze to the comforter. My heart races out of control in my chest and my cheeks burn. If it really was five years ago and a man like Sawyer told me I was gorgeous, I would have flirted with him without a second thought but now... I have no idea what to do or who to be.

"What? No compliments for me?" he asks, moving the hand on his stomach to cover his heart. "I'm hurt. Is it my hair? Does it look like shit in the mornings?"

He ruffles a hand through his hair before trying to comb it all over to one side and I laugh despite the butterflies trying to escape from my belly. Pushing it all down, I summon a little piece of that girl I was five years ago and give him a little shove before turning to swing my legs over the edge of the bed.

"You're all right, I suppose," I fire back, peeking back at him as I fight a smile. "But I need to go get ready."

He laughs. "Yeah, all right. I'll load up the truck while you're getting ready and we'll hit that diner before we take off."

I nod and push off the bed before grabbing my bag and slipping into the bathroom. When the door is locked, I turn to the mirror and stare at my reflection again as my heart rate slows to a normal level and my cheeks go back to their usual tan color. Good Lord, what is going on with me? I've never felt anything like this in my life and I can't decide what is real and what is just a result of this crazy situation I'm in.

"Be rational, Jules," I whisper to myself as I shake

my head. I met the man a total of seven hours ago and most of that time was spent asleep so there is absolutely no way in hell that I actually feel anything for him. Do I think he's cute? Hot, even? Absolutely and I do think he is kind for agreeing to this plan in the first place but that's it. Except I don't know if that's true…

There is this nagging feeling that I'm finding harder and harder to ignore telling me that this time is different. But then again, I can't remember the past five years of my life so what the hell do I know? Sighing, I drop my head for a second before meeting my gaze again. I can't keep doing this. If this whole thing is going to work, if I'm going to get the answers I so desperately need, I have to follow my heart and just do what feels right. Even if that means flirting with a man I just met. I can't fight it anymore and I have faith that someone out there has a plan for me, that all of this is happening for a reason.

Confident in my conclusion, I nod to my reflection and turn to my bag before opening it and pulling out a pair of dark jeans and a casual t-shirt. It's cute but perfect for sitting in a truck all day long as we make the drive back to Baton Rouge. Once I'm dressed, I fix my hair into a cute messy bun and throw on some mascara and lip gloss. Satisfied with my look, I pack everything back into my bag before stepping out into the room again. Sawyer is sitting on the edge of the bed, looking at his phone and he glances up.

"Ready to go?"

My stomach growls as if on cue and I laugh as I

nod. "I think that's a yes."

"Let me take your bag," he says, reaching for the duffle in my hand and I pass it to him. As we head for the door, I feel his hand at the base of my spine, gently guiding me out of the room and for some reason, it makes me feel so safe. He's literally got my back and I feel like nothing bad will happen to me as long as he's around. Well, hell... I guess Mercedes might have been onto something when she called the club. When we get to the truck, he opens my door for me and I flash him a smile as I climb inside.

"I'm just going to do one last sweep of the room, okay?" he asks and I nod. He sets my bag in the back of the truck before heading back into the room. I dig my phone out of my purse and consider calling Mercedes while I sit in the truck but decide to wait until we're about to leave. Surely Gavin has found my note by now and I don't want to risk him finding a way to track me down before I even make it out of the city. What would I even say to him if he did track me down? It's not like I can go back to that apartment and pretend to be his fiancée with no memories. Thoughts of him finding the note and the ring on the kitchen counter this morning fill my mind and my teeth sink into my lip as I wonder how he took it. Was he angry? Did he understand why I need to do this? I'm sure that either way he is hurting but I just hope he will be able to see my logic and look at this situation from my perspective. The door to the truck opens and I jump as it jerks me out of my thoughts. Sawyer's brow arches as he slides behind the wheel.

"You okay?"

I nod. "Yeah."

He studies me for a second before nodding in agreement and starting the truck. The engine rumbles to life, sending vibrations from my feet all the way to my chest and I sigh as I lean my head back against the seat as he pulls out of the parking lot. The sun is just starting to peek up over the ocean, casting hues of pink and purple across the sky as we drive down the street in our quest to consume the best pancakes in the county. Sawyer pulls the truck into the parking lot and I scan the area. There are a few cars in the lot but it's empty for the most part which isn't surprising since it's barely six thirty. I press the back of my hand to my lips as I yawn and Sawyer chuckles.

"Not a morning person?" he asks as he pulls into a parking spot and I shake my head.

"Nope. Night owl. You seem...perky, though."

He barks out a laugh that makes my heart flutter. "Perky? You know... I don't know that anyone's ever used that word to describe me."

"Do they not have eyes? Or are they also unusually perky morning people?"

"Neither," he answers, his smile falling away as he drops his gaze into his lap and shakes his head. I scowl, studying him as I lean forward and place my hand on his arm.

"You okay?"

He meets my gaze. "Yeah... It's just... if I told you

what I was thinking right now, you'd think I was crazy."

"You might be surprised," I mutter under my breath. I'm certain that, right now, my story is all kinds of insane and would beat whatever he is holding back but I'm not about to tell him that.

"Yeah? Wanna tell me about it over pancakes?"

I suck in a breath as I sink back into my seat. Shit. He wasn't supposed to hear that and damn if the way he's looking at me right now isn't making me want to spill all my secrets. I shrug as I turn away from him and open the door.

"Maybe."

I hop out of the truck without waiting for him and as I walk to the front, I hear his door open and close behind me. Glancing up, I watch him as he closes the distance between us and just as I'm turning to go into the diner, he grabs my elbow. His touch is so gentle but it sets me ablaze and I take a deep breath as I turn back to him.

"If you're in some kind of trouble," he whispers, his eyes are begging me to let him in. "You can trust me. I won't let anything happen to you."

I study him for a second before nodding. "Let's go eat. I'm starving."

He nods and as we walk into the diner, he places his hand at the small of my back again just like he did at the hotel. It's insane how safe one simple little gesture can make me feel or how easy it is to be around Sawyer especially when I was with Gavin for a week and never felt at home. What does it mean though?

Hell, maybe it's nothing - one of life's great mysteries as my mom used to say. Maybe I'm searching so hard for answers about everything in my life right now that I'm looking into this too much and overthinking everything. More than ever, I wish I could remember the last five years. If I knew who I am, or who I was, then all of this wouldn't be so hard. Or maybe it would. I don't know.

"Good mornin', you two," a cheery older waitress says as we stop in front of the counter. She reaches for the menus. "Anyone else joining you for breakfast?"

I shake my head.

"No, just us," Sawyer says and she flashes us a grin. The heat of his hand seeps through my clothes and warms my skin. My body begs me to lean back into him but I manage to stop myself as she pulls two menus out of the cubby and motions for us to follow her. Sawyer's hand moves, slipping around to my waist and he pulls me into his side. I suck in a breath and his grip tightens. She leads us to a little booth in the back corner of the diner and smiles as she sets our menus down and moves out of our way so we can sit down. The table is just big enough for the two of us and as Sawyer sits across from me and lays his arms on the top, his hand skates dangerously close to mine.

"Can I start y'all off with something to drink?"

I smile up at her. "Coffee, please. Lots of cream and lots of sugar."

"You got it, sweetie," she answers before turning to

Sawyer.

"Coffee, black."

She nods and slips her notepad back into the pocket of her apron. "I'll give you two a minute to look over the menu."

"Thank you."

She flashes me a kind smile before walking away and I sigh as I pick up my menu and open it. There is a giant block smack in the middle of the menu talking all about their pancakes and the various toppings you can get. My stomach growls as I read over the options before deciding on something. When I close my menu and set it down on the table, I glance up and meet Sawyer's eyes. It's like the rest of the room melts away and it is just he and I here, lost in whatever the hell this is and even though I can't identify what this is, it feels damn good.

"You never answered my question outside," he murmurs and I scowl as I try to remember what he asked me outside. Oh...right. It's not even like I could answer the question if I wanted to. I mean, sure, I think I'm safe but the trouble is I don't know what I don't know and my stolen memories could hold a whole treasure trove of secrets. I open my mouth to reply to him before snapping it shut and sliding my chair back.

"I need to use the restroom. If she comes back to take our order, can you get me the pancakes with bananas?"

He nods, his face the picture of frustration. "Sure."

I stand up and grab my bag from the floor before

running away from the table as fast as I can without actually looking like I'm running. Weaving through the various other diners seated around the dining room, I pull my phone out of my pocket and turn it on. As it springs to life, I slip into the bathroom and plop down on the love seat positioned in one corner of the room. It is surprisingly nice and clean in here for a diner bathroom and I suck in a breath as I dial Mercedes' number. It rings in my ear and just when I think it's going to go to her voice mail, I hear a click.

"Jett?" she asks, her voice full of sleep. "Are you okay?"

I nod as my knee bounces in front of me. "Yeah, I'm good... I'm just wondering how much you told the club when you asked them to help me."

"Just that you needed a ride. Why?"

I pinch my forehead and blow out a breath. "I don't know... it's just... I don't know anything and he's asking me if I'm in trouble and I don't think I am but obviously I don't know that since I can't remember anything for five goddamn years and somebody *did* just run me and my dad off the road and I don't know how to act or who I am anymore."

"Whoa, slow your roll, girl. You're spinning out of control."

"Yeah, you're tellin' me," I whisper as I try to focus on calming myself down.

"I think the important question is how much do you want to tell him?"

I shake my head. "I don't want to tell him anything.

It's nice that I can just be around him without worrying about who I'm supposed to be now."

"Juliette... you don't need to be anything other than who you are. You've always had good instincts so follow them and just do what feels right... hold on, I've got another call coming in."

I nod as I wait for her to check her caller ID, her words churning around in my head. It's not like I didn't already know that was the answer but it helped to hear her say it.

"Uh... Jett? Why is Gavin calling me this early in the morning?"

I wince. "Um... probably because I snuck out in the middle of the night."

"And you didn't tell him you were leaving?!"

"No, I did... just not in person."

She sighs. "Explain."

"I kind of broke up with him in a note I left on the kitchen counter."

"Jesus Christ!" she exclaims and I let out a huff.

"Well, what else was I supposed to do, Mer?" I ask, shaking my head. "Do you really think he would have just let me leave?"

"Why wouldn't he?"

Sinking back into the couch, I wrap my arm around my belly. "What would you do if someone you loved, who lost all of their recent memories told you they wanted to leave?"

"All right. Fair point."

"Just don't tell him anything, okay? I know he's

probably going to find me eventually but I'm serious about figuring out who I am and getting my memory back and I can't do that in Miami."

She's quiet for a moment before sighing. "Okay. I won't say anything but you have to keep me updated. Are y'all leaving now?"

"As soon as we're done with breakfast. Sawyer just *had* to try this diner that proclaims to have the best pancakes in the county."

"Oh, I love that place. We always hit it up at least once whenever I come to visit and get the banana pancakes."

A smile tugs at my lips. "Really? That's exactly what I ordered."

"See, Jett? The memories are there and you'll get them back."

"You have no idea how much I needed to hear that," I tell her, tears stinging my eyes but for the first time since I woke up in the hospital, I feel a spark of hope that maybe my memories aren't completely lost.

"I'm glad to help but right now, I want to go back to bed."

I nod. "Right. Sorry. I'll let you sleep."

"No worries, babe. Call me from the road, okay? I've got meetings until late tonight but we can grab lunch tomorrow. What hotel are you staying at?"

"I'm not sure yet. I'll let you know."

She makes me promise to keep her updated about our trip again before we say good-bye and I sigh as I tuck my phone back into my pocket and look up at my reflection in the full length mirror attached to the wall. My renewed hope is written all over my face and I flash myself a smile before standing up and marching out of the bathroom.

Sawyer looks up from his phone as I approach our table, his brows knitted in concern. "Everything okay?"

"Yeah, sorry," I answer with a nod as I sink into my seat. "I just had to call Mercedes and let her know we're leaving as soon as we finish eating."

He nods. "I ordered for you and she said it should be up soon."

Before I can answer him, our waitress walks up with two steaming plates of pancakes. She sets mine down on the table in front of me and the aroma hits my nose, stirring up something in my mind. It nags at me, begging me to remember but it's like there is a film over the memory and no matter how hard I squint, I can't see through it.

"Here you go. Can I get you two anything else?" she asks as she sets Sawyer's food down in front of him. We lock eyes across the table before he glances up at her and shakes his head.

"No, I think we're good for now. Thank you."

Nodding, she turns and leaves us to our food. I grab the syrup from the middle of the table and pour some over my pancakes before glancing up to offer it to Sawyer. He's staring at me, his brows drawn together and his gaze intense in a way that makes me feel like he knows all my secrets and like he wants to eat me alive at the same time.

141

"Syrup?" I whisper, my heart thundering in my chest as my skin prickles with awareness. He nods, not taking his eyes from mine as he takes the dispenser from my hand. When he looks away to coat his pancakes, I breathe a sigh of relief but as soon as he's finished, he's looking at me again.

"What?"

He shakes his head. "I'm still waiting for an answer to my question."

"Which question is that?" I ask, dropping my gaze to the table as I buy myself a few more seconds. He sighs.

"Are you running from something... or someone?"

I scowl. "No. Why would you think that?"

"It's kind of my job to think that. The Devils - we do a lot of work with battered women and children, domestic violence situations and things like that so I have to ask."

"No." I shake my head. "It's nothing like that. I just wanted to go home to Baton Rouge and Mercedes didn't want me traveling alone."

"Smart," he replies as he grabs his fork and cuts into his pancakes. "What brought you down to Miami?"

I shrug as I grab my cup of coffee and take a sip. "It's complicated."

"Well, lucky for you that you've got my undivided attention for the next thirteen hours then, huh?"

"Okay," I breathe, seeing no way to get out of giving him at least some kind of explanation. "So, I was born in Baton Rouge and we lived there until I was nine

142

before we moved to Miami. I ended up going to school back in Louisiana but wanted to be closer to my dad so I moved back here about five years ago."

"So why are you leaving now?"

I suck in a breath as tears sting my eyes. "My dad passed away a little over two weeks ago."

"Oh, Juliette," he breathes, my pain mirrored in his eyes and I can't look away. "I'm so sorry."

I nod. "Thank you."

"What about your mom? Is she back in Baton Rouge?"

"No," I whisper, shaking my head and dropping my gaze to the table. "She died when I was nine which is what prompted the first move to Florida. Mercedes is pretty much the only person I have left and this place..." I look out of the window and sigh. "It just doesn't feel like home anymore."

He reaches across the table and takes my free hand, giving it a squeeze. My heart skips a beat and I meet his eyes again. "I can't say that I understand what you're going through but I'm so sorry."

"Thank you," I whisper and he nods.

"I don't want you to worry about a thing, okay? I'll get you back home safely and... just, you don't have to feel alone, either. I know I just met you last night but if you ever need *anything*, you've got me. Okay?"

I suck in a breath, my heart pounding in my chest as I nod. Just like before, the rest of the world falls away as I stare into his eyes and I can't help but feel like there's something more going on between us. Beneath the seemingly normal conversation and heated looks, lies so much more and if I shut out all the noise,

143

turn off my mind, and just listen to my heart like Mercedes told me to do, I have to admit I'm excited to find out what it is.

Never Let Me Go
Chapter Ten
Sawyer

"Good morning, sleepyhead," I call to Juliette as she begins to stir in the passenger seat. She groans and throws her arms over her head to stretch, huffing in annoyance when they hit the roof of the truck. Bending her body, she finds a new position and her shirt rides up her belly, showing off soft, tan skin and my grip on the wheel tightens as I suck in a breath and turn back to the front door of the little burger joint right off the interstate I'm parked in front of. As soon as we climbed in the truck after breakfast, she was out like a light. In fact, I don't even think I made it on the interstate before her cute little snores were filling the cab. Not that I mind all that much. Turns out she talks in her sleep and that combined with the faces she was making as she dreamed kept me pretty entertained. "Hungry?"

She perks up and looks around. "Yeah, I could eat."

"I've been staring at billboards of this place for the

past ten miles. That sound good?" I ask, peeking over at her. She inspects the front of the building and nods.

"Yeah," she answers around a yawn before flashing me a smile. God, she's fucking gorgeous. I mean, I knew that as soon as I laid eyes on her in that diner parking lot last night but the more time I spend with her, the more beautiful she becomes. Not to mention, that her unwillingness to talk about herself and her past is driving me up a fucking wall. Most girls I meet can't wait to tell me all about themselves and their past and it's cliché as fuck but the air of mystery surrounding her turns me on.

"God, I can't believe I slept so long."

I smirk. "To be fair, you did warn me that you weren't an early bird."

"Actually, I haven't been sleeping all that well lately and I think it all just caught up with me." Her eyes are full of pain as she turns away from me to stare out of the window and my heart seizes in my chest. I hate that sadness in her eyes.

"What's keeping you up at night?"

She shakes her head. "Just can't get my head to shut up some nights."

I study her for a second before nodding and turning the truck off. As much as I want to ask about her comment, if our breakfast conversation taught me anything this morning, it's that she has her secrets and she has no intention on revealing them to me. Fuck. That just intrigues me even more though. I know it hasn't even been twenty-four hours since I met her but the urge to help her and keep her safe is stronger than I've ever felt and I can't do that if she won't open up to me.

My phone rings and I sigh as I dig it out of my pocket. Blaze's name pops up on the screen and I show it to Juliette.

"Why don't you run inside and grab us a table? I've got to take this."

She nods as she grabs her bag and opens the door of the truck. "Sure. Want me to order you something to drink?"

"I'll take a Coke," I answer and she nods again before hopping out the truck. As soon as she closes the door, I accept the call. "What's up, boss?"

"Just checkin' in. How's the drive?" he asks as I watch Juliette walk around the truck to the front door of the restaurant, my gaze glued to her ass as it sways with each step she takes and I imagine gripping her hips and pulling her into me.

"Good. We're just outside Gainesville now and stopping for lunch."

"Everything go well with Cora yesterday?"

I nod as she slips into the restaurant. "Yep. She's safe and sound with her sister. We still got an eye on Freddie?"

"Oh, yeah." Blaze laughs. "Boy is straight up losing his shit over Cora."

"Has he made any moves?"

Blaze scoffs. "Besides sitting outside her old apartment and talking to a few of her neighbors, no."

"I guess it's good we moved her stuff out in the middle of the night then."

"Yeah," he agrees. Juliette meets my gaze through the window as a waitress leads her to one of the booths along the windows and I nod to let her know I'm almost done.

"What do you know about Juliette?"

"Mercedes' friend?" he asks. "Nothing more than I've already told you. Why?"

I shrug. "I don't know. Just get the feeling that she's running from something."

"We talked about this, Moose. You gotta stop searching for danger in every scenario and live sometimes. I appreciate your dedication to the club's mission but I don't want it taking over your life."

"Yeah," I sigh. "I hear you, boss."

"Hold on." His voice drifts away from the phone for a second. "Oh, for the love of God... Streak wants me to ask you if she's as hot as she looks online."

"He looked her up?" I growl, my chest burning. I swear to God, I'll rip that little fucker limb from limb if he tries anything with her. "Tell him..."

"Goddamn it," Blaze says, his voice fading. "I'm not a goddamn secretary."

"So," Streak cuts in. "Is she hot?"

"None of your fucking business," I snap and his laughter fills the line.

"I'm gonna take that as a yes, Moosey-boy," Streak says and I shake my head. "Maybe I should introduce myself once y'all get to town."

"Over my dead body."

"Streak, get the fuck out of here," Blaze snaps and Streak's laughter fades away as Blaze sighs. "Is this what I think it is?"

I scowl as I watch her look over the menu. "What are you talking about?"

"Well, you sound pretty damn possessive…"

"It's not like that."

"Mmhmm, that's becoming a real common phrase around here and you see how it all worked out for them." I'm reminded of what Cora said yesterday as we finished our trip into Miami and the more I think about it, the more I know she's right. I do want something real like what my brothers have found but I've been burned before and I'm not sure how to let someone else in. Except since meeting Juliette, I keep thinking that I could try. Shit. It's crazy to think about since it hasn't even been twenty-four hours since we met but I've seen how fast some of the other guys in the club have fallen so I know it's not impossible. "How long has it been?"

"How long has what been?"

He sighs. "Since Molly."

"A while," I answer, gritting my teeth. Just the mention of her name and it feels like the clouds have filled the sky and blocked out all the light. It's been a while since I thought of Molly and now I wish I hadn't. "Listen, I've got to get going but I'll keep you updated."

He reluctantly agrees before saying good-bye and as I hang up, I open my door and step out of the truck, trying desperately to shake off thoughts of a darker time. It has been six years since Molly walked out of my life but the pain and destruction she left behind still haunts me.

Shaking my head, I walk into the restaurant and my gaze lands on Juliette. The last thing I want to be thinking about when I'm with her is my ex. She glances up and our eyes lock as she smiles and waves me over. Like magic, as I close the distance between us, the sun begins to shine again, peeking through the dark clouds and banishing my issues with a flash of brilliant light.

"I was about to eat without you," she teases as I slide into the booth across from her.

"I'm sorry that took so long. Blaze wanted updates on the drive and the girl I dropped off yesterday."

She shakes her head. "I was just teasing. She hasn't even come to take our drink order yet."

As soon as the words are out of her mouth, the waitress walks up and stops chomping on her gum long enough to flash me a flirty smile. "Hey there, darlin'. Can I get you something to drink?"

"We'll both have a Coke," Juliette snaps before I can say anything and I turn to her, biting back a grin as she glares at the waitress. I can feel the waitress's gaze trained on me as I keep my eyes locked on Juliette, waiting for her to get the hint but she seems a bit slow to catch on. Juliette glances at me before turning her attention back to the waitress and clearing her throat. "Two…Cokes… please."

"Be right back," she mutters as she rolls her eyes

and walks away. When she's out of earshot, Juliette makes a noise of frustration and slaps her hand against the table.

"So fucking annoying."

"You seem jealous," I say, fighting back a grin at the fire dancing in her eyes. Fuck. Why does the thought of her being jealous over me make me want to beat my chest like some kind of goddamn caveman? She scoffs.

"No, it's nothing like that." She glances away for just a second but it's long enough to tell me that she's lying. "I just hate it when people are rude."

I nod. "Mmhmm."

"So, this girl you were helping yesterday," she says, playing with the frayed corner of the menu. "Why was she coming down to Florida?"

"This guy started stalking her back in Baton Rouge and she needed to skip town before things got too intense."

She narrows her eyes, studying me. "Do you guys deal with things like that a lot?"

"I guess, yeah. More than we'd like to and definitely more than we should need to but we've been on a mission to help those who can't help themselves."

"Why, though?" she asks, shaking her head. "I mean, don't get me wrong, I think it's amazing but it's a lot to handle and y'all don't have to do this."

"It is a lot but we all have our reasons for why we do this. Each one of us has experienced the horrors of domestic violence in one way or another and now we just want to do our part to help."

She stares at me for a second before looking at the table and shaking her head. "Do you wanna hear something crazy?"

"Sure."

"I have to keep reminding myself that we haven't even known each other for twenty-four hours because when I'm around you it just feels so easy. I feel like I could talk to you about anything."

I nod, wondering why she feels she needs to be cautious around me and hold herself back. "You're not the only one feeling that way."

"So if I ask you why it is that you do this work, would you tell me?" She looks up at me with hope in her eyes and a blush staining her cheeks as her teeth sink into her full bottom lip. It's a tantalizing picture and I find myself fighting the urge to tell her my entire life story.

"Maybe someday," I answer instead.

She flashes me an adorable pout. "But not today?"

"No, not today."

Before she can reply, the waitress walks up to the table and practically slams our drinks down in front of us. Juliette and I stare at each other with wide eyes as she rips her notepad from her apron and gives us an expectant look.

"What do you want to eat?" she asks, practically snarling at us. A defiant look flashes in Juliette's eyes as she reaches into her purse and yanks her wallet out. I watch in amazement as she pulls out a hundred dollar bill and slips out of the booth before bringing her thumb and middle finger to her lips. A loud whistle pierces the air and the restaurant falls silent, every single patron and employee staring in our direction as she climbs up on the seat and waves the money in the air.

"This goes to anyone who wants to take over our table and give us *polite* and *professional* service."

"What the fuck?" the waitress hisses as I hide my smile behind my hand. A murmur ripples through the crowd but I can't take my eyes off Juliette. She's fucking magnificent. Another waitress sets a stack of plates down on the counter and steps out into the dining room. Our waitress turns to her with a death glare. "Seriously, Kitty?"

Kitty shrugs. "My kid needs braces."

"This is bullshit," she whispers, turning away from our table and shoving Kitty with her shoulder as she passes her. After she disappears into the back, everyone else turns back to their meals as the chatter resumes and Juliette sits across from me again.

"I'm so sorry about that, y'all. Robyn can be…"

"A bitch?" Juliette provides and Kitty laughs.

"Well, yeah. What can I get you two to eat?"

Straight ahead of me is a glass door that leads into the gas station connected to the restaurant and I smile.

"Actually, let's get out of here."

Juliette turns to me with a scowl. "Why?"

"I have an idea. Just trust me," I say. She studies me for a second before nodding and handing the hundred dollar bill to Kitty who starts shaking her head.

"I can't accept that. I didn't do anything."

Juliette grins and forces the bill into Kitty's hand. "Sure you did! You made Robyn go away and that's well worth a hundred dollars. Well... ninety-five dollars once you take out the cost of our drinks."

"I..." Kitty snaps her mouth shut and shoves the bill into her apron pocket. "Thank you."

She turns and heads back into the kitchen as we stand up and I hold my hand out to Juliette as I flash her a grin. After grabbing her bag, she slips her hand into mine and a feeling of peace settles over me as I lead her into the gas station.

"What are we doing in here?" she asks, scanning the small store.

"Finding food."

We walk through the aisles, holding hands and grinning as we grab chips, sandwiches, drinks, and candy before carrying our haul up to the cashier and dumping it all on the counter. He rings us up and tosses everything into a bag before handing it over to me. Once we've paid, we walk back out to the truck and I release Juliette's hand to lower the tailgate.

"Ta-Da," I say and she laughs.

"What am I looking at?"

I set the bag of food down. "A picnic... on the side of the interstate."

"A picnic?" she asks, arching a brow at me and I shrug.

"Or we could go back inside and let sweet Robyn wait on us."

She stares at the door of the restaurant for a moment before grabbing my hand and climbing in the bed of the truck. As soon as she's situated, I climb up behind her and start passing out our food.

"So," she prompts as she unwraps her sandwich. "What do you do when you're not out saving women?"

"I work at the club's bike shop."

"And that's your dream job?" she asks before taking a bite of her sandwich and I tilt my head from side to side.

"Kind of... I'd really love to build custom bikes and restore old ones."

She nods. "That's really cool and it sounds like something you could easily incorporate into the work you already do. Would your president be on board to add another aspect to the business?"

"I think he would be but I haven't asked."

"Why not?" she asks and I sigh as I grab a chip, popping it into my mouth as I look up at the interstate.

"I don't know... not good timing, I guess."

"That's bullshit," she proclaims. I whip my head toward her and narrow my eyes as she covers her hand with her mouth. "I'm sorry. That probably sounded really bitchy but in my opinion that's just something you tell yourself to feel better about the fact that you haven't gone after what you want."

I flinch at her honesty as I clench my fists. "What do you do then if you've got all the goddamn answers?"

"I run my own company," she answers, challenging me with her gaze to be rude to her again and I suck in a

155

breath and let it out before running my hand through my hair.

"Shit. I'm sorry."

She nods. "It's okay. I'm sorry if I was harsh but I meant what I said."

"Understood," I say, nodding in agreement. "What does your company do?"

"I'm a jewelry designer."

My eyes widen as I look up at her. "Yeah? Anything I would have heard of?"

"You been buying a lot of nice jewelry lately?" she asks, arching a brow before she drops her gaze to her food. I laugh and shake my head.

"Uh... no, not exactly."

She shrugs. "Probably not, then."

"That's cool, though," I reply as I lean back against the side of the truck bed. "I'd love to see some of your designs."

Meeting my gaze, the corner of her lip twitches. "Not today."

"Touché."

"You know about art?" she asks as she mirrors my pose, leaning back against the side of the truck, and studies me. I shrug.

"A little bit. My mom is an artist."

"Yeah?" She sits forward, her eyes lighting up. "What does she make?"

"All sorts of things - pottery, jewelry, paintings, sculptures... the list goes on. My dad built her a little shop in their backyard and she's got it full to the brim with stuff."

She grins. "That's so cool. Does she sell her stuff anywhere?"

"Yeah. She's got a little table at the artists market on the weekends. Does pretty well for herself actually. Not that she cares. She's a total hippy - all about the joy of creating."

"She sounds a lot like my mom," she replies, sadness creeping into her tone and I reach over to grab her hand. She blinks and her gaze meets mine, almost as if she was pulled from her memories by my touch.

"What was your mom like?"

A wistful smile tugs at her lips as she looks over my shoulder. "Amazing. She was a musician, a business woman, and like I said, a total hippy but to me, she was just the woman who tucked me into bed at night, danced around the kitchen with me while we baked cookies, and told me everyday that I could do anything I dreamed up. She always urged me to reach for the stars. My dad always says that she would light up any room she walked into and people just adored her."

"Oh, so that's where you get it from," I whisper and her gaze snaps to mine as tears gather in her eyes.

"Thank you for saying that."

I nod. "I meant it. There's something special about you, Juliette. I'd have to be blind and stupid to not see it."

"Funny," she muses, her gaze flicking over my face like she's trying to memorize me and my heart pounds in my chest. "I was just thinking the same about you."

157

A.M. Myers

Never Let Me Go
Chapter Eleven
Juliette

"I'm bored," I whine, scrunching up my face as I
lean forward and turn the music down. Sinking back
into my seat, I turn to the window. We've been back on
the road for a few hours now but my ass hurts from this
seat and I can only stare at the trees along the side of
the road for so long before I lose my mind. Sawyer
laughs, drawing my attention back to him with the
warm, addictive sound.

"Is there something you'd like me to do about
that?"

I flash him a grin. "Let's play twenty questions."

"Oh, God," he groans as he throws his head back
and rolls his eyes. Arching my brow, I cross my arms
over my chest and pin him with a look. He may be
perfectly content with not talking as he drives us back
to Louisiana but since I'm not able to turn my phone on
and I didn't think far enough ahead to bring a book with

me, I need him to help entertain me. Glancing over at me, he sighs. "Fine, but no stupid questions."

"And what exactly constitutes a stupid question?"

"What's your favorite color?" he asks, imitating a typical teenage girl voice as he grabs a lock of his hair and twirls it around his finger. I throw my head back and laugh.

"What's your sign?" he continues. "What's your favorite food? Shit like that."

Once I get control of my giggles, I nod and meet his gaze as I try to make my face serious, giving him a mock salute. "Got it. No stupid questions and absolutely no fun will be had in this truck."

"You're lucky I'm driving and can't do anything about that comment," he growls through the grin on his face and my heart thunders in my chest as the heat builds in his eyes. From just one look, I'm imagining myself stripping naked in front of him and letting him have his way with me. My nipples pebble and warmth flushes over my skin as I clamp my lips together, pretending to be thinking of my first question.

"Okay," I whisper before clearing my throat. A question pops into my mind and I flash him a smile. "If everything in your house had to be one color, what color would you choose?"

He glances over at me with wide eyes before shaking his head. "You sassy little shit."

"What?" I ask, trying my best to look innocent as I fight back laughter. "It wasn't one of your banned questions. Answer, please."

"It absolutely was one of my banned questions!"

I shake my head. "No, I remember clearly. You said I couldn't ask you your favorite color and I didn't."

"Semantics," he scoffs and I bite my lip to keep my laughter at bay.

"Not really. It would actually be a smart idea to not pick your favorite color. I mean, if you had to stare at it all day long everywhere you went, you might get sick of it so that's why you would choose..."

"Like a gray-ish blue, I guess," he grumbles and I can't help but laugh as I reach across the cab and nudge him. He shakes his head. "What?"

"You can totally tell that your mom is an artist just from that answer."

He scowls at me. "How?"

"Most guys would say gray or blue but you got real specific."

"My turn," he replies, ignoring my comment and I roll my eyes as I nod. "Name a cheesy ass song that you have memorized."

"Oh, this one is easy," I say as I turn toward him more and start singing. "*Maybe it's intuition, but some things you just don't question, like in your eyes I see my future in an instant and there it goes, I think I found my best friend...*"

"What the hell is that?" He laughs, looking at me like I've lost my mind but also... kind of like he likes it.

"Are you kidding me?" I exclaim, trying my best to look horrified through the silly grin on my face. I feel weightless each time he flashes me that grin of his and it feels impossible that we just met because talking to him is so easy and feels so right. "It's "I Knew I Loved You" by Savage Garden. Classic nineties love ballad."

He shakes his head. "You and I listen to very different music from the nineties. I like good stuff."

"Hell no. You can't judge it before you listen to the whole thing," I say as I grab his phone and look up the song. As the music begins playing, I hold the phone up above my head and sway back and forth as I sing the lyrics again. When the chorus hits, I clench my fists and really sell it. "*I knew I loved you before I met you, I think I dreamed you into life. I knew I loved you before I met you, I have been waiting all my life.*"

"All right, I think that's enough," he says, grinning as he grabs the phone from my hand and shakes his head. He turns the music off and glances over at me. "Your turn."

Keeping in theme with my first question, I flash him a mischievous look. "If you could only eat one food for the rest of your life…"

"Nope," he interrupts. "Ask something else."

"Come on," I urge and he shakes his head, looking amused but the look in his eyes tells me he's not going to give in. I sigh. "Okay… If you found a suitcase full of money, what would you do with it?"

"Give it to the club so we could help more people."

I tilt my head to the side as I study him. Most people would choose taking it to the police or keeping it for themselves but I really like that he would choose to help others. My thoughts drift to the amount of money currently sitting in my bank account. Maybe once we get to Baton Rouge, I can donate some money to the club. Back when I was in college, I remember hearing stories about how the Devils had turned things around and it's nice to see that they were true.

"Is it my turn?" he asks, pulling me out of my thoughts and I nod. "What are you thinking right now?"

"I was thinking about the stories I used to hear about y'all back when I was in college. When we lived in Baton Rouge when I was kid, the way people talked about the club… they were terrified. You'd never catch certain people on that side of town but I love how much has changed and I'm kind of overwhelmed thinking about all the girls you've helped."

"I get that way sometimes, too," he replies. "It'll hit me out of nowhere how many lives we've had a hand in saving and it makes the ones we couldn't help just a little bit easier to bear."

"Have there been a lot?" I ask, reaching across the truck and laying my hand on his arm. He glances down at it before sucking in a breath.

"No, not a lot but more than we'd like." Sadness and regret clouds his eyes as he stares out at the interstate, almost like he is somewhere else right now and I want to do something to help him.

"I think it's my turn to ask another question."

He glances over at me and offers me a grateful smile. "Shoot."

"Where would you rate yourself as a kisser on a

scale from one to ten?" I ask and his brows shoot up as a slow smile stretches across his face, all hints of pain gone.

"You been thinking about kissing me, sweetheart?"

I shake my head. "No. Who said that? I just asked if you were good at it."

"Mmhmm. Well, I've never had any complaints," he says and I roll my eyes as I cross my arms over my chest. My eyes fall to his mouth for just a moment before meeting his eyes again but from his wide smile, I know he caught me.

"That doesn't mean anything. Maybe all the girls you kissed before were just polite and didn't want to hurt your feelings."

"Maybe," he muses, his gaze flicking between me and the road. "Guess you'll just have to test it out yourself to really know for sure."

Heat rushes to my cheeks and goose bumps break out along my flesh. "I suppose so."

"Now it's my turn." He flashes me a wolfish grin and butterflies flap around in my stomach as I nod. Oh, God. What is he going to ask? "What are your three favorite places on your body to be kissed?"

My lips part and I suck in a breath as a shiver works its way down my spine. Without warning, an image of him leaning in and pressing his lips to my neck fills my mind and I squirm in my seat. "You're going to go there?"

"Oh, no, darlin'. You went there, I'm just following along." He arches a brow in challenge and I stare at him, debating my answer as I chew on my bottom lip. Even though I started our conversation in this direction, a mix of emotions run through me as I drop my gaze to my lap. The more time we spend together, especially in this truck, the more I like him. My mind drifts back to Baton Rouge and I remember going out to clubs with Mercedes before Rick and I started dating. I always felt a little bolder around her so I summon a little bit of that now as I meet his gaze with a smirk.

"I guess you'll just have to find out for yourself."

He grins, his gaze falling down my body before quickly returning to my face and a slight blush stains his cheeks. Well, hell. Who would have guessed I could make the biker blush? "I'm really looking forward to that."

"Okay," I breathe, my cheeks heating and my nipples pebbling as I turn to look out of the window in an effort to cool down. "I think it's time to change the subject."

"I've got a question for you."

I turn back to him. "What?"

"It's an important one," he teases and I nod as he pins me with a serious look. "Name your top three favorite movies."

"Okay," I say as I start counting them out on my fingers. "*Selena*, *Titanic,* and *Hope Floats*."

He scoffs. "How about a recent movie?"

"I liked *Guardians of the Galaxy*," I tell him.

"Babe, *Guardians of the Galaxy* came out a while ago."

My mind goes blank and my eyes widen as I stare at him, my heart beating out of control in my chest. Oh, God… I was so happy and caught up in our conversation that I completely forgot about the fact that I know nothing about the last five years and the fact that I'm hiding that from him. Jesus. What a fucking mess! His gaze flicks between the road and me, demanding an answer. Swallowing my fear, I turn away from him and shrug.

"I haven't been to the movies in a while."

"Hey," he whispers and as I turn back to him, he reaches across the truck and nudges me under the chin, forcing me to meet his gaze. "What did I do?"

I shake my head. "Nothing."

"Come on, Juliette. I may be a "dumb guy" but I'm not an idiot. Tell me what I said to make you so upset so I can fix it."

This man is going to be the death of me.

"Nothing," I assure him, grabbing his hand and holding it between mine. I hope he believes me because the last thing I want to do is ruin this by telling him the truth. "I promise."

He studies me for a moment before nodding. "You want to keep playing? I think it's your turn for a question."

"Actually, I think I get two now since you stole an extra one."

"Lay 'em on me, baby," he replies with a smile and I push away my past once again to focus on us. In a few hours, he'll be dropping me off at a hotel and then who knows if I'll ever see him again. I don't want to spend the last few hours I have with him stressing about everything I left behind. Not when I have him.

A.M. Myers

Never Let Me Go
Chapter Twelve
Juliette

"What kind of girls do you usually go after?" I ask, fighting back a smile as he turns to me, his brows creeping up into his hairline. What started off as twenty questions has just turned into hours of conversation and the rest of the drive has gone by in the blink of an eye. He scoffs and shakes his head as he glances across the cab.

"The wrong ones."

I arch a brow. "What does that mean?"

"Someone recently suggested that I sabotage myself." As he peeks over at me again, he looks so damn vulnerable that my chest aches.

"Is it true?"

He shrugs. "They might have been on to something."

"Why do you think you do that?" I ask, studying his face as he scowls. It breaks my heart to think about him stopping himself from being happy because of some kind of pain in his past. After a second, he glances over at me and forces a grin to his face.

"Well, if I knew that…"

"No," I interrupt. "Don't do that. If you don't want to tell me, that's fine but don't lie to me."

"The way you call me out on my bullshit should be infuriating but I just can't seem to care with you…" He shrugs as his words fall away and I grin at him as I tilt my head to the side.

"It's a gift."

He laughs before his face turns serious. "I don't talk about this kind of stuff with anyone but I feel like I can tell you anything."

"You can," I whisper, reaching across the cab to grab his hand. He glances down and smiles as his gaze flicks back to the road. It's quiet for a few seconds before he sucks in a breath.

"A couple of years after I joined the club, I met Molly; she was putting herself through college by working at a bar downtown and I was smitten from the first moment I laid eyes on her. I asked her out and to my surprise, she said yes. It didn't take long for me to fall in love with her. Everything between us was so good, you know? And after dating for nine months, I decided I was going to propose to her."

Oh, no.

The pain in his eyes hits me right in the chest and I squeeze his hand.

"I went out and spent weeks finding the perfect ring

and finally I stumbled across it in an antique shop. On the night I was going to pop the question, I came home and found a note on the kitchen table and all her stuff was gone."

Guilt swarms me as I think about the note I left Gavin only yesterday. "What did the note say?"

"Just that she couldn't do this anymore. That's the thing that haunts me the most - I have *no idea* what I did wrong, no idea how to *not* make that same mistake again."

"So you ruin things before anyone else can," I whisper and he glances over at me with a curt nod.

"Yeah, sounds stupid, huh?"

I shake my head. "No, it doesn't sound stupid. Have you ever thought that you didn't do anything wrong at all?"

"What do you mean?"

"I mean, maybe she left because of something that was wrong with her, something she needed to figure out."

"You sound like you speak from experience," he says and I shrug. "It's only fair to ask what kind of guys you usually go for since you asked me."

"Honestly?" I ask, thankful that he opened up to me a little bit. He nods.

"That would be preferable."

Heat creeps up my cheeks as I pull my hand away from his. My heart thunders in my chest as I take a deep breath and meet his gaze. "I usually go for guys… like you."

"Oh," he replies as a slow smile stretches across his face. "Is this one of those things where you say guys like me aren't good for you and you need to pick someone better?"

I shrug, avoiding his eyes as I fiddle with my hands. "In the past, guys like you haven't been good for me but…"

"But what?"

I shake my head. "Nothing."

"Oh, come on, Juliette. I've been nothing but honest with you about everything." He meets my eyes with a challenge and I sigh.

"My past is… complicated but being with you today… I don't know. It feels like I've known you so much longer than that and I don't know the right thing to say or do."

He reaches across the truck and grabs my hand. "Just be honest. You're not the only one feeling something so it doesn't matter how crazy it seems to the rest of the world if it makes sense to us."

"You feel different. This," I say, motioning between the two of us with my hand. "This feels different to anything else I've ever felt but then I remind myself that it hasn't even been twenty-four hours since I first laid eyes on you and I have to wonder if I'm losing my mind."

"If you are, then so am I."

Our eyes meet and I suck in a breath as warmth rushes through me and butterflies flap around in my belly. My heart pounds and my skin aches to feel his hand creep up my arm. The truck vibrates as we hit the rumble bars on the side of the road and he rips his gaze from mine to turn back to the road but he doesn't release my hand. City lights dance in front of us as he pulls into Baton Rouge and I smile, a feeling of peace settling within me. After rolling my window down, I lean back in my seat and let the sounds and smells of my city greet me. A different kind of warmth radiates from my chest and I sigh like I've just been wrapped up in a warm blanket. Every cell in my body knows that I'm home.

"Home sweet home," Sawyer says. I open my eyes and find him already staring at me so I flash him a grin as I nod and squeeze his hand.

"It feels amazing to be back."

He smiles. "Where are you staying?"

"Oh." I release his hand and pull my phone out of my pocket before turning it on. It comes to life and as soon as it's ready, I pull up the internet where I was searching for a hotel at a gas station along the way. It looks... not the nicest but I only have a limited amount of money if I want to keep where I am a secret for now so it'll have to do. Grabbing his phone off the stand, I enter the address into the GPS and set it back down. He studies the map for a second before turning as instructed by the automated voice.

"I don't want to be too forward," he says as we drive down quiet streets. "But given our last conversation, I'm just going to go for it. I'd really like to see you again... like, as soon as possible."

I smile, feeling giddy as I nod. "Yeah, I'd really like that, too."

"Get over here," he commands, grabbing my hand again and yanking me across the bench seat until I'm tucked into his side. My heart pounds and my belly flips as he throws his arm over my shoulder and I cuddle into his side. God, this feels so damn right. We cuddle together in a comfortable silence as we drive to the hotel and the closer we get to the ETA on the GPS, the more my chest aches. It sounds crazy but I don't want to leave him.

"Um…" he mutters as the GPS declares that we've reached our destination. The motel stretches out in front of us and I do my best not to recoil. The photos online didn't look great but I thought I could make it work. Now, I'm not so sure. Small groups of people hang around outside, smoking, drinking, and talking as music pumps through an open door. A breeze blows trash across the parking lot and up on the second floor, two people are going at it pressed up against the window while a group of guys whoop and holler from below. "No."

"No, what?" I ask, peeking up at him and he flashes me a stern look.

"There's no way in hell I'm leaving you here."

I glance back up at the hotel and suck in a breath, dread weighing me down. Staying here isn't exactly an idea that I'm fond of but with only nine hundred dollars left, the forty-five dollar a night price tag is enticing.

"I'll be okay," I assure him, sounding a whole lot

more confident than I feel. He shakes his head and pulls me tighter into his side.

"Over my dead fucking body."

"Sawyer," I prompt, laying my hand on his leg. "I can take care of myself."

He shakes his head, glancing down at me like I'm crazy. "There's no damn scenario where I leave you here alone. Absolutely not. You can come stay at my house."

"I can't do that."

"Why not?" he growls as he surveys the parking lot. I swear, the more I look at it, the worse it gets and my stomach rolls. Why can't I go stay with him? Well, there's the fact that I just met him… and I haven't been completely honest with him… "I'm not going to take no for an answer."

"Sawyer," I breathe.

"Come stay with me," he urges, his voice softer this time. "I need to know you're safe and we already decided we want to spend more time together."

I sigh and squeeze my eyes shut.

God… am I really going to do this?

"I'm not sleeping in the same bed as you."

"I have a spare bedroom," he replies, relief in his voice as he flips the truck around and starts driving away from the hotel.

"I didn't say yes, yet!"

He scoffs, his gaze meeting mine for a second before he turns back to the road. "I told you I wasn't taking no for an answer. I wasn't playin' around."

175

"Oh, no, sir! I am a grown ass woman, you don't make decisions for me," I snap and he blinks in surprise before nodding.

"Okay. I'm sorry." He pulls the truck over to the side of the road and turns to me as he cups my cheek in his hand. "Will you please come stay with me?"

My teeth sink into my bottom lip as I search his eyes for a second before nodding. "Yes."

"See? Wasn't that so much easier?" With a grin on his face, he turns back to the wheel and tucks me into his side before pulling back onto the road.

"Wait, before we get to your place, is it a bachelor pad? Am I going to find something disgusting when I walk in?"

He laughs. "No. My house is perfectly clean."

"Hmm," I hum. "I think I'll be the judge of that."

"I always keep it clean in case I need to take one of the girls we help there to lay low. It's also why I have a spare bedroom with a nice bed in it."

I smile up at him. "You went out of your way to set up a room for the girls you help?"

"Yeah. I just figure they've already been through so much that they should, at least, have a nice, safe place to sleep."

I lay my head on his chest as I stare out of the windshield, unable to wipe the smile off of my face. His heart… it's just so pure and warm and as crazy as it sounds, I'm already feeling something for him. I hesitate to call it love since we haven't known each other for that long but it's…something. Something powerful, all consuming almost. Something that fills me up and makes me feel happier than I can ever remember being and something that I'm terrified to lose. How is that possible? How can I be so attached to whatever these feelings are after only a day? It defies all logic and reason which is maybe why Mercedes told me to just follow my heart. But how could she have known that he and I would have such a connection?

"Here we are," Sawyer says, cutting into my thoughts and I blink, turning to a cute little Tudor-style brick house as Sawyer pulls his truck into the driveway. There are stones leading up to an enclosed front porch and bright flowers line the base of the house on both sides as well as adorable bay windows that I just want to spend all day reading in.

"This is your house?"

He nods, a slight blush staining his cheeks. "Yeah. Do you like it?"

"I love it," I answer, turning back to the house. It feels stately despite its small size and still manages to evoke a feeling of home in me that puts me completely at ease. Sawyer turns off the truck.

"Come on. I'll show you around."

He takes my hand and threads his fingers through mine as he opens his door and steps out, pulling me along behind him. Once I'm out of the truck, he shuts the door and leads me up the front walk as his thumb brushes the back of my hand and electricity zips up my arm. I feel lightheaded and weightless, like I'm floating along next to him and every time he glances down at me to flash me a shy smile, my heart thumps a little bit harder.

We walk up onto the porch and a piece of paper taped to the front door catches my eye at the same time that Sawyer sees it. He scowls and rips it off the wood before unfolding it. As he reads whatever it is, his face grows more irritated and I study him, my heart sinking at the look on his face.

"Everything okay?"

He glances over at me and nods as he hands me the paper. "Yeah, just an issue with… well, I guess you could call her my ex."

"You want me to read this?" I ask, staring up at him with wide eyes and he nods. My thoughts are sluggish as I try to wrap my head around why he would give a girl he just met yesterday a note from his ex-girlfriend to read. "Why?"

"Because I like you, Juliette. And I'm not about to ruin this by not being one hundred percent up front about everything."

Where in the world did this guy come from? And why the hell did just the word "ex-girlfriend" make me feel all kinds of jealous and possessive? I stare at him for a second, trying to work through my confusing thoughts and emotions, before turning to the note in my hand and sucking in a breath as I unfold it.

Never Let Me Go

Moose,

I've been trying to reach you for a couple days to apologize about our last phone call. I didn't mean anything that I said and I want to talk to you. Please reach out when you get back from your trip.

T

"Um... I, uh... I don't know what I'm supposed to say here. You don't owe me any kind of explanation..."

"I know," he says, squeezing my hand. "Remember earlier when I said I picked the wrong women? Well, she was one of them and I'm showing you this note because I meant what I said. I like you, Juliette, probably more than I've ever liked anyone and I know Tawny well enough to know that this probably won't be the last time we hear from her but I'm telling you now, nothing is happening there and it never will again. I don't want her."

"Okay..." I breathe, still unsure of what to say. "I'm not... You don't have to... We..."

He turns to me and unlaces his fingers from mine before taking my hand and pressing it to his chest. "Look, I'm not crazy, okay? I know this is happening fast and I'm sure your head is spinning just as much as mine is but more than anything I want to explore this feeling..."

My fingers flex against his chest as his heart thunders against my palm, almost matching mine in its intensity and I nod, struggling to breathe.

"Is that something you want, too?"

I nod again. "Yes."

He flashes me a brilliant smile that lights up his entire face and his blue eyes sparkle as he stares down at me and closes the distance between us, his other hand cupping my cheek as he leans down and presses his lips to mine tentatively. My entire body comes alive and I melt against him as a soft moan slips out of me. He releases my hand but I don't move it, gripping his shirt to pull him closer as his large arms wrap around my waist and pull me into his body and his tongue flicks against my lips. I give in, allowing him to take all of me as a hand slips into my hair and grabs a chunk of it. He doesn't give it a tug or use it to control me like most men but just holds it almost like he's saying that he's got me and if we fall, we're going down together.

Never Let Me Go
Chapter Thirteen
Juliette

I walk into the office of Champagne Dreaming, the blog Mercedes told me she started when I spoke to her on the phone last night and marvel at the marble floors and sleek furnishing. Not that I'm all that surprised. Mercedes has always been just a little… extra when it comes to her work and home spaces. She used to say that our apartment was a retreat so it should look like one.

"Can I help you?" a young woman with bright red hair asks as she glances up at me from behind the large oval shaped desk. I smile and nod.

"I'm here to see Mercedes Richmond."

She nods. "Your name?"

"Juliette Shaw."

"And is she expecting you?" she asks as she picks up the phone and I nod.

"Jett!"

I whirl around as Mercedes struts into the lobby, looking every bit the successful, sexy mogul she is on her way to becoming in her pale pink pencil skirt and black v-neck shirt. Her honey blonde hair hangs in waves around her face and I swear, she hasn't aged a day since the last time I remember seeing her.

"Oh my God, Mer!" I exclaim, abandoning the girl behind the desk as I close the distance between us. "Look at you! You look incredible."

As soon as I'm within her reach, she reaches out and pulls me into a hug, squeezing me tightly to her body and a wave of relief washes through me. My life may be a complete mess right now and I may not be able to remember anything since I moved away from this city but at least this, our friendship, never changes.

"Me? Look at you," she parrots as she pulls away and grips my shoulders to inspect my face. "You're fucking glowing, babe."

I fight back a smile as heat rushes to my cheeks and the kiss Sawyer gave me last night plays through my mind. Her brow arches.

"Oh, I definitely want to know what that look was all about." Her gaze drops to the bag in my hand. "Is that lunch?"

I nod. "Yeah. I stopped by Nina's and picked up our favorites."

"Oh my gosh, I haven't been to Nina's since you moved away. Let's go eat in my office," she says, looping her arm through mine as we walk into a large room with a long oval table right down the middle of one side and individual cubbies on the other side. Along the walls on either side of me are doors and windows leading to more private office spaces and at the very back of the room is an office decked out in gold.

"Gee, let me guess which one is your office," I tease and she grins at me.

"Good taste never dies, Jett."

I laugh, shaking my head at her as she leads me into the office and clears off one of the chairs for me. After handing her the bag of food, I sit down and turn to look out the window at the hustle and bustle in her office.

"This place is amazing, Mer. I'm so proud of you."

She beams at me as she passes me my sandwich. "Thank you but I want to hear about you."

"Oh? What about me?"

She shakes her head as she points a finger at me. "Don't play with me, Jett! You call me three days ago to tell me that you don't remember any part of your life and now you're sitting across from me eating lunch plus I'm certain that there's something going on between you and Sawyer and I need every single detail."

"Okay." I laugh. "What do you want to know?"

"Start at the very beginning."

My eyes widen. "Waking up back in the hospital?"

She nods enthusiastically as she takes a bite out of her sandwich and I sigh as I launch into the story, telling her how I heard Gavin's voice calling out to me but it felt like I was just floating through darkness.

"That sounds terrifying."

"It wasn't, really. It was actually kind of soothing, like falling to sleep, except for when I did want to communicate and couldn't."

She flashes me a sympathetic look. "What did you do when you woke up and there was a stranger beside you?"

"Honestly, I think I just stared at him. It was so disorienting, Mer. I mean, I knew I was in a hospital but I couldn't figure out how I got there and then trying to piece together the last thing I remembered..." I shake my head. "And then they told me my dad was dead and I was engaged to the man next to me."

"It's so crazy," she whispers. "Why do you think that night we went out to celebrate your move is where your memories cut off?"

"I have no clue. Maybe I was unhappy in Miami and I wanted to be back here."

She purses her lips together. "Yeah, maybe... So, what about when you went home? Was it better then?"

"No, just a different kind of weird."

"What do you mean?"

I explain to her how the apartment was so unlike me and my personality and all my things were tucked away in boxes in the closet and she scowls.

"What are you talking about? Your place is full of pictures and little trinkets from all the places you've travelled."

I stare at her, trying to piece together what she's saying. "No... there was nothing. It was like the whole place was devoid of life... Why would Gavin put everything away?"

"Maybe he didn't," she answers with a shrug. "Or maybe he thought he was helping."

"It just doesn't make any sense," I whisper as I take a bite of my sandwich. She brushes it off as a smile stretches across her face.

"We can figure all that out later. Tell me all about Moose."

I scrunch my nose up. "Why does everyone keep calling him that?"

"You haven't heard the story?" Amusement shines in her eyes and I shake my head. What kind of story ends with Sawyer earning the nickname 'Moose'? "Oh, Lord. Okay, the way I heard it, Sawyer was dating this girl who was cray cray, right?"

I nod, Sawyer's words about always picking the wrong woman coming back to me.

"Anyway, he realized that this chick was off her rocker and broke things off with her. Well, this bitch got it in her head that she was going to kidnap him to get him back."

My eyes widen and I cough as I choke on my food for a second. "What?"

"Right? So anyway, she showed up to a party at the clubhouse and when Sawyer went upstairs to go to bed or something, she cornered him in the hallway and shot him with a tranquilizer dart. Apparently, as he was passing out, he started moaning like an animal and the boys dubbed him "Moose"."

"Poor Sawyer," I muse, scowling at my sandwich

185

and she sucks in a breath.

"Oh my God, you really like this guy, don't you?"

Heat rushes to my cheeks as I meet her eyes and nod. "You have no idea how much."

"Wait. What happened between Miami and here? Tell me everything."

"It was instant, Mer," I tell her, my mind drifting back to seeing him in the diner parking lot as I shake my head. "Like from the moment I laid eyes on him, there was something there but at first, it was easy to push away. Then, we shared a hotel room and when we woke up the next morning, I was in his arms and God, I don't even know…"

"Jett… I've never seen you like this about a guy."

I arch a brow. "Not even with Gavin?"

"No." She shakes her head. "I mean, don't get me wrong, you were in love with Gavin and I think you were truly happy but it wasn't this look you've got in your eyes right now. What happened after the hotel?"

"We spent the day together driving to Baton Rouge and we talked… about everything. Once the conversation started, it didn't stop and for lunch we stopped at this restaurant but the waitress was so rude that we left and he made a picnic in the back of his truck."

"Stop it!" she squeals. "That is so cute."

I nod. "I know. Like how am I supposed to not like him when he's doing stuff like that?"

"Did anything else happen?"

I tell her about how he wouldn't let me stay at the

sketchy hotel and how he showed me the note from his ex when we got to the house.

"Thank God, he didn't let you stay at some gross motel. Why would you even suggest that?"

I shrug. "I only have nine hundred dollars unless I take more out of the ATM but if Gavin's looking for me, that will tip him off."

"Oh, Gavin's looking for you. I've gotten at least three calls a day since you left and he's losing his mind."

"Shit," I whisper, my chest feeling tight as I set my sandwich down. "I really hate that I'm hurting him."

"I mean, you did break up with him, right?"

I nod. "Yeah. In my note I told him I needed to go and I wanted him to move on and find happiness. I also left my ring there."

"I feel like you left a pretty clear message. If he can't accept it, that's on him." She takes a bite of her food. "Besides, the look on your face when you talk about Sawyer… it's everything."

"It's crazy, though. Right?" I ask, my cheeks burning. "I mean, I met the man two days ago."

She shrugs. "If I came to you and told you about this new man I met but the whole time, I couldn't wipe the smile off my face and my eyes were shining and you'd never seen me happier, would you think it was weird?"

"I suppose not."

"You wouldn't," she urges. "In fact, I think you would encourage me to go after it so that's what I'm doing. I think the biggest question is does Sawyer feel the same way about you?"

My teeth sink into my lip. "I think so. He told me he really wants to explore the things he's feeling and he kissed me last night."

"He kissed you and you're just now telling me?" she shrieks and my eyes widen as I glance over my shoulder to see if anyone heard her. A few people are milling around near the conference table but they don't look our way.

"Will you keep your voice down?"

"I'm sorry," she whispers, shaking her head. "But this is huge news. How was it? Sexy? Sweet? Steamy?"

I shake my head. "Life changing."

"Giiirrll," she drawls breathlessly as she falls back into her chair. "Life changing?"

"Yep." I nod and she stares at me for a second before laughing and shaking her head. I narrow my eyes. "What?"

"I was just thinking that maybe all of this happened for a reason. Like as awful as it is that you got in the accident and your dad died and you lost your memory, maybe there was a purpose in it."

I smile. "My mom would be thrilled to hear you telling me that the universe brought me here for a reason."

"I mean it," she says with a laugh. "I really think this all happened for a reason and with the way you're feeling now, can you really disagree?"

"No." I shake my head. "I can't."

"So I take it you're going to continue staying with Sawyer?"

I nod. "Yeah, for the time being."

"Well, just remember that you can always come crash at my place but I'm secretly hoping you and Sawyer fall in love, get married, and have cute little babies."

"Noted." I laugh. "What about you? How's Andrew?"

Her face falls, pain springing into her eyes. "Oh, God, you don't remember, do you?"

"What? What happened?" Back in college, Mercedes and her boyfriend, Andrew, were inseparable - the ultimate power couple - and I always assumed that they'd get married some day and have gorgeous blonde haired, blue eyed babies.

"Andrew," she says, his name sounding like a curse as it leaves her lips. "Dropped me like a bad habit as soon as he was picked up by the NFL."

My heart breaks as she fights back tears. "Oh, Mer. I'm so sorry. I wish I had known. I didn't mean to cause you any pain."

"No," she says, shaking herself as she looks up at the ceiling to dry her tears. "It's okay. You just caught me by surprise and it's been so long since I even thought of him."

"Mer," I warn, seeing right through her bullshit and she sighs.

"He was my soul mate, Jett. I still believe that and now I get to live the rest of my life without him."

I shake my head. "What a fucking prick."

"I second that."

Pushing out of my chair, I round her desk and pull her out of her seat before wrapping her up in a hug. She shudders and tears sink into my shirt for a moment before she pulls away and fans her eyes.

"God, I'm not going to do this today. I'm done crying over that asshole."

I grab a tissue out of the box on the table and hand it to her so she can fix her mascara. "I have half a mind to find his number and rip him a new one."

"Oh, you already did, Hon. The first time around. Even did it right in front of his new teammates. It was glorious." She laughs at the memory and I smile, fighting back the sadness that overwhelms me as I wish I could remember it, too.

"I could do it again. You know, as an exercise to get my memory back."

She throws her head back and laughs. "As much fun as that sounds, I don't want to give him the satisfaction of knowing how much I still love him and probably always will."

"Okay. I'll restrain myself then."

"Thank you," she says, flashing me a smile as she sinks back into her chair and I walk around the desk and sit down again. "So, what are your plans now that you're here?"

"I suppose I need to call my assistant, Nico, and see if she'll be open to coming here so we can get back to work."

She scowls. "But you don't remember anything about your company, do you? Or what designs you've already done?"

"No, but Nico has kept pretty good records and she can help me figure all that out. I need to do something other than sitting around and thinking about how much I want my memories back."

"Can we trust her?" she asks, studying me intently. "Will she tell Gavin?"

I shake my head. "I don't think so. Speaking of Gavin though, what have you told him?"

"Nothing. I either don't answer the call or when I do, I tell him that I haven't heard from you but I can tell he's not buying it." Her phone starts ringing on her desk and she shakes her head as she glances down at the screen. "Speak of the devil."

"Gavin?"

She nods.

"Answer it," I tell her and she nods again as she presses the button to accept the call before putting it on speakerphone.

"Hi, Gavin."

Even through the phone, I can hear his sigh of relief. "Hey, Mercedes. Please tell me you've heard from her."

I wave my hands to get her attention and she mutes the call as her brows knit together.

"Tell him I called you and I'm fine but you don't know where I am."

She nods.

"Mercedes?"

She unmutes the call. "Sorry, someone walked into my office to ask me a question but Jett called me last night."

"Oh, thank God. Where is she?"

"I don't know. She wouldn't tell me," she says, meeting my gaze and I nod. "But she's okay."

He growls. "I need to find her, Mercedes. She needs to come home."

"Listen, Gavin… I don't mean to step on toes here but she's been through a hell of a lot lately *and* she told me that she ended things with you when she left so I think maybe you should just let her do whatever soul searching she needs to do."

"She's not in her right mind!" he bellows into the phone and an image of him raking his hand through his hair pops into my mind. I scowl. Why would I think of that? Did he ever do that when I was around him?

"Just because she doesn't remember what's been going on over the last five years doesn't mean she's crazy. If you love her, you will respect her wishes."

Something crashes on the other end of the call. "Bullshit. It's because I love her that I need to find her. Are you lying to me?"

"All right. I've been more than understanding during this situation but now I'm done. You don't get to call me a liar and bombard me with multiple calls a day. If Juliette wants to speak to you, she'll reach out. Good-bye."

She hangs up and shakes her head as I release a

breath.

"He sounds…"

"Out of his ever-lovin' mind? Yeah, he does."

"Maybe, I should call him…"

Shaking her head, she slaps her hand down on the desk. "Absolutely not. You made your feelings clear and I just reinforced them but he doesn't care. Calling him only tells him exactly where you are."

"Do you think he already knows?"

"I think he suspects," she says. "It's the first logical place that you would go especially considering where your memory cuts off."

My teeth sink into my lip. "How long do you think before he figures it out?"

"I don't know," she sighs. "I would keep an eye out if I were you. He could already be here and coming to see me at my office probably wasn't the best idea."

Shit.

"I'll be careful," I assure her with a nod. She sighs as she looks over at the calendar on her desk.

"All right. I'd better get back to work but call me if you need anything, okay? And we'll get together again soon."

I stand and toss the trash from my lunch in the basket next to her desk. "Actually, there is one thing you could do for me."

"Name it, babe."

"I need to rent an office for my business down here."

She smiles. "Well, wouldn't you know, my tenant

upstairs just moved out."

"Here?" I ask, glancing up at the ceiling. She nods.

"Yep. What do you say? Want to see it?"

"Absolutely."

She stands and walks around the desk before linking her arm through mine and leading me back to a long hallway next to the lobby with two elevator doors. She presses the up button.

"So, the footprint of the second floor is basically the same as this and below us is the employee parking garage so you won't have to pay for parking somewhere else."

I nod as the doors slide open and we step in the car, excitement coursing through my veins. It will be so nice to get back to work, not only because I need something to do in my day but because I'm so eager to learn all about this business I've put my blood, sweat, and tears into for the past five years.

"What do you know about my company?" I ask her and she glances over at me with a wide smile on her face.

"I know you're freaking killing it and I've even seen some of your pieces on some of the upper class women here in Baton Rouge."

My eyes widen. "Really?"

"Oh, yeah. But I would expect nothing less after you got your work into a certain store that favors a little blue box."

"Are you talking about Tiffany's?" I breathe, my heart hammering in my chest and butterflies flapping around in my stomach. She nods and I press my hand to my heart. Oh my God. It's so major that I can't even wrap my mind around how much I've been able to accomplish in the five years I lost. "That's crazy."

"You should have heard your voice when you called to tell me. You could barely get the words out and you were crying. I was so proud of you."

I grin as the elevator doors slide open, revealing a sleek lobby just like the one below us. Beyond that is a set of glass doors that lead into a wide open space. Mercedes guides me over to the doors and pulls them open.

"Right now, you just have this huge open room but you can do whatever you need to do to make it work for you. I know you need room for shipping and that might be the only thing we can't accommodate here but I can help you look into other properties that might work for that."

Staring around the room, a vision starts to unfold in front of me and I can see exactly how I can make this space work. Turning back to Mercedes, I smile.

"How much?"

"For you? Three thousand a month."

My grin widens. "I'll take it."

"Yay!" she exclaims, clapping her hands together. "I'm so excited that you're going to be working in the same building as me."

"Me, too. I'm so ready to start building a life here."

"So, that's it, then? You're not going back to Miami."

I shrug. "I don't see why I would. It's not like there is anything left for me there, you know?"

"Besides Gavin," she says as she links her arm through mine and we start back for the elevator. I shake my head.

"Obviously, I can't say this for certain since my memory still hasn't come back but I don't think it matters. This feels like home and what I feel with Sawyer… it's…"

"Epic," she supplies, arching a brow as we reach the elevator and she presses the button. I laugh.

"Yeah, maybe."

The doors open and as we step inside, she releases my arm to pull her phone out. "I'm writing myself a note to call the lawyer and I'll get the rental agreement sent over to you as soon as possible. What are you thinking on term?"

"Let's go month to month for now and see what happens."

"Smart. You might hate renting from me."

I laugh. "Or I might be a terrible tenant and you'll be itching to kick me out."

"Hey, anything is possible."

We're both giggling as the doors slide open and we walk into the lobby where she wraps me up in a hug.

"Okay, I really need to get back to work but I'll let you know when all this is ready and let's do lunch again soon."

I nod as I pull away. "You got it."

"Love you."

"Love you, too."

She waves as she turns to head back to her office and I watch her disappear before I turn toward the door and pull my phone out of my pocket. I dial Nico's number and step outside.

"Jules!" she yells into the phone. "Where are you? Are you okay?"

"Are you with Gavin?" I ask, stopping and leaning back against the building.

"No... Why?"

I sigh. "I assume you've spoken to him though?"

"Yeah, of course. He told me that you went missing."

I pinch the bridge of my nose and suck in a breath. "That's not exactly what happened. I left him."

"Why?" she gasps.

"Because I need to figure things out and I couldn't do that in Miami."

"Oh," she whispers, understanding in her voice. "You're in Baton Rouge."

I nod. "I am but you can't tell anyone."

"Of course, Jules. I'll keep my lips sealed."

I push off the wall and begin walking away from the building. "I also wanted to ask you how open you are to the idea of moving."

"Uh... I'm open to it, I guess. Are you not coming back to Miami?"

"I just don't think it's for me anymore. I feel really good here and I think this is where I want to build my life."

She's quiet for a moment and my belly flips as I wait for her response.

"But what if you change your mind once your memory comes back?"

"Well, I'm only doing month to month on my rental so if something happens, we can readjust but for now, I'd like to have you here with me to set everything up."

She sucks in a breath and slowly lets it out. "Okay. Let me wrap up a few things around here and set everyone else up to run without us for a while and then I'll be down there."

"Thank you, Nico."

"Of course."

"And please, *please* don't say anything to Gavin. I know he's hurting but I ended things. I've asked him to move on and he's choosing not to."

She sighs. "I promise I won't say a word and if he calls me again, I'll tell him to let it go."

I thank her again and she promises to get in touch soon to let me know when she will get to town before we say good-bye. Releasing a sigh, I slip my phone back into my pocket and glance up as I turn to where I parked Sawyer's truck. A large man in a black SUV catches my attention as he pulls a camera away from his face. Even behind the sunglasses, I can feel his eyes boring into me and my belly flips as my heart rate quickens.

Shit.

Did Gavin find me already?

I have no idea what the new me would do in this

situation but the old me, the girl I remember, would never take something like this laying down. Sucking in a breath, I march up to his car and arch a brow.

"Can I help you with something?"

He shakes his head, completely unfazed. "Nope. I was just waiting for someone."

"Then why the hell are you taking pictures of me?"

"I wasn't."

I point to the camera in his lap. "I saw you."

"I was taking pictures of the city. Not you." There is something sketchy about him and I don't believe him for a second but without proof, what else can I do? I suppose I could demand to see his camera but that is a little too much for me. Sucking in a breath, I take a step back and nod.

"Sorry."

He flashes me a grin. "No problem."

I back up and turn away from the car with my cheeks burning, my stomach sinking like a stone and hoping against hope that my time isn't up.

A.M. Myers

Never Let Me Go
Chapter Fourteen
Sawyer

"Heard you ended things with Tawny," Storm, the club's VP, says as he plops down on the couch across from me with a bottle of beer in his hand. I take a sip of my own as I nod.

"Yeah. She's not getting the message, though."

He arches a brow and a shit eating grin spreads across his face. "Oh? We got another Hysterical Hoover situation on our hands?"

"For the love of God," I growl, shaking my head and clenching my fist. "Y'all need to stop bringing that shit up and no. I can handle her."

"You sure about that?" He laughs. "I heard about her parting words to you."

I shake my head and down a third of my beer. "Those weren't her parting words. She called me incessantly on my trip and when I got home from Miami, there was a note from her on my front door."

He laughs again but before he can say anything, Blaze steps out of his office to bellow "Church" before disappearing again. Thank fucking God. The last thing I want to do is listen to more jokes about how badly my relationships go. Then again, maybe I just met the one who is going to change all that.

Sighing, I stand up and follow Storm into the war room before taking my seat near the back of the room as Storm sits on the other end. The rest of the guys begin to trickle in, some taking their seats while others stand around bullshitting with each other.

"How was the trip, by the way?" Storm asks. I set my bottle of beer down on the table and lean back in my chair as I nod and I fight back a smile, my mind consumed with thoughts of Juliette and our drive back from Miami.

"Good."

He narrows his eyes, studying me, but before he can say anything, Blaze walks into the room and a hush falls over our group as everyone sits down and faces the front of the table where Blaze sinks into his chair and sighs.

"All right. Let's get started, Smith," he says as he nods to Smith, our sergeant at arms. Smith nods and glances down at the paper on the table in front of him.

"We've got one rescue this week but it's going to be super tricky and we probably need a couple of back-up plans."

Kodiak crosses his arms over his chest with a scowl. "How is it tricky?"

Never Let Me Go

"Peyton is basically a prisoner in her own home. Her boyfriend, Dustin, went a little crazy at their local tech store and installed cameras and motion sensors all throughout the house. He watches her during the day to make sure she doesn't leave and if she even opens a door to accept a package, he gets a notification on his phone. When you add in the fact that he only works a mile away from their house, it makes getting her out of there a challenge."

"Try impossible," Chance says, shaking his head as he leans back in his chair. We all stare at each other, trying to come up with a plan that could possibly work, but no one says anything.

"Streak, could you disable the cameras and sensors?" Blaze asks and Streak, our tech guy, nods.

"Most likely but it would tip him off immediately if everything went dark. I might be able to run a loop. You guys would have to be quick and we'd have to pray he doesn't just decide to pop on home for something."

"How did we even find this girl?" Storm asks and I nod in agreement. It seems odd that she was able to reach out for help if she can't even open the front door of her house.

"The one person she's allowed to speak to is her mother and that's who reached out to us," Smith answers, shaking his head. "The other issue is we haven't been able to have any contact with Peyton but her mother has agreed to pass along the message when we're ready to move."

Blaze nods. "Streak, why don't you look into the security system and we'll develop a plan once we know more?"

"Sure thing, boss."

"Anything else?" Blaze asks, his gaze flicking around the room. When no one says anything, he grabs the gavel and bangs it on the table once, dismissing us. We all head back into the main room and Streak heads upstairs to his lair while the rest of us gather around the bar.

"Heard you got another stage five clinger," Chance says as he walks up behind me and slaps me on the shoulder. These guys really should have better things to do than sit around and gossip like a bunch of women and yet, they all seem to know what's going on in my life. Well… mostly. My thoughts drift to Juliette and the way she felt in my arms last night as I pushed her up against the front door and kissed her like my life depended on it. Quite frankly, I'm not convinced it didn't.

I shake my head as he grabs a beer. "Naw. I've got it all under control."

"Mmhmm," he hums. "Let's just hope she's not as crazy as Courtney or we'll have to find you a new road name."

"Fuck off," I growl, turning away from them. I hate how much they are always doggin' on me. I mean, yeah, I've made some mistakes when it comes to women and relationships but they aren't fucking saints either. Shit. Chance was married to a stripper for a while and Storm didn't date at all before he met his wife.

"Moose. Kodiak. Fuzz," Blaze calls as he walks out of his office with his phone in his hand. "With me."

I set my beer down on the bar and clap Chance's shoulder to say good-bye as I follow behind Kodiak and Fuzz. Blaze leads us outside to the line of bikes.

"What's up, boss?" Kodiak asks. Blaze shakes his head as he grabs his helmet and puts it on.

"Not sure but Rodriguez just called and said there's something he needs to show us. It sounded urgent."

That's all we need to hear.

We all nod before going to our bikes and following Blaze out of the parking lot. The club met Detective Rodriguez five years ago when he was involved with a case we were working on. After everything went down, we were able to develop a friendship with him and it's proved beneficial to both of us. When things fall beyond our reach, he steps in to give us a hand and anytime he ever needs our assistance, we are there to help. It's unconventional but it's been a fruitful relationship and has resulted in more lives saved which is all we both want.

As we drive through the streets of Baton Rouge, my mind drifts to Juliette and that intense kiss on my front porch last night. I've thought a lot about what Cora said on my trip down to Miami and even if I can't admit it out loud to anyone other than Juliette, I know she was right. I hold myself back and don't invest in anything as a coping mechanism and to prevent myself from getting hurt again but this thing with Juliette... I have never felt anything like this so I don't give a fuck how much it scares the shit out of me - I'm not letting her go.

Red and blue lights bounce off of buildings as we slow to a crawl. Police tape stretches out, blocking off the street as a crowd of people start gathering around, trying to get a peek and my stomach sinks. Why the hell would Rodriguez be calling us to a crime scene? Blaze pulls his bike off to the side of the road and we all follow behind him. As we park and dismount, we exchange worried glances. Rodriguez has never called us to a crime scene like this before so I have to assume that it has to do with someone we know but who? I look at Kodiak and Fuzz, my thoughts racing out of control.

"Let them through," a voice calls out as we approach the police tape and an officer in uniform lifts the tape, allowing us to walk under it as Rodriguez makes his way over to us, his face strained. "Sorry to bring you out here, guys."

"What's going on, Diego?" Blaze asks, his gaze sweeping over the scene and I do the same. There are drops of blood in a line along the sidewalk and when I follow them, I suck in a breath. What I can only assume is a body lies on a gurney at the end of the trail, covered in a white sheet. My thoughts screech to a halt as I stare at it and then a list of names begins running through my head - anyone that means anything to us.

Tatum.
Emma.
Nix.

Carly.
Ali.
Quinn.
Brooklyn.
Daisy.
Addilyn.
Alice.
Tucker.
Trey.
Juliette…

My breath rings in my ears and my heart pounds as the world around me warps and fear creeps up my spine. Rodriguez calls out to two men standing near the body and as they wheel the gurney over, my stomach rolls. I want to leave, turn away from what I know is coming, but I can't move no matter how hard I try. The men stop next to us and Rodriguez pulls the sheet back.

"Sammy," I breathe. A sense of relief shoots through me, quick as a flash, before the pain descends and I take a step back, tears stinging my eyes as I stare at her bruised and bloody face. Memories come rushing back from my past and another wave of pain crashes into me, this one older and weathered from years of tormenting me.

"What happened?" Blaze asks, snapping me out of my daze and I take a step forward as I push the pain away, ready to funnel all my energy into examining the scene around us. Rodriguez shakes his head as he covers her with the sheet again.

"We're not sure yet but it appears someone lured

her out of her apartment and attacked her from the cover of the trees." He points over my shoulder and I turn, studying the thick patch of foliage behind me. "She stumbled out of there and made it into the street before she collapsed."

"How did she die?"

Rodriguez glances over at the gurney. "We don't have an official cause of death yet but it looks like someone literally beat her to death."

"Jesus," Kodiak hisses, shaking his head. "Poor girl."

"We just saw her," Fuzz adds, looking as shell shocked as I feel. It's insane. Only a week ago, we were helping her move boxes into her new place and now she's dead. But how? The man who hurt her, the man we saved her from, he's gone. None of this makes any sense. Blaze runs his hand through his hair.

"How did you know to call us?" I ask. When we saved Sammy from her captor, we never involved Rodriguez in that part of it so there's no way he could have known that we had helped her.

He grabs an evidence bag and presents it to us. "This was on top of her body."

My eyes widen as I stare at our business card, covered in blood and Fuzz releases a stream of curses. We gave her a couple of our cards but the placement doesn't make any sense. The only way that it would have been laying on top of her body would be if the killer put it there himself.

"Do you have any witnesses?" Kodiak asks and

Rodriguez shakes his head.

"I have officers canvasing the area but it's not looking good."

"So you don't have any leads?"

Rodriguez sighs. "I just started the investigation, Blaze, but I promise I'll keep you guys updated."

Blaze nods and shakes his hand. "Please do. We'll let you get back to work."

Rodriguez nods and turns back to the crime scene as Blaze ushers us back to our bikes, all of our questions hanging over us like a cloud.

"Who would do this?" Kodiak asks as we stand on the sidewalk, watching the police work. Blaze shakes his head.

"I don't know. After all that girl survived..." He blows out a breath. "She deserved better than this."

Something nags at me and I scowl as I watch them load her body into the medical examiner's van, unable to put my finger on it. We had such a run of bad luck lately when it comes to the girls we help and I can't help but feel like we're failing in our mission.

"Something more is going on here," Fuzz says and Blaze's eyes narrow.

"What do you mean?"

He shakes his head. "I mean, this is the second girl to die after we helped her in the past year or so and with Dina, we all assumed her ex did it but Sammy's abuser is dead so..."

"The only other connection is us," I whisper.

"No," Kodiak snaps, taking a step back as he shakes

his head. "That's insane. Who would do that?"

I smack his chest with the back of my hand. "Think about all the women we've helped, then think about all the men who would have a reason to hate us. Surely one of them is mad enough and crazy enough to do something like this."

"There could be other things that we've missed, too," Fuzz adds, his face grave. "We need to get Streak to start looking into this and we all need to start going over old cases as well but we need to do it quietly."

Kodiak holds his hands up. "Hold on. Two times is a coincidence, not a pattern."

"And if you're wrong? Are you really willing to let another girl die before we start looking into this?"

"This is insane," I breathe, tipping my head back and squeezing my eyes shut for a second before blowing out a breath and meeting their gazes. My thoughts keep swirling back to Juliette no matter how hard I try to think of something else and the thought of her getting hurt kills me. "We've got too many important people in our lives to take the chance that this isn't connected."

"And let's say it is connected and we start looking into it and only end up pissing whoever it is off more. Then what?"

"Enough," Blaze says, his voice full of authority and we all turn to him. "You all have valid points. We'll start looking into this but we'll do it carefully and quietly. The last thing we need is to lose anyone else."

Never Let Me Go

Chapter Fifteen

Juliette

Butterflies flutter around in my belly and each breath I take rings in my ears as I smooth my trembling hands down my jeans and glance up at the clock. Before he left this morning, Sawyer told me he would be home at five and I have just about five minutes to finish this up before he gets home.

God, why am I so nervous?

After my lunch with Mercedes today, I decided to run to the store and grab what I needed to throw together a quiet little dinner for Sawyer and me so I could thank him for letting me stay here. It was just supposed to be casual and allow us to start exploring our feelings like we talked about last night and I thought I would be okay but now that he's almost here, I feel like I am about to go on my first date all over again. I have never cooked for a man, at least I don't think I have, and since I didn't want to ruin the surprise, I couldn't exactly ask him what he liked or if he is allergic to anything. This whole thing could really blow up in my face.

Burying my face in my hands, I groan. What the hell was I thinking? This is going to be a disaster, I just know it. My heart jumps in my chest and I take a deep breath before shaking out my hands. This is crazy. How does he affect me so much? Granted I don't remember a huge chunk of my recent past but I don't ever remember feeling like this before meeting Sawyer. He lights a fire inside me. A fire that is just as warm and comforting as it is exciting and I can't imagine ever giving it up. But I'm still lying to him and I have no idea what he's going to do when the truth comes out.

Maybe I should just tell him. Maybe I should just open up and let him in to the horror of my life for the past two weeks but the way I feel around him feels too damn good and I'm quickly becoming addicted to it. What if his feelings for me change once he knows the whole story? I honestly don't know what I would do or how I would cope if he decided he wanted to walk away from me.

How can one man consume so much of my life in such a short amount of time?

Sighing, I straighten the silverware and light the candles in the center of the table before taking a step back and pursing my lips. Maybe the candles are too much. I mean, I want us to have a nice dinner but I also don't want to put too much pressure on him. What if his feelings have changed since last night? We were both swept up in whatever it was we were feeling in the truck yesterday but what if, today, in the cold light of day, he realizes that he was acting crazy? Closing my eyes, I picture the two of us on his front porch last night and rub my palm with my thumb in the exact same spot

Never Let Me Go

I felt his racing heartbeat before he kissed me.

No.

There's no way that wasn't real - daylight or not.

I stare at the candles for another couple of seconds before deciding to leave them. My heart races as I peek up at the clock again on my way into the kitchen.

He should be here any second...

To distract myself from incessantly staring at the door, I stir the Shrimp Alfredo I made for us. It's about the only thing I know how to make, besides boxed mac and cheese, so I really hope he likes it.

Shit.

What if he doesn't?

I'm pretty sure I'd die on the spot. Shaking my head, I grab the plates off the counter and scoop food onto each one before carrying them to the table and sitting down in one of the chairs as I release a breath and check the time on my phone.

5:06 p.m.

Nodding, I lean back in my chair and try to slow my breathing as my knee bounces out of control. God, I hope he likes this and doesn't think it's weird. He won't think it's weird, right? Fuck. I'm losing my mind. I snatch my phone off of the table and dial Mercedes' number.

"Hey, babe. What's up?" she answers and I release a breath.

"Um, well... I'm losing my mind."

She laughs. "Why?"

"So, after I left your office, I thought it would be nice to cook dinner for Sawyer to say thank you for letting me stay, you know?"

"Uh-huh."

"And now I'm just sitting here waiting for him to get home and I'm so nervous."

"Oh my God," she shoots back. "You like him *so* much."

"Shut up. That's not helping at all."

Her laughter echoes across the line. "Did you cook your famous Shrimp Alfredo?"

"Um... yes. How did you know that? And why are you calling it famous?"

"It's the same thing you made for Gavin to get him to sleep with you. We learned it at the cooking class we took in Miami."

I scowl. "What cooking class?"

"Jett," she gasps. "We took that class during your lost memories."

"Oh," I whisper, staring at the plate of food in front of me. How could I remember how to make this if I can't remember anything else from my life? All damn day, I've been trying to remember anything from my life in Miami and this is what I get? "Wait... you said I made this for Gavin?"

"Yeah, the night y'all had sex for the first time. You made a whole plan to seduce him."

I shake my head and pinch my eyes closed. "Well, did it work?"

"Um, yes." She laughs. "Have you seen yourself? You could have taken him to bed just by looking in his direction."

"Stop it," I beg her as my cheeks burn and she laughs again.

"Is Sawyer late?"

I glance up at the clock. "Yeah. He said he'd get home ten minutes ago."

"Want me to kick his ass?" she asks, sounding almost eager and I laugh as I shake my head.

"No. I'm just nervous."

"I bet," she replies, a hint of tease in her voice. "I would be, too, if I was waiting on another life changing kiss."

Groaning, I pinch the bridge of my nose. "I never should have told you that."

"No, no, it's okay. I only have a minor case of jealousy."

"Maybe you should think about getting back out there," I suggest and I swear, I can feel her shudder through the phone.

"I think not. Not right now, at least. I have way too much work to do to deal with a man."

"Mmhmm," I hum as a noise by the front door catches my attention and I sit up straight. "Oh, shit. I think he's here."

"Have fun! Don't do anything I wouldn't do!"

"You realize that doesn't take much off the table, right?"

"Yeah," she answers. "Sounds like a fun night."

Laughing, I say good-bye to her and promise to call her tomorrow before setting my phone down just as the door swings open and Sawyer stumbles into the house. His gait is uneven and he smashes his knee into his couch, hissing a string of cuss words. Jesus Christ, is he drunk? Glancing up, he stops and blinks bloodshot eyes at me before examining the table. His eyebrows shoot up.

"Oh, what's this?" he slurs, a goofy smile

stretching across his face as he stumbles further into the room and almost trips over a rug. I bolt up from my chair and meet him in the living room, wrapping my arm around his waist to keep him from falling. He hums and buries his nose in my hair. "You smell good."

"I cooked us some dinner," I prompt, pointing to the table and his smile grows. He looks down at me with a look that makes me feel all warm and gooey inside.

"You're amazing."

"And you're drunk," I say, my eyes burning from the smell of alcohol wafting off of him. "You didn't drive, did you?"

"Nope. Uber."

I nod in approval as I guide him to a chair and push his big body into it. He lands with a thud and grabs my arm, pulling me into his lap before I can stop him.

"Sawyer!"

He grins. "I really like the way you say my name. Do it again."

"Sawyer," I say, smiling as I relax into his arms. "We should get some food in you."

"No. Don't leave me. I like you right here," he says, his grip on me tightening and I nod as I reach up to cup his cheek.

"You always come home three sheets to the wind?"

He shakes his head. "Only on really bad days."

"What happened?"

"Someone died," he whispers, tears filling his eyes as he looks away from me and my heart aches in my chest, stealing my breath as tears sting my eyes and thoughts of my mom and dad flash through my mind.

"I'm so sorry, Sawyer."

His gaze meets mine and he traps a lock of my hair between his fingers as he shakes his head. "I can't believe I met you."

"Why not?" I ask, trying desperately to keep up with the ever changing topic.

"I said I was done. I wasn't gonna date anyone else until I fixed my shit and then there you were... like an angel. My angel."

Tears fill my eyes at the pain in his voice. "Sawyer."

"It's gonna hurt like hell when you leave me. I don't want to let you go."

"Who said I was leaving?" I ask, trying to guide his gaze back to mine but he shakes off my hand.

"You will. I'm not good enough for you."

I push out of his arms and the panic in his eyes breaks my heart as I turn and straddle his legs, placing my hands on his chest. "Why would you think that?"

"I'm never enough, Juliette. Never good enough to save them. Never good enough to love...just never enough."

I shake my head and cup his cheek, forcing his gaze to mine as my chest hurts fiercely. "I think you're everything, Sawyer."

We stare at each other for a moment before he scoffs and picks me up with ease. He stands and sets me back down in the chair before disappearing into his room without another word and slamming the door. The sound reverberates through the house and tears spring to my eyes as I stare at the floor, wondering where the hell I went wrong but the more I replay what just happened in my head, the less sense it makes. Sucking in a breath, I wipe my tears and start cleaning off the table to distract myself.

Once everything is cleaned up and the food is in the fridge for later, I grab my phone and walk down the hallway to my room directly across from his. Pausing outside his door, I press my hand to the wood and my lips wobble. My mind is a jumbled mess after everything that just happened and as much as I know it's going to haunt me tonight, I also know that we won't be able to solve anything until he's sober. If there is even anything left to solve.

*   *   *   *

I pull my sweater tighter around my body to ward off the morning chill as the sun begins peeking through the trees, making the world around me glisten. Fighting to keep my eyes open, I press the back of my fingers to my lips as I yawn and shake my head. Last night was awful and I spent hours tossing and turning before giving up around four a.m. The house was so quiet that I had to get out so I just started walking and stumbled onto this cute little park a couple of blocks away from Sawyer's house. There's a small fountain in the middle surrounded by a gorgeous garden full of bright, colorful flowers. Leading away from the fountain are walking paths that stretch into the woods and I would be tempted to go explore if I wasn't so damn exhausted. Birds chirp sweetly from the trees and the sound of bubbling water washes over me, melting away my stress. It's so serene that I may just never leave.

"All right, woman," a voice says from behind me and I turn as Mercedes walks up to the bench with a drink carrier and a paper bag in her hands. "You wanna tell me why you have my ass out here at six in the morning?"

I take one of the coffees from the drink carrier and flash her a smile. "Maybe I just like your company."

"Bullshit. No one likes my company at six in the morning. What's going on? How did last night go?"

"Oh, just peachy," I answer as I roll my eyes and she nods as understanding washes over her face and she takes a sip of her own coffee.

"Ah, I see. What happened?"

"Nothing."

She sighs. "Again with the bullshit. Give me all the deets. What happened after you called me last night?"

I take a sip of my coffee and shake my head, irritated by her persistence. "So, after I hung up with you, he stumbles into the house, drunk and when I said drunk, I mean *druuunnnk*."

"Oh." She purses her lips in disapproval and I nod, staring at the fountain in front of me.

"Yeah. And then he tells me that someone died yesterday but when I tried to get him to tell me who, he just started calling me his angel and saying that it was going to suck when I left him."

She arches a brow. "What the fuck?"

219

"Exactly." I dig a donut out of the bag and take a bite. "Then, I ask him who said I was leaving and he says I will because he's not good enough for me and that he's not good enough for anyone."

"What did you say to that?"

I shake my head as my cheeks burn. "I told him that I thought he was everything."

"Aw."

"No, not aw, because he stormed off to his room and left me and the dinner I made for him sitting in the dining room."

"Have you talked to him at all today?" she asks and I shake my head as I take a sip of coffee. I feel so stupid that I was so giddy and happy about this man when the truth is, he is a stranger. For all I know, the man I saw last night is who he really is and he has been putting on one hell of a show since I met him.

"No. I couldn't sleep all night because I was worried about him and wondering who had hurt him so badly. Around four, I just got up and started walking until I found this place." I motion to the park and she sighs, taking a sip of her coffee as she relaxes into the seat next to me.

"Well… what do you want to do about him now?"

I shake my head. "I don't know yet. I'm tempted to just go pack up my shit and use my credit card to get a hotel."

"And let Gavin find you?"

"I think he already has," I tell her, shrugging my shoulders and she scowls at me. Why is it that on my list of problems, Gavin finding me seems so much less important than what happened last night? I mean, I was engaged to Gavin but the idea of him finding me and trying to convince me to come back to Miami just doesn't bother me and I can't decide if it's because I feel like I'm home here or because of Sawyer.

"How do you know?"

"There was a man outside of your office yesterday taking pictures of me."

She gasps. "Are you fucking kidding me?"

"Nope."

"Oh, hell no. I'll hire security for you or something, babe."

I shake my head, flashing her a look. "I don't need security. It's just Gavin."

"And what if he shows up here? What are you going to do then?" she asks and I tilt my head to the side as I think over her question. So what if Gavin does show up here? I'm not going back to Miami and I'm done feeling guilty for that. Baton Rouge is my home and where I'm supposed to be. My mind drifts back to Sawyer and I sigh.

"If he shows up here, I'll tell him to go back home."

"I don't know if it will be that easy," she says and I turn to look at her. "He called me two more times after you left yesterday."

I shrug. "Let him come. What is he going to do? Force me back to Miami? I don't think so."

"You know, I was really worried about you when you first told me you lost your memory but look at you, kicking butt and taking names."

"Do I remind you of the old me?"

She shakes her head. "Yes and no. I don't think you should be so concerned with who you were and just focus on who you want to be now."

"I couldn't agree with you more."

Before she can say anything else, the roar of a bike fills the air and we both turn toward the street, watching for a second before a man I recognize all too well pulls into one of the parking spaces.

"Oh, here we go," Mercedes whispers like she is settling in to watch her favorite guilty pleasure TV show. I shake my head as I cross my legs and watch him climb off of his bike and grab a colorful bouquet of flowers off the back of the bike. "Two points for pretty flowers."

"Are you grading his apology?" I ask, trying not to laugh and she glances back over her shoulder and nods, a grin on her face. We both turn back to Sawyer, who looks like he's about to shit a brick as he approaches us. But damn if he doesn't still look like I could eat him alive - a perfect mixture of swaggy bad-ass biker and the kind of guy you can see yourself settling down and having babies with.

"Two points for the very convincing "I'm sorry I'm a piece of shit" face," she whispers and I smack her in the back.

"Stop it."

Sawyer meets my gaze and my heart leaps into my throat, pounding like a bass drum as butterflies flutter through my belly.

Aw, hell.

"Juliette," he murmurs, the rich texture of his voice coating me like a blanket and I nod, studying him as he tries to subtly wipe his hand on his jeans. God, he looks nervous and it's breaking my heart. Wait… why is it breaking my heart? One, I barely know him - a fact that was made all too clear to me last night - and two, I have every damn right to be angry after the way he acted. Then again, I understand the pain he was in yesterday all too well.

"Sawyer."

He sucks in a breath. "Can we talk?"

"Sure," I answer and his gaze flicks to Mercedes.

"Alone?"

"Nope," Mercedes answers, shaking her head as she lifts her coffee cup to her lips and takes a sip. "You want my girl back, you can grovel... in front of an audience."

"Mercedes," I whisper as I give her a little nudge. Usually, I appreciate her attitude but the look on his face is killing me right now and I don't know how much longer I can sit here before I give in. Every cell in my body is screaming to get up and give him a hug but I force myself to remain in my seat.

"No, it's okay," Sawyer answers. "I'll do it here."

He drops down on one knee and Mercedes and I both suck in a breath as our eyes widen.

"Eight points for the grand sweeping gesture," she whispers, her voice full of shock but I'm too stunned to say anything in response or tell her to knock it off. What is he doing? I meet Sawyer's eyes and shake my head in confusion.

"What are you doing?"

"Juliette," he says, his voice a perfect mixture of confident and nervous as he holds the bouquet of flowers out in front of him. "I know I really screwed things up last night. The dinner you planned and cooked for us was so beautiful and I really wish we could have eaten it together. You'll never know how much I'll regret ruining it."

I shake my head but he doesn't let me say anything.

"And I know this isn't an excuse for my behavior but the club lost one of our girls yesterday, she was murdered, and I didn't handle it well. Partly because I take the work we do so seriously and partly because of my past which I really hope I get a chance to tell you about."

I scoot to the end of the bench and set my coffee down on the pavement before reaching out for him but he shakes his head as he leans back. I can't decide if I admire his commitment to his apology or if I just wish he'd let me forgive him already.

"I meant what I said last night… you are my angel and all that other shit… it is stuff I'm really trying hard to work through. I just hope you'll give me time and another chance to do this right."

"Um…" Mercedes says. "Not to break up a super romantic moment but what *exactly* are you asking her?"

His eyes never leave mine as he smiles and I melt into a puddle of goo. "I love having you at the house, love knowing that I get to come home to you, so I really hope you don't want to go stay somewhere else but I understand if you feel like that is what you need to do. And if you do decide to leave, I just hope you'll still let me take you out on a real date and show you that everything I said the night we first kissed was the truth. So, what do you say? Will you get all dressed up and let me show you off to the world?"

How the hell is a girl supposed to say no to a request like that?

My heart thunders in my chest and a smile creeps across my face as I nod. "Okay."

A wide smile stretches across his face as he jumps up and grabs my hand, yanking me up off of the bench and into his arms. Warmth radiates through my body as I tilt my head back to meet his gaze and he leans down, sealing his lips over mine. I gasp at the electricity that races through my body as I circle my arms around his neck and pull him closer, unable to get close enough. He holds me tight to his body and kisses me like he's never going to let me go and a small part of me, the irrational, whimsical part that believes all this could be real, hopes that he never does.

A.M. Myers

Never Let Me Go
Chapter Sixteen
Sawyer

Grabbing my beer off the bar, I turn and scan the room. Fuzz is hunched over a table, files scattered all across the surface as he scowls and I shake my head before crossing the room and sinking into the chair next to him.

"What are you up to, brother?"

He glances up at me. "Going over old cases and looking for a pattern."

"You realize you aren't a cop anymore, right?" I ask and he glares at me as he pulls out another sheet of paper and shoves it in my face.

"Just look at this. It's a pattern."

I study the paper in my hand as I take a sip of my beer. There are five names written down, three of them grouped together at the bottom and the two other off on their own with numbers in parenthesis next to them. "What am I looking at?"

"In the eight years that we've been doing this work," he says, pointing to the paper. "We've lost five girls. One, the year after we started. The second one during year three and then three in the past two years."

"Three? I thought it was just Dina and Sammy."

"And Laney."

My eyes narrow. "That was Rodriguez's case."

"That he called us in on," Fuzz exclaims. "Plus, one could argue that Rodriguez is so connected with the work that we do that anyone who had a grudge or vendetta against either of us would likely come after either one of us… or both."

"Look, I…"

"Three in two years, Moose," he cuts in, shaking his head. I nod.

"Yeah, it's been a bad couple of years but…"

"No, it's more than that."

"Fuzz," I sigh, tossing his paper back on the table. "I know you've been struggling with Sammy's death. We all have but it's just a coincidence."

He shakes his head, turning back to the files. "No, there's a connection here. I just know it."

Sighing, I watch him as he scans the paper in front of him, his brows knitted together in concentration. We're all struggling with the people we've lost lately and I know each of us deals in our own way but Fuzz's obsession with finding a hidden plot against the club is dangerous, a cancer that will spread and drive all of us to hysteria if we buy into it.

The door to the clubhouse opens and I glance over

my shoulder as sunlight streams into the room and Tawny walks in.

"Fuck," I hiss, turning away and shaking my head. What are the chances that I pretend like I didn't see her? Not that it will matter for long.

"Sawyer," she purrs, walking up behind me. "Just the man I was looking for."

"What do you need, Tawny?"

She places her hands on my shoulders as she stops behind me. "Can we talk somewhere more private?"

"Nope," I answer, rolling my shoulders to try and get her hands off me. "We can talk here."

"Aw, come on, baby," she whispers, leaning down so far that her mouth brushes the shell of my ear. I shudder in revulsion. How the fuck did I ever find this woman attractive? "Let's go upstairs. I think we'll need a little privacy."

My restraint snaps and I stand up before turning to face her. "What the fuck makes you think I want to go upstairs with you?"

"Sawyer," she whispers, blushing as the guys all start looking in our direction. Funny how she finally uses my real name now that she wants something from me. "I know you got all my messages and I'm sorry for the way things went down but let's go upstairs and fix this."

"I don't want to *fix* this, Tawny. I broke up with you, remember?"

She places her hand on my chest and I glance down at it. "Well, maybe I can change your mind."

"No." I laugh, lifting my bottle of beer to my lips. "You can't."

Her hand starts dragging down the front of my body and I choke on my drink as I grab it and push it away as I shake my head.

"Don't ever do that again."

"I know you love my mouth," she whispers, taking a step toward me and leaning in to kiss my neck. "And all the things I can do with it."

I dodge her advance and slip out of her grasp as I finish off my beer. Fuck this shit. No more trying to be nice. No more letting her down easy because I'm not going to risk losing Juliette just to protect Tawny's feelings, especially when she can't take a hint. She spins around to face me and smirks. A few chuckles ring out behind me as she starts stalking toward me and I back up like a cornered animal.

"We don't have to be anything more than we were before. We can just go back to being fuck buddies. Isn't that what you want?"

I shake my head as my back hits the bar. "No. The only thing I want from you is to leave me the hell alone."

"You don't mean that. I know you have to be getting lonely, baby."

"I met someone else," I snap and she screeches to a halt, staring at me with wide eyes. I can feel every set of eyes in the room on me.

"What?"

"You heard me - I met someone else and it's

serious."

She starts to shake as rage stains her cheeks. "You cheated on me?"

"No. I met her in Miami," I say and her color quickly returns to normal as she laughs. Storm nudges my arm and I glance over at him.

"Seriously?"

"Yeah."

He nods and as I turn back to Tawny, I catch sight of Smith and Chance sitting at one of the other tables, laughing as they watch the scene unfold. Motherfuckers.

"How serious could it be if you just met her?" Tawny asks. "We have history."

I shake my head. The last thing I want is Tawny and our history but I have a feeling nothing short of marriage will deter her. Sucking in a breath, I cross my arms over my chest and say the first thing that comes to mind.

"I'm claiming her."

Tawny gasps, taking a step back. "What?"

"I'm fucking claiming her," I say louder, surprised by how right it feels. "Y'all heard me, right? Juliette Shaw is my old lady."

"You son of a bitch," she hisses, charging at me. Storm and Kodiak step in front of me, blocking her path as Blaze stomps into the room with his phone in his hand.

"Moose, Kodiak, and Storm, get over to Peyton's house now. Something is going down."

The three of us jump up and Tawny stumbles back as we push past her to get to the door.

"Seriously?" She calls after us but she's the last of my priorities, now or ever. We rush out to our bikes, working like a well oiled machine as the roar of bikes fills the air and we peel out of the parking lot. Peyton's house is about three miles from the clubhouse but to get there, you have to go through a busy part of town so we stick to backroads and perform some less than legal maneuvers as we weave through traffic.

When we pull up in front of Peyton's house, everything looks normal which only increases my unease as I scan the neighborhood. As we climb off our bikes, the front door opens and a small little thing with mousy blonde hair steps out of the house with a suitcase in her hand. She has bruises all over her face and arms as well as a nasty cut down the middle of her lip. Kodiak glances at me with a questioning expression and I shrug.

"Peyton?" Storm calls and she nods as she steps out onto the sidewalk. "Where's your boyfriend?"

She points over her shoulder. "Sleeping."

We all exchange a glance.

"I think we're going to need a little more explanation," I tell her and she sighs as she glances back at the house. The door is still wide open and I wonder if the motion sensor is just continually going off in there while we stand around outside.

"I'm happy to do that but can we not do it here? Also, I'm really hungry."

Storm nods, taking control as he steps forward. "Yeah. Have you ever ridden a bike before?"

She shakes her head.

"Okay. Let me show you the basics."

As Storm leads her down to his bike and explains what to do, I take her bag and secure it to the back of my bike as Kodiak closes the front door. Once we're all ready, Storm turns to us.

"Let's take her to that restaurant we passed on the way here."

I nod. He climbs on his bike and helps Peyton get on behind him before pulling away from the curb. As I follow them, I check my mirrors obsessively to make sure we're not being followed. The whole situation is weird. From everything we've heard, her boyfriend is super obsessive so why is he just missing all of the sudden? I mean, I don't want to accuse her of anything but you got to wonder if he's really lying dead on the kitchen floor or something. It wouldn't be the first time one of these women snapped and did something crazy after years of torture and abuse.

Folks turn to look at us as we pull into the parking lot of the restaurant Storm suggested, their gazes bouncing from each one of us to Peyton's battered face before turning back to us with disgust. You'd think after years of doing this work in Baton Rouge, people would know what it meant when they saw a Devil with a woman who had been knocked around but they always just assume we had something to do with it. Sometimes I wonder if we'll ever get to a place where we can lose our old reputation and be known as a beacon of good in this town but maybe that's too much to ask.

"I don't want to hang out here for long," Storm murmurs to me as we climb off our bikes and I nod, scanning the street again.

"Agreed."

Storm guides Peyton into the restaurant with Kodiak and me guarding his back. We bypass the hostess stand and walk over to the booth all the way in the corner. He lets Peyton slide onto the seat closest to the door before sitting next to her and Kodiak and I sit across from them, watching the door. A flustered waitress rushes up to our table and pastes a smile on her face.

"Hi. Can I get y'all anything to drink?"

Storm nods to Peyton. "Go ahead and order whatever you want. To go."

Nodding, she looks up at the waitress and orders a root beer, a cheeseburger, and fries. The waitress looks to each of us, silently asking if we want anything and we all shake our heads. The faster we can get out of here the better.

"Okay," Storm says as the waitress walks away to put Peyton's order in. "Why don't you tell us what happened?"

Tears well up in her eyes and guilt swamps me. We have been going over how to best help her for days but we couldn't agree on anything and in the end, she was on her own to deal with his abuse.

"Yesterday, I got distracted while I was cooking dinner and accidentally burned it." She shudders. "It sent him into a rage and when he was finished beating me, I couldn't even get up off of the floor. He realized that I was seriously hurt so he picked me up and carried me to the car before taking me to this friend of his who was a medic in the Army. He examined me and stitched up this cut on my arm." She points to a nasty gash on the underside of her arm that I didn't notice before and my stomach rolls. "This guy, I think he felt bad for me, so he slipped me some painkillers that he had left over when Dustin wasn't looking and I hid them in my bra."

"So what happened today?" Kodiak asks, his voice soft.

"He ordered me to make him his lunch and I remembered that I still had the pills in my bra so I snuck off to the bathroom and crushed them up and put them in his drink."

Storm meets my eyes. "Is he...uh..."

"Alive?" she asks, nodding. "Yes. He's just passed out."

"And that's how you were able to sneak out of the house?" I ask. She shakes her head.

"No. That's how I was able to get his phone and unlock it with his fingerprint. The code for the security system is saved in his notes so I found it and called you guys."

I stare at her for a second before I start laughing and the guys join in.

"I'm sorry," I tell her. "I know it's not funny but..."

She shakes her head. "No. It is funny and I'm sure I will think it's even funnier when it doesn't hurt so much to laugh."

"We can get you into a doctor to make sure nothing is broken."

Sighing, she practically deflates in front of us. "I would appreciate that."

"Please tell me you left your phone at the house, too," Kodiak says and she grins as she nods. Despite all she's been through, there is a bit of a sparkle in her eyes and it makes me smile to see how strong she is.

"Both of our phones are currently sitting at the bottom of a toilet bowl."

We all laugh.

"I just…" she says before clamping her lips shut and taking a deep breath. "I need to thank you guys. Two weeks ago, I was ready to die and a big part of me was convinced that was my only option and then my mom told me she had contacted you all and it gave me the strength to fight again."

"Is that where you're going to go? To your mom's?"

She nods. "About a month ago, she sold her house and moved two hours away so he has no idea where to even look for me."

"Have you spoken to her to let her know you're on your way?"

"No," she answers. "I didn't want to have a call to her on my phone in case he finds some way to access my call log."

Kodiak nods. "Well, I suppose he'll find the call to us first and if he does we'll be able to give you a heads up."

"Oh… no, he won't find the call to you." She giggles at our confused looks. "I called you from his phone. He'll be so obsessed with going over everything in my phone that he won't even think to check his."

"That's brilliant." Kodiak laughs as the waitress stops by our table with a bag of food and a drink for Peyton.

"Here y'all go and here's your check." She rips off a piece of paper and lays it face down on the table before telling us to have a good day and walking away. As Kodiak grabs the bill and goes to the counter to pay it, Storm and I lead Peyton out to the parking lot.

"Just how many pills did you give that man and how long do you think he'll be out?"

She snorts. "Three and for a while. He doesn't even drink so he's a total lightweight."

Nodding, I climb on my bike and relax into the seat, feeling a little more at ease knowing that her ex isn't out there chasing us down right now. Kodiak meets us outside and after he climbs on his bike, we head back toward the clubhouse, my mind racing with thoughts of my date with Juliette tonight. I'm fucking lucky as hell that she accepted my apology after the shit I pulled the other night and I'm damn sure not going to make a mistake like that again. I meant everything I said to her and as much as I'm struggling to push past the fear that I have kept buried for so many years, I am determined not to lose her. She's fucking everything I always wanted and then some and I'll do whatever it takes to convince her that I can be everything she needs and wants in a man. I check my watch as we pull into the clubhouse parking lot and scowl.

Two p.m.

We don't have plans until six and it's not like I could swing home and just hang out with her since she's at her new office, working to get everything set up and running. She was so excited when she told me about the office space she found above Mercedes and I love that she is so close to Storm's wife, Ali, and Chance's wife, Carly. If anything ever went down and we needed to assign protection to the girls, it helps to have them all in one place. Plus, I can worry about her just a tiny bit less knowing there's someone there who would call me immediately if something happened to her.

Or they will now, at least, since I claimed her today. Shit.

I'm gonna have to explain that to her and we technically haven't even had our first date.

Hopefully, she won't be too mad at me.

I park my bike next to Storm's and climb off before helping Peyton down off Storm's bike as he holds her food. She smiles up at me in gratitude and grabs her food from Storm.

"Moose!" a voice screeches and I flinch, my heart jumping into my throat as I turn toward the door as Tawny charges across the parking lot. "Is this her? Is this the little slut you left me for?"

Jesus Christ.

"What the fuck are you still doing here, Tawny?" I ask, stepping in front of Peyton to block her path. She slams into me and pounds her fists against my chest as I roll my eyes.

"You motherfucker! I can't believe you did this to me."

"For fuck's sake, Tawny. I didn't do anything to you. Dial it down."

Her fists pause as she looks up at me with wide eyes. "Did you just tell me to calm down? After you left me for this ugly skank?"

"Enough!" Blaze says, his voice booming out across the parking lot and Tawny jerks back and almost shrinks into herself. "Tawny, you are banned from this clubhouse from here on out. If I see you anywhere around this place or my guys again, that photo we talked about will find its way to Detective Rodriguez. Are we clear?"

She nods. "Yes."

"Leave," he orders and she glances up at me before turning back to him. "Now!"

With a huff, she turns and marches toward her car but not before throwing me a look over her shoulder that clearly says "This isn't over". We watch her go before Storm and Kodiak lead Peyton inside and I turn to Blaze.

"What do you have on her, boss?"

He laughs. "A photo of her doing blow off of some

chick's thigh."

"Can she be prosecuted for a photo?" I ask and he laughs again as he shrugs.

"Dunno but she doesn't know that." He turns back to me and claps my shoulder. "Keep an eye out for her, you hear? She's trouble."

I nod, watching her car as it disappears down the street and he turns back toward the clubhouse before spinning around again.

"Oh… congrats on your girl, by the way. But I thought it wasn't like that? Isn't that what you said when I called you on your trip?"

I laugh and give him a little shove. "Yeah, go ahead. Rub it in. I was wrong and you were right."

"Naw, I'm happy for you, Moose. Really."

"Thanks, boss."

He nods. "Go ahead and get out of here. We've got this handled from here."

Shit.

You don't have to tell me twice.

I slap his shoulder and turn back to my bike, more than ready to get back to my girl… even if she doesn't know that she is my girl yet. On second thought, I better use this time to prepare something that will really blow her away. I won't consider this night a success unless I walk away with her heart.

Never Let Me Go
Chapter Seventeen
Juliette

My heart hammers against my rib cage as I step into
the living room in my simple, white, fit and flair dress
that hits me right at the knee and makes me feel like a
glowing goddess. Sawyer's broad back greets me as he
runs a hand through his hair and I clear my throat.
Spinning around, his eyes widen and his jaw drops. His
gaze rakes down my body but I'm too consumed with
oogling the fine man in front of me to pay attention to
that. He looks so goddamn handsome in his black suit
pants and the white button up shirt he decided on for
the evening. The first two buttons of the shirt are
unbuttoned, giving just a tease of his massive chest and
his sleeves are rolled up to his elbows, playing peek-a-
boo with his tattoos.

"Sawyer," I breathe, taking a step toward him and
laying my hand on his chest as he wraps me up in his
arms.

A.M. Myers

"You are so fucking gorgeous, baby." As he meets my gaze, I melt at the tender look in his eyes. He lifts his hand and drags his knuckles down my cheek like he can't quite believe I'm real and my heart aches with something I can't find a name for. "My angel."

Closing my eyes, I suck in a breath and try to get a handle on my emotions but it's useless when he leans forward and presses a kiss to my forehead.

"You're ruining me."

His lips stretch into a grin against my skin. "Good."

"You look so handsome," I tell him as I open my eyes and lean back to meet his gaze. He smiles, a slight blush staining his cheeks that I find so endearing and I lean in to steal a quick kiss. When I pull away, he groans and tightens his grip, pulling me closer as he goes in for another one.

"Do we have reservations?" I ask as I lift and turn my head to the side so his lips connect with my neck and a shiver runs down my spine.

"Nope."

He kisses my neck again and I suck in a ragged breath. "Fuck."

"Jesus Christ, woman. You keep talking like that and we won't be leaving the house at all."

"Okay," I whisper as I catch a hint of his cologne. Warmth floods my body and I arch my back, rubbing myself against him. Groaning, he tightens his grip again before releasing it.

"Shit. You have no idea how much I wish I could throw you over my shoulder right now but we have

242

plans."

I nod, leaning into him and pressing a kiss next to his ear. "Later."

"Fuck," he growls as he steps away from me and takes a deep breath. His gaze traces the contours of my body before he meets my eyes and flashes me the kind of grin that could melt the panties right off a nun. "You're going to be the death of me."

"What a way to go," I answer with a shiver and his smile grows as he holds his hand out to me. I take it, lacing our fingers together and letting him pull me to his side.

"You ready to go?"

I run my finger along the edge of my bottom lip and turn to him. "How's my lipstick?"

"Perfect," he answers as he reaches up and drags his thumb under my lip. I grab it before he can pull it away and scoff at the red smear of product on his skin.

"How is it perfect if you had to wipe some off?"

"Baby," he mutters, shaking his head like I'm ridiculous. "You could color that shit all over your face like an excited three-year-old and you'd still be perfect."

"Thanks. I have a cavity now from that line," I quip and he throws his head back in laughter as I fight back a smile. I love hearing him laugh like that. Each time he does, I get the odd feeling that it doesn't happen often and I should cherish it but when he's around me, I feel like we're always laughing.

"Come on, smart ass," he says, releasing my hand to

place his at the small of my back. "Dinner is waiting."

I peek back at him as we walk to the front door. "Where are we going?"

"It's a surprise."

I purse my lips as I watch him lock the door before he's back at my side, guiding me with a gentle hand on my back to the truck. He opens my door and holds his hand out to help me climb inside before shutting it and walking around to his side.

"If I ever meet your mama, make sure I don't forget to compliment her on your excellent manners," I say as he climbs behind the wheel and he laughs.

"Oh, don't worry. I won't let you forget."

My heart flutters in my chest as Sawyer glances across the cab of the truck and smiles, holding his hand out to me. I take it and he pulls me closer before lacing his fingers with mine and I can't wipe the damn smile off my face. He backs the truck out of the driveway and I settle into his side, content in a way that I can't remember ever feeling before and as I peek up at him, I desperately want to tell him the truth about my past.

What will he think?

What will he do?

Fear swarms through me and I push it back down as I take a deep breath. I'm not going to tell him tonight. I can't. But soon I will spill all my secrets to him and hope to God that he can accept them.

"We're here," he says as he pulls into a parking spot a couple blocks down from the house and I scowl at him before turning to the scene in front of us and gasping.

"Sawyer."

We're at the little park where he apologized to me yesterday but all the benches have been taken out and a round table sits right in front of the fountain. Twinkle lights are strung through the trees and across the garden, bathing everything in a golden light.

"I can't believe you did this," I whisper, glancing over at him. "It's incredible."

He blushes. "I'm glad you like it. At first, I planned to take you to the nicest restaurant in town but then I remembered our impromptu picnic on the road. I thought we'd recreate it and make it an official date."

"I love it. Honestly, it's perfect."

Grinning, he opens his door and gets out before turning back to me and holding his hand out. I take it and let him pull me to the edge of the seat. He wraps his hands around my hips and effortlessly lifts me out of the truck before setting me down at his feet and slipping my hand through the crook of his arm. As he leads me up to the table, I notice more details and realize just how much time he spent putting this together. There are little orb lights stuck into the ground amongst the flowers and candles lined up along the outer ring of the fountain as soft music plays from a speaker set up behind the fountain. A man steps forward out of the trees and sets a cooler down at his feet. Sawyer nods in approval and without a word, he walks out to the street and jumps on a bike.

"Who was that?"

Sawyer rolls his eyes as he peels away. "Rooster. He's a prospect for the club."

"A what now?"

"A prospect. Basically, it means he's doing his trial period with us now and then we'll decide if we want to welcome him into the club."

I nod as I glance over at the street where he was a moment ago. "Is he going to make it?"

"Honestly, I hope not. He's kind of an asshole... but enough about him. Let's get back to our date."

"Okay," I reply, looking down at the cooler. "What did you bring for us?"

He grins. "Have a seat and I'll show you."

Following his instructions, I sink into my chair and fight back a grin as he opens the cooler with a flourish and starts pulling out sandwiches, chips, soda, and candy bars. It's everything we had at our picnic along the side of the road and I can't help but laugh.

"Sawyer, did you get me all dressed just to eat sandwiches?"

He shakes his head. "Hell no. I got you all dressed up so I could look at you while we eat sandwiches."

"Mmhmm. I suppose I'll let it slide since I get to look at you like this all evening," I say, motioning to his outfit and he grins as he sits across from me, his face lit up by candlelight. I turn to look out at the garden and shake my head as I sigh. "I can't believe you did all this for me."

"I can't believe you are so easily impressed."

"I'm not," I answer as I shrug and grab one of the

sandwiches off the table before unwrapping it. When I glance up, he's staring at me with an expression that is hard to read. "What?"

He drops his gaze to the table and shakes his head before meeting my eyes again. "Nothing."

"You finally going to tell me what happened on the day you came home drunk?"

"Yeah, about that…" he sighs. "A couple of months ago, we helped this girl named Sammy out of a bad situation and right before I left for Miami, we had gotten her set up in a new apartment and were helping her look for a job, basically rebuilding her life for her."

I nod, studying him as I take a bite of my sandwich. "What happened?"

"We got a call from this detective we work with and he said we needed to get down to this scene he was at. When we got there, he told us someone had beat her to death in the middle of the street and our business card was sitting on top of her body."

"Oh my God, Sawyer," I whisper, my eyes wide in horror and he sighs.

"We should talk about something else. This isn't great first date conversation."

I reach across the table and grab his hand. "I disagree. I want to know you, Sawyer, the real you, inside and out and this is something that really affected you."

"I just hate failing these girls, you know?" he says, meeting my eyes and the pain staring back at me breaks my heart. "Plus, we've lost two other girls this year so it's been extra rough."

"Is that normal?"

He shakes his head, his lips flattening into a line. "No, it's not. Fuzz was just showing me our stats the other day and since we started doing this eight years ago, we've lost five girls including the three this year."

"Okay, before I forget, I have to ask what the hell is up with these names? Fuzz? Moose?"

He rolls his eyes and falls back into his chair. "For fuck's sake. Who told you that story?"

"Mercedes but don't worry. I don't ever see myself calling you Moose."

"Thank God," he sighs and I can't help but laugh. "What do you say we stop talking about death and sadness and get back to proper first date activities?"

"What did you have in mind?"

He stands up and walks around the table to me before holding his hand out. Heat creeps up my cheeks as I take it and let him pull me out of my chair and away from the table to the side of the fountain where we can hear the music better. With a shit eating grin on his face, he wraps one arm around my waist while he pulls his phone out of his pocket and after a second, "I Knew I Loved You" by Savage Garden starts playing.

Throwing my head back, I laugh.

"Classic nineties love ballad, right? That's what you called this?" he asks as he slips his phone back into his pocket and wraps his other hand around my waist as I lay my arms across his shoulders. We begin swaying back and forth and I meet his eyes.

"Don't make fun of my music."

He shakes his head and takes one of my hands before pulling it up to his chest. "I'm not. In fact, this song is really growing on me lately."

"You're so full of it," I quip and he laughs as he pulls me closer, dancing with me under the stars as the chorus begins playing and I can't help but feel like it's so perfect for the way I feel about him. He's everything I could have asked for and more and I don't ever want to let this feeling go. "In fact, I'm going to change your ringtone to this song and call you while you're with the guys so everyone can see *just* how much this song is growing on you."

"Go for it, baby. I'll gladly make a fool of myself for you."

Sucking in a breath, I lean back to look in his eyes. "My mom used to talk about these moments in life where everything lines up, everything makes sense, and you finally understand that everything you went through was to get you to where you are, you know?"

"Yeah," he answers, his voice full of gravel as he smiles down at me. "I do."

"I have been having that feeling a lot since meeting you."

He nods. "Me, too, sweetheart."

"It's crazy, though, right?" We met five days ago but I really feel like I've known him forever, like he's always been a part of my life and it's so intense that I'm having such a hard time wrapping my head around it.

"If you shut out all the noise, does it feel crazy in

your heart or does it feel crazy because of other people's expectations? Because, I gotta be honest with you, I couldn't give two shits what anyone else thinks." He releases my hand to reach up and skate his thumb over my cheek. "I've never felt this way about anyone and it doesn't matter if it's been a week or ten years."

"That's a really good answer," I whisper and he grins as he strokes my cheek again and leans down, pressing his lips to mine. Under the twinkling lights, with the sound of trickling water and a classic nineties love ballad drifting through the air and Sawyer's lips against mine, I feel like I'm truly home for the first time in weeks. As much as I love Baton Rouge, I get the feeling that it wouldn't feel as comfortable and meaningful without Sawyer by my side.

He pulls away and stares down at me with something that looks an awful lot like love and my heart kicks in my chest. "There's something I should tell you."

"Oh?" I whisper. "What's that?"

"Tawny, that girl who left the note on my front door, swung by the clubhouse today and well, long story short, I ended up claiming you as my old lady in front of everyone."

My mouth pops open as I squint up at him. "I'm sorry... what?"

"My ex, Tawny..."

"Yeah, no, I got that part," I say, interrupting him as I wave my hand through the air. "But please explain the part about claiming me and me being an old lady."

He laughs. "Basically, it means that I told the club that you're mine, you're off limits to anyone else who may have been thinking about…"

"Oh, hell no…."

He slams his lips down on mine again for a quick kiss, shutting me up.

"Just listen. It means that you're one of the most important people in my life and it also means that any one of my brothers would die to protect you, just like I would for someone they care about. It means I choose you, I want you."

I suck in a breath. "Oh."

"What the fuck?" he growls and I jerk back to look up at his face. He's staring out at the street and I follow his gaze to a black SUV that I recognize from outside Mercedes' office. Oh, no. Sawyer plants a kiss on my forehead before gently shoving me away from him. "Stay here."

"Sawyer," I call but it's too late. He storms across the grass, looking intimidating as hell as he closes in on the P.I. and my stomach rolls. Once he gets to the open driver's side window, he starts yelling. It's loud enough that I can hear his voice but I can't make out what he is saying as he gestures wildly before pointing to me.

Oh, Lord Almighty.

After a couple more tense seconds of angry conversation, Sawyer shoves the guy and backs up onto the sidewalk before pointing down the street in a clear order to leave. The SUV backs out of the space and races off. He watches it leave before turning around and marching back to me as he scans his surroundings. When he stops in front of me, he runs his hand through his hair and pulls me back into his arms.

"It's a goddamn P.I. and he's watching you."

"Oh," I whisper like I didn't already know that.

"He wouldn't tell me who he's working for, though. Son of a bitch. Maybe I can get Streak to hack his phone or something to get us some answers."

Squeezing my eyes shut, I consider telling him everything but when I open my mouth, that's not what comes out. "I've seen him around before…"

"What?" he bellows, stepping back to look in my eyes. "And you didn't tell me?"

"I didn't know for sure," I reason, shaking my head. "And when I confronted him, he said he was just taking pictures of the city. I didn't know what to do."

He shakes his head. "Why would someone have a P.I. following you around?"

"I don't know," I lie, my hands trembling and the words burning as they spill out of my mouth. He takes a deep breath and pulls me back into his arms almost like he needs the comfort as much as I do.

"Listen, I have a little cabin out in the middle of nowhere. What do you say we go get lost for a few days and then when we get back we can figure all of this out?"

I nod, relief flooding me at the thought of being away from Gavin's prying eyes for a little while and I promise myself that after we get back, I'll tell him everything.

Never Let Me Go
Chapter Eighteen
Juliette

"Just Got Started Lovin' You" by James Otto spills out of the speakers in the truck as we wind down a back country road on the way to Sawyer's cabin and I smile as I lay my head back on the seat and close my eyes. My feet are up on the dash and the windows are down, letting the sun warm my skin and the wind whip through my hair and away from the prying eyes of Gavin and his lackey, as all my stress melts away. After the abrupt end to our date last night, we went back to the house and I helped Sawyer pack up supplies before I called Nico to see when she thought she'd be down in Baton Rouge. She said she has a few things to wrap up in Miami and she should get into town in three days which gives us the perfect opportunity for a mini getaway to the woods. I turn my head to the other side and smile across the cab at Sawyer. He peeks in my direction before grinning and returning his gaze to the road.

"You're gorgeous."

Turning to face forward, my smile widens. "Flattery will get you everywhere, sir."

He laughs as he slows down and turns on his blinker. Dropping my feet from the dash, I lean forward and scan the tree line. There's a little dirt road nestled in there, almost hidden from view and my belly does a little flip as he turns down the road.

"I can't wait to see your cabin."

He shakes his head. "Fuck, I'm nervous. I've never brought anyone out here."

"Not even Molly?"

He sighs. "No… Molly wasn't really into this kind of thing."

"What? Nature?" I ask, laughing and he glances over at me with a nod. "Oh."

"She couldn't stand the thought of being in my little two room cabin and lord help you if you mentioned the bugs out here."

I scowl. "So, what? You always just did what she wanted to do?"

"Pretty much but I didn't mind. Making her happy made me happy."

Oh my God.

How has this sweet, perfect man not been taken by another woman yet? How does he not know how perfect he is?

"Did she make you happy?" I ask as the trees open up slightly to reveal a cute little log cabin and he scowls as he parks the truck.

"You know, before I met you, I would have said yes without even thinking about it but now, I don't know… I mean, it's not like she never did anything for me or that I was at her beck and call."

I reach across the cab and grab his hand. "It's okay. You don't have to stress it."

"Is that what you're doing? Just coming out here with me to make me happy?"

"Yes and no. I really do love being out in nature. Get me next to a lake and I'll be a happy girl. Plus, I'm never going to say no to spending alone time with you. You are very quickly turning into my favorite person."

He grins, a look of vulnerability in his eyes. "Yeah?"

"Oh, yeah," I agree with a nod as I scoot across the bench seat and straddle his legs. He grips my hips gently and I lay my hands on his chest. I can't help rocking my hips against his denim covered cock and he groans softly before shaking his head at me.

"You know… if you walk through those trees over there," he points over my shoulder and I glance behind me, "you'll find the lake you were talking about."

I beam as I turn back to him. "Really?"

"Yep."

"Will you show me?"

He glances down at his lap and manipulates my hips with his hands, rubbing my core against his growing erection. "You sure you don't want to check out the cabin first?"

A.M. Myers

"On second thought, that sounds like a better idea," I whisper as he rotates my hips again. My fingers dig into his chest as warmth rushes through me and I gasp. "Sawyer."

"Fuck… I think that's my favorite way I've heard you say my name, angel."

My eyes roll back as he does it again and my nipples pebble, aching to be touched. "Take me inside."

"I thought you wanted to check out the lake?" he asks, flashing me a very convincing confused puppy look as he forces my hips down at the same time that he thrusts up and groans. Jesus H. Christ. I'm going to die, combust right here in his truck if he doesn't stop doing that. I shake my head.

"Later."

His hand slips under my tank top and skates up my back. When he gets to my shoulders, he pushes me down to meet his lips and I moan, my hips moving on their own now as his fingertips dig into my skin.

"Sawyer," I moan, ripping away from his kiss and he groans as he leans in and nips at my neck while he reaches over to fumble for the door handle.

"Fuck."

He finally gets the door open and he grabs my ass, holding me up as he stumbles out of the truck. Grabbing his face between my hands, I steal desperate kisses as he carries me to the cabin and up the stairs of the front porch before he presses my back against the wall.

"Shit. My keys are in the truck." He lowers me to

256

my feet and smacks my ass. "Don't you go anywhere."

I glance around as he jumps to the ground, skipping the stairs completely, and smile as I strip my tank top over my head and unbutton my jeans before he turns back around with the truck keys in his hand.

"Don't you dare take anything else off without me," he growls, charging back toward me with a predatory look and I let out a giggle as he wraps one arm around my waist and unlocks the cabin with his other hand. Inside, he sets me down and as I walk over to the bed, I shove my shorts down my legs. He sucks in a breath and I grin.

"You trying to put on a show, baby?"

I peek over my shoulder at him. "Maybe. Do you want me to stop?"

"Absolutely not," he groans, his eyes glued to my ass as he unbuttons his jeans and shoves them down his legs before leaning back against the closed door and wrapping his hand around his thick cock. Holy fuck. Pure, undiluted desire races through my bloodstream and steals my breath as I turn to face him and watch as he slowly strokes his hand up and down his shaft.

"Sawyer."

He closes his eyes, his face bathed in pleasure, as he nods. "Say it again."

"Sawyer," I purr, taking a step toward him as I reach behind my back and unhook my bra. He opens his eyes just as it falls to the floor. Hunger and need rage in his blue eyes as he rips his shirt over his head, displaying his damn near perfect body and making me feel so powerful. His eyes never leave me as I close the distance between us and smile before dropping to my knees and peeking up at him.

"Juliette," he breathes. I lick my lips and wrap my hand around his length, giving it one quick stroke, as he shudders and slides his hand into my hair. The anticipation on his face fans the fire burning inside me and I lean forward, letting my lips hover just above the head while he watches and his body tenses. When I pull back again, he relaxes with a frustrated groan. "Juliette."

"Oh, I think that's my favorite way I've heard you say my name."

He shakes his head and closes his eyes before knocking his head back against the door and I take advantage of the distraction, leaning forward and running my tongue along the underside of his cock from his balls to the tip. The hand in my hair tightens and he hisses, his hips bucking forward.

"Turn about is fair play, angel," he warns me and my heart skips a beat at the thought as I lean in again and take him into my mouth. A loud groan rips through him as he throws his head back and I resist the urge to smile as I close my lips around his length and suck.

"Motherfucker," he breathes, tugging on my hair a little and moisture pools between my thighs as he takes control, thrusting his hips forward as he holds my head steady. He hits the back of my throat and groans again as another shudder runs through his body. As he thrusts again, I wrap my hand around the base and tease the underside of his cock with my tongue before sucking hard and I swear, his knees almost buckle. I glance up and meet his eyes. He hisses a curse, pulling his length out of my mouth before yanking me to my feet and wrapping his arm around my waist as he slams his lips to mine.

Moaning, I hook my leg over his hip as his tongue tangles with mine and he grabs the other leg, effortlessly lifting me into his arms. My skin tingles with need as he grabs my ass in his hands, his fingers so close to my pussy but just out of reach, driving me crazy. I buck my hips, trying to convey what I need to him and he grins as he gently skates his fingers over my panties.

"Yes," I gasp, tearing my lips from his and he groans into my neck as he carries me over to the bed. He lays me down on the bed with my ass right at the edge before dropping to his knees in front of me and hooking his fingers into the waistband of my panties as he meets my eyes. His expression screams raw, primal need and makes me moan as I drop my head back on the bed and close my eyes. The light brushes of his fingertips against my skin as he slowly lowers my panties down my legs heighten every single sensation until I'm on the verge of screaming.

I need relief…

I need this.

I need him.

"Sawyer," I beg and he moans as he climbs up my body, kissing and licking a path across my skin as he goes and my heart thunders in my ears as my hands shake.

Oh, God.

He kisses up my neck, sending goose bumps racing across my flesh, before he claims my lips again, kissing me like he owns me, like I'm his to do with as he pleases, and I have no trouble complying with that. Not when it feels this damn good to have him on top of me. Planting one last quick kiss on my lips, he starts kissing down my body again and I whine as I reach for him, trying desperately to get him back where I want him but he just laughs as he slips between my legs and runs his hands up the inside of my thighs.

"You want some relief, angel?" he asks and I cry out as I nod.

"Yes."

I can feel his breath on my pussy as he brushes his thumb over my clit and my entire body jerks like I have been electrocuted, sounds like I've never heard spilling from my lips. He nips at my thigh with a groan and just when I think he's going to tease me some more, his mouth is on me. I scream, my entire body bowing off the bed and he presses down on my hips as he starts flicking my clit with the tip of his tongue.

"Oh, fuck. Oh, fuck. Oh, fuck," I chant, digging my fingers into his hair as he sucks the sensitive bundle of nerves into his mouth and my hips buck again. "Sawyer, please."

It's too much.

My body is swamped with too many sensations to

name or try to pin down and it's skirting dangerously close to torture.

"Sawyer," I cry again when he seems intent on continuing his torment. He growls and climbs up my body, dragging his hands over my damp skin as he goes and I struggle to breathe as my pussy throbs with need and my skin aches to feel his touch. I look up and meet his gaze. "Fuck me. Please."

With a groan, he presses his lips to mine as his cock brushes against my core and I lift my hips off the bed but he moves away.

"You have no idea how much I love hearing you beg me," he whispers and I close my eyes as I shake my head back and forth.

"No more, please. I need you." When I open my eyes again, a tear trickles down my cheek and he moans as he kisses it away.

"I need a condom," he says, jumping up from the bed and running to his jeans by the door before grabbing one and coming back to bed. He stands over me, stroking himself a few times before he rips the packet open with his teeth and slides the condom on. When he's back between my legs, he leans down and kisses me again, softer this time like I'm the most precious thing in his life and I gasp as he slowly buries himself inside me. My body arches off the bed and my eyes close as I try to cling to him, my hands slipping across his skin.

"Shit," he hisses, pulling back to look down at where we're joined together as he pulls his hips back

and sinks in again, enraptured. He meets my gaze.
"You're perfect."

I nod, ignoring his comment as I reach for him.
"More."

He flashes me a grin before plunging into me
harder. My body clenches down around him and
pressure builds in my belly as he keeps the same pace
and leans down to kiss me. It's such a contradiction to
the animalistic motion of his hips and I'm obsessed,
well and truly ruined for any other man because no
other man will ever be able to compare to this. He
touches me like I'm glass and indestructible at the same
time.

Fire and ice.

Heaven and hell

Black and white.

It's a perfect contrast designed and executed to
drive me out of my mind.

I scrape my nails down his back and he rears back
with a groan before grabbing my wrists and pinning
them to the bed as his hips thrust into me a little bit
harder.

"You're not being very nice, angel."

I shake my head. "Neither are you."

"Oh. Did you want to come?" he asks, punctuating
his question with a couple of quick thrusts and I cry out
as I nod my head.

"Yes."

He nods and releases my hands before reaching
between us to rub his thumb over my clit. "Go ahead,

baby. I want to feel you come on my cock."

"Sawyer," I moan as my release overwhelms me, white lights exploding behind my eyes as my body clamps down on him and shudders. He groans. Gripping my hips, he thrusts into me for a few more seconds before his eyes close and he stills, releasing something between a moan and a sigh as his body jerks above me. He sighs again as he opens his eyes and meets my gaze with a silly grin on his face. I laugh.

"You're a tease," I accuse him and he laughs as he rolls to the bed next to me and drops the condom in a trash can.

"Oh, angel," he muses, pulling me into his arms. "You ain't seen nothing yet."

A.M. Myers

Never Let Me Go
Chapter Nineteen
Sawyer

"Wake up, sleepyhead," her sweet voice says as she cuddles into my side and I hum, wrapping my arms around her and pulling her closer. She skates her fingers down my stomach. "It's time to wake up."

I peek one eye open. "Why don't you keep moving that hand of yours down? That sounds like a pretty nice way to wake a man up."

"He says like he didn't fuck her four times last night before they finally passed out."

"Your point?" I ask, biting back a laugh and she shakes her head.

"My point is it's time to get up." She swings her leg over my hips and her tits hang in my face as she reaches toward the nightstand for something. Growling, I grip her hips and try to bury my face between them as she squeals. "Stop it. I have hot coffee."

"No," I whine, closing my eyes. "It's too early."

She laughs. "It's almost nine."

"We're on vacation."

"Which means we should probably try and spend some time together," she argues as she holds my coffee in her hand and tilts her head to the side. The early morning sunlight frames her silhouette and she flashes me a smile that smacks me right in the chest.

"You're fucking gorgeous, angel."

She blushes but shakes her head. "Time to get up."

Before I can stop her, she climbs off of me and sets my coffee down on the nightstand again. I watch her as she grabs my t-shirt and pulls it over her head. As she turns and struts away from me, I sit up and lean back against the headboard with a grin. I bite my lip as her ass sways back and forth in her tiny little pair of lace panties. Fuck, she's perfect.

"Come on, baby. Turn around and come back to bed," I say, thrusting my hips into the air as the words roll off my lips and she rolls her eyes.

"If I come back to bed, it's to sleep, not fuck," she warns, arching a brow in my direction and my cock twitches at her dirty mouth. "Between the multiple orgasms, your snoring, and a nightmare, I didn't get much sleep."

I frown. "What did you have a bad dream about?"

"Oh, it wasn't me. It was you," she says as she sits down at the table and picks up a pencil. My dream from last night plays out in my mind and I wince as a shudder runs through me. It all started out fine - Juliette and I were in bed at home when I looked out of the window and noticed a black SUV, the same one that we saw at the park and when I turned back to tell Juliette, she had vanished. I was in a panic, searching for her everywhere but no matter how hard I tried to find her, I came up empty. Then, it morphed into some kind of weird haze from my past and I found her dead on the living room floor. I push the image out of my mind as I pick up my coffee and take a sip

Ever since we left Baton Rouge, I've really been trying to not focus on all the questions I have about Juliette but it's getting harder and harder. My initial feeling was right all along and there is something going on with her but I just can't put my finger on what it is. What the hell does she have going on that is so bad she feels like she can't talk to me about it? This is what I *do* and I've claimed her in front of the whole damn club. There isn't anything I wouldn't do for her and it kills me to think that she can't trust me with this. God, I want to ask her so fucking bad but I promised her we'd wait until we got back to the city and I'm going to honor that. That doesn't mean I didn't ask Streak to look into it for me, though.

"What are you working on over there?" I ask, watching her as she scowls at her paper and drags the eraser across it, her cute little nose crinkling in displeasure. She looks up.

"Just doodling."

I scoff and throw the covers off of my legs before climbing out of bed and after walking across the room, I sink into the chair next to her in my birthday suit. "Let

267

me see."

"No making fun of me."

"Why would I make fun of you?" I ask, throwing my arm over her chair and pulling her closer. She shrugs as a blush stains her cheeks.

"I don't know. I just hate showing my designs to people before I feel like they're perfect."

"I bet it already is perfect."

She shakes her head as she fights back a grin. "Your approval is not the one I need."

"Well, let me look anyway."

She passes over the notebook and my brows shoot up as I study the "doodle" she's thrown together. It's a necklace, dripping in diamonds, and all I can imagine is her wearing it around her pretty little neck with nothing else on as she rides my cock.

"What do you think?"

I turn to her and my gaze falls down to her nipples as they press against the fabric of my t-shirt. "I think you'd look fucking amazing in this… and nothing else."

"Fucking pervert," she scoffs, giving me a little shove as she turns away to hide her smile. My chest aches as I watch her.

This woman fucking owns me.

"Tell me I'm wrong," I whisper as I lean in and let my lips brush against her neck as I breathe in her scent. She shivers.

"I can't."

I grin. "See? Now come over here and kiss me."

Never Let Me Go

"Only because I like you so much," she murmurs as she gets up and straddles my legs. I wrap my arms around her and pull her closer as she runs her fingers across my chest with a sigh. "You going to tell me what your bad dream was about?"

"It was about you."

Surprised eyes meet mine. "Me?"

"Yep. I dreamed about you going missing and mystery black SUVs."

"Oh," she whispers with a nod as she stares down at her lap. "That."

Reaching up, I cup her cheek and force her gaze back to mine. "Why won't you tell me what's going on, baby? Do you not trust me? Is it that bad?"

"It's…complicated. And I *am* going to tell you as soon as we get back to Baton Rouge but I just want to enjoy spending time with you *before* things get complicated."

I tighten my grip and sigh. "Are you in danger?"

"I don't think so."

"What the fuck does that mean?" I ask, studying her as my mind spins.

"I told you it was complicated."

I scoff as I turn to look out of the window. "Yeah, you did…"

"Sawyer… I hope you know that no matter what I have to tell you when we get back, my feelings for you are real. I want you. I want us."

"Okay," I say, nodding despite the voice in my head that is screaming at me that she's lying. "Let's just table it for now."

She nods and turns to look over at her drawing. After a minute she starts chewing on her bottom lip and I can practically see the wheels turning in her head.

"What are you thinking about so hard? I thought we were gonna drop it."

"Actually, I was thinking about doing your idea for the advertisement. I think it'd be gorgeous."

I jerk back. "You absolutely will not."

"Excuse me?" she hisses, her brow arching as she turns to glare at me. "What did you just say?"

"I said there's no way in fucking hell I'm going to let you pose naked for the whole goddamn world to see," I snap and her eyes widen. She stands up so suddenly that she almost knocks the chair over and before I can grab her, she stalks over to the bed and grabs a pair of shorts.

"Where the fuck are you going?"

She stands and pulls her shorts on, glaring at me the whole time. "I'm going for a walk."

"No, you're not."

"Listen here, you fucking cave man, I'm tired, I'm hungry, and I'm very likely going to kill you if you keep saying shit like you aren't going to let me do this or that so I'm going for a walk. End of discussion."

After slipping her feet into her tennis shoes, she marches past me and I try to grab her hand but she rips it from my grasp without even looking back at me. The screen door slams as she stomps down the stairs and a scream of frustration rips through the air, echoing through the trees around us. Scrubbing my hand over my face, I sigh.

Well, that could have gone better.

What the hell was I thinking? I know better than to try and tell a woman what to do but the thought of millions of men staring her naked body, especially after everything that we shared last night, made me fucking homicidal. And now I can't even apologize to her. Turning away from the door, I scan the cabin and stop on the refrigerator. I guess I could cook something for her. She did say she was hungry and maybe if I feed her she won't be so damn mad at me. Sighing, I get up and grab a few things out of the fridge. I'm not a great cook but I can fry bacon and whip up some eggs, at least and then when she gets back, we'll talk this out. There is no other option because she's right, I know how she feels about me and I know there's no way in hell I'm walking away from her.

As I grab the pan from the cupboard, a loud bang rings through the trees and every muscle in my body tightens as I turn toward the door. That sounded like a gunshot... With my heart pounding in my ears, I throw on my jeans and rush out to the front porch as I scan the property for any sign of Juliette but the trees are blocking most of my view. Another bang echoes through the trees and my stomach drops as I jump off the porch.

"Juliette!" I yell, running into the trees before I stop to listen for her.

Come on, baby.

A.M. Myers

Let me hear you.

"Juliette!"

Silence greets me and I take off in one direction, hoping I run into her at some point. The forest is silent, too fucking silent, or maybe I can't hear anything over the thrashing in my ears as I scan the area around me for any sign of her. Either way, it's fucking torture.

"Juliette!" I scream, stopping and bringing my hands on my knees as I suck air into my lungs. My chest feels tight and my hands shake as fear runs rampant through me.

Please, baby...

Say something.

I remember she wanted to check out the lake so I turn in that direction and take off again, praying with every ounce of strength that I have that she's okay but images of her bleeding out on the ground won't leave me alone.

"Juliette!"

"Sawyer?"

I skid to a stop.

Her voice is a sweet relief and I turn toward the direction it came from before taking off again. Come on, gorgeous. Where are you? She bursts through the brush with tears in her eyes and crashes into me, almost knocking both of us over. As soon as she's in my arms, a sob tears through her. I step back to look her over as I run my hands down her arms.

"Are you okay?"

Her eyes meet mine, full of fear as her hands shake

272

and she struggles to breathe. "I heard the bullet… it hit a tree right next to me… I could have died…"

"Shh, baby," I whisper as I pull her into my arms and close my eyes, thanking God that she is okay. "It's okay. I've got you."

"The second one…" she continues, speaking quickly in between sobs. "I felt the air from it on my face… It was so close and… it just missed me."

My stomach rolls thinking about how close I came to losing her. I rub my hands all over her body, wishing I could wrap her up so tight that she'd feel safe again as I scan our surroundings. My nearest neighbor is three miles away and for someone to come that close to hitting her, they had to be on the property.

"Why would someone be shooting a gun out here?" she asks, pulling back to look up at my face and I shake my head.

"I think we should head back to the city."

Her eyes widen. "You think someone was actually shooting at me?"

"I don't know but that's the most likely scenario and I'm not okay with staying here if it's going to put you in danger."

"Why?" she whispers, shaking her head. "Why would someone shoot at me?"

"I think it's time you told me everything, angel."

She stares up at me for a second before nodding. Relief rushes through me that I'm finally going to get some answers but I won't rest easy until I know for sure that my girl is safe.

A.M. Myers

Never Let Me Go
Chapter Twenty
Juliette

My stomach is in knots as Sawyer sets our bags
down on the living room floor with a sigh and glances
over at me. We spent the drive back from the cabin in
silence but he never once took his arm off my shoulder,
holding me close to his body. I know we're still really
shook up after what happened at the cabin but he was
there for me anyway. It was a relief, to be honest. Who
knows how much of a mess I would have been after
what happened in the woods if he had been cold and
distant to me. Sinking into the couch, I stare at my
hands, which haven't stopped shaking since the shots
started. Closing my eyes, I remember hearing that first
bang and the way the bark on the tree right next to me
exploded as the bullet made impact. I stood there,
frozen in fear as my heart thundered in my chest and
tears gathered in my eyes, unable to do anything as I
cried out for Sawyer. When the second bullet ripped

through the air, I felt the force of it against my cheek and my stomach rolls as I think about how close it came to hitting me. I've never felt fear like that in my life but I still can't wrap my head around the idea that someone wants to hurt me.

It doesn't make any sense.

Sawyer walks into the kitchen and comes back a few seconds later with a beer in his hand before he sits in the chair across from me and nods. "Time to start talking, angel."

I nod.

"Why don't we start with who hired that P.I. out front?"

Wincing, I shake my head. "Can we start with something else?"

"Like?" he asks, arching a brow. His gaze is hard and the longer he stares at me, the more I see him shutting down and throwing up walls to block out the pain he thinks I'm going to cause him. God, why didn't I just tell him the truth from the beginning? Would he really have treated me differently? I suck in a breath as I wring my hands together.

"Do you remember when I told you that my dad just passed away in a car accident?"

He nods. "Yeah."

"Well, I was in that accident, too…"

"What?" he whispers, concern flashing in his eyes as he studies me. "Why would you lie about that?"

"Because it put me in a coma for a week and when I woke up, I was missing the last five years of my memories."

His entire body freezes and his eyes widen. "Are you serious?"

I nod.

"Again, why wouldn't you tell me that?"

"Because I had no idea who I was supposed to be and I didn't want you to treat me differently. Then, once we started getting to know each other, I was just scared."

He sucks in a breath and scrubs his hand over his face. "What about now? Can you remember anything from your past?"

"Not really, no."

Blowing out a breath, he leans forward and shakes his head. "What does that mean?"

"Well, you know that dinner I made you the night you got drunk?"

He nods.

"Apparently, I learned that in a cooking class with Mercedes in Miami. I remember the recipe but I don't remember the class at all."

Sighing, he rubs his temple with his fingertips. "Anything else you remember?"

"I don't think so."

"Right," he scoffs, bringing his beer to his lips and chugging half of it before turning to look at me again with narrowed eyes. "How does that lead us to the man following you around?"

My heart hammers out of control and my stomach rolls as I suck in a breath. "When I woke up in the hospital, there was a man there. I didn't recognize him but he told me that he... was my fiancé."

"You're engaged?" he roars, jumping up from his chair and I shake my head as tears prick my eyes.

"No. I was engaged in my old life and before I left Miami, I broke things off with him but as you can see, he's not exactly taking no for an answer."

"Jesus Christ," he hisses as he begins pacing in front of me and running his hand through his hair. "Is there anything else you're lying to me about?"

I wince and he stops.

"What?"

A tear slips down my cheek and I quickly wipe it away. "Have you ever heard of O'Shaw Records?"

"Of course," he answers, flashing me a blank look before it fades to recognition. "Holy shit. Are you telling me that you're the Shaw in O'Shaw Records?"

"No. My dad was."

"Holy fuck!" he exclaims as he resumes his pacing and I resist the urge to burst into tears. This is so much harder than I thought it would be and it kills me to see the pain in his eyes from my deception. I shouldn't have lied. My teeth sink into my lip as I stare at my hands and another tear slips down my cheek.

"Sawyer..." I whisper and he barely glances at me as he passes by me and turns to go back the other way again before he stops and throws his body back in the chair. Leaning forward, he braces his elbows on his knees.

"I'm fucking terrified to ask but anything else?"

I shake my head. "Not unless you're concerned with my net worth."

He balks. "I didn't even think about that... it's a lot, isn't it?"

"Yes." There's no point in beating around the bush anymore. If I'm going to tell him the truth, then I'm going to tell him everything.

"How much?"

I open my mouth to respond when he holds his hand up and shakes his head.

"You know what... I don't want to know."

My fingers twitch with the urge to reach out and touch him but I know I can't bring him any comfort right now. "Are you sure you don't want to know?"

He scoffs. "Am I sure? No, I'm not sure about anything anymore. I can't decide if I should believe you or if there is still more you're hiding."

"I'm putting everything out on the table, Sawyer. I want to build a future with you."

He falls back in his chair and shakes his head. "I just don't know if I can do that anymore."

"What?" I whisper, my heart stalling as tears burn my eyes. He meets my gaze and pain shines back at me, amplifying my own.

"I think I need some time to think about all this."

A weight settles into my stomach and my chest aches as I nod. "Okay..."

"Go get your things and I'll drive you over to the clubhouse. They have some rooms you can crash in until you figure something else out," he says, refusing to look at me and it would have been kinder if he punched me in the gut. Nodding, I push off the couch and practically run to the guest bedroom where I've been staying before shutting the door and gasping for air as the tears run down my face.

I knew he would be upset.

I knew he would be mad.

But I had hoped that we had built something strong enough to withstand this. Guess I was wrong.

Through my tears, I throw all my clothes back into my bag before going into the attached bathroom and tossing everything I can find in my toiletries bag. I toss it on top of my other bag as I plop down on the edge of the bed and sob into a pillow. Memories from the past week and a half play out in my mind and I struggle to breathe as the tears refuse to let up. The thought of sitting next to him in the truck as he drives me to a hotel sounds like torture and I know I can't do it. Tossing the pillow aside, I try to wipe the tears from my face as I pull my phone out of my pocket and text Mercedes.

Me:
911. I need you.

I barely set the phone down on the bed next to me when it starts ringing and I suck in a breath as I answer it.

"Hello?"

"What's going on?" she asks, her voice panicked and my bottom lip wobbles as I try to keep it together.

"I need you to come get me."

"Why? What happened?"

I press my fingers into my forehead. "Please, Mer. I promise to tell you everything, just not right this second."

"You at Sawyer's house?"

"Yes."

"I'm on my way."

After hanging up, I toss the phone on the bed next to me and brace my hands on either side of my body as I wonder if this is truly the end for Sawyer and me. He said he needed time to think but I can't help but think what he really needed was to get me out of his house so it would be easier to end things with me. Closing my eyes, I remember our first kiss on the front porch and my chest burns, pain rushing over me like a tidal wave.

Sawyer is the one.

I think I knew it from the moment I laid eyes on him but now, because of my mistakes, I'm going to lose him.

"You ready?" he asks, knocking on the door and I jerk up and quickly wipe the tears from my cheeks as the door opens.

"Mercedes is coming to get me. I didn't want to put you out more than I already have."

He nods, staring at the floor. "Right."

"Sawyer," I whisper, more tears dripping down my

cheeks. "I'm so sorry. I never meant to hurt you. I was only…"

He turns away from me. "Make sure you leave your key on the counter."

Before I can say anything else, he disappears and I wince as his bedroom door slams shut, echoing down the hallway and I can't help but think it sounds like the book closing on our relationship. This is it. After a whirlwind of ten days, this is all I'm left with.

My phone pings with a message.

Mercedes:
I'm outside.

Shoving my phone in my pocket, I stand up and grab my bags before leaving the key to the house on the dresser. I step out into the living room and the closer I get to the door, the more it hurts. There's a part of me, albeit a very little part, that is hoping he will realize this is a mistake and we belong together before he rushes out of his room and begs me to stay but the closer I get to the door, the more that fantasy dies. As I grab my bag from our trip to the cabin, I turn and look back at the house before sucking in a breath and opening the door. There's no use in prolonging the pain and the more I put this off, the harder it will be to force myself outside.

Mercedes jumps out of her car and pops the trunk

before helping me with my bags, her worried gaze inspecting my face. I can only imagine what I look like right now with tear tracks dragging mascara down my face but I don't care. Once my bags are in the trunk, she shuts it and wraps me up in a hug.

"What happened, sweetie?"

I shake my head. "Later, Mer. I have to get out of here."

She nods as she lets me go as I glance up at the house, meeting Sawyer's gaze in his bedroom window. My heart cracks wide open, pleading and crying for him, but he turns away from me and pulls the curtain over the window. Slipping into the car, I let out a sob and Mercedes reaches across the console to grab my hand as she pulls away from the curb.

"You're coming over to my house."

I shake my head. "No. Just take me to a hotel."

"Okay," she answers brightly. "We'll have a sleepover. Maybe we can even go to the spa and relax a little."

"Mercedes," I whisper, a dull ache beginning to form in my forehead. She shakes her head and flashes me a stern look.

"You are in obvious pain and you have zero chance of getting rid of me tonight so we can go to my place or we can sleep over at a hotel. Your choice."

"Hotel. I need somewhere that doesn't have memories tied to it."

She nods. "Okay. You ready to tell me what happened?"

I suck in a breath and nod. I'm not really ready to tell her but I'd rather just get it over with so I spit everything out - the P.I. crashing our date, disappearing to the cabin, someone shooting at me, and telling Sawyer the truth.

"Oh, honey," she whispers, squeezing my hand. "I'm sure he'll come around once he gets a chance to think it all through. That's a hell of a lot for any person to deal with, let alone over a three day period."

I nod. "I know but you didn't see the look on his face. He used to look at me like I was the only one he could see, like I shined and stood out among the rest of the world."

"And how did he look at you just now?"

"Like I was just like the rest of them," I answer as a sob rips through me and I close my eyes. The look in his eyes as he stood in the window… it will haunt me for the rest of my life. "Do you think I should have told him the truth from the start?"

She sighs. "Yes and no. I understand why he's hurt but I also know you were just trying to protect yourself and figure out who you are. Plus, I'm not convinced that he would have been open to the feelings you two have for each other and your connection if he had been looking at you like someone else he needed to protect."

"Damned if I do and damned if I don't."

"Exactly."

My phone starts ringing and my heart jumps into my throat as I fumble for it. I finally manage to grab it and my face falls as I stare at the screen.

Never Let Me Go

"Who is it?" Mercedes asks and I turn it to show her Gavin's name on the screen. She sighs. "Just get it over with, girl."

Nodding, I answer it. "Hello?"

"Jules," he breathes, relief coursing through his voice. "I'm so glad I finally got ahold of you. Where are you, baby?"

"Stop playing games, Gavin. I know you have a P.I. following me."

He sighs. "Look, can we meet up? Maybe grab some dinner and talk?"

"No, I have plans."

"What about tomorrow? Lunch, maybe?"

I shake my head. "I don't think that's a good idea."

"Juliette, please," he pleads and a sliver of guilt slips through my armor.

"I'm really sorry, Gavin. None of this is your fault and I realize that you got put in a shitty situation but the accident changed everything for me and I'm not the same person I was."

"I understand that. I was just hoping that maybe we could start over again. You fell in love with me once, you know, it could happen again."

My teeth sink into my lip as I shake my head. "No, it couldn't."

"Why not?"

"Because I'm already in love with someone else."

He scoffs. "No, you're not."

"Yes, I am."

"It's not possible. You just left. Two weeks ago,

285

you were my fiancée."

I shake my head and sigh. Maybe any other day I would be gentler and explain to him that what Sawyer and I have is just too big, too powerful to ignore but I don't have the energy for it right now.

"Maybe I was before the accident but I don't know you anymore."

"You haven't even given me a chance!" he bellows and I pull the phone away from my ear for a second before sucking in a breath. "If you did, we would fall in love all over again."

I shake my head. "No, we wouldn't. My future is here, in Baton Rouge. I'm sorry and I really wish you the best but this is over."

He protests on the other end of the line but I pull my phone away from my ear and hang up. For the first time in weeks, my mind is completely clear and even without my memories, I know what I want.

"Oh, I know that look," Mercedes says, her gaze flicking between me and the road. "What's the plan, Jett?"

"Tonight, we're going to eat ice cream, watch terrible movies and cry, and then tomorrow, I'm going to get my man back."

Never Let Me Go
Chapter Twenty-One
Sawyer

Sighing, I walk into the hotel and ignore the woman behind the front desk as she smiles at me, scanning the lobby for the bar Mercedes told me to meet her in. It's tucked in the corner near the elevators and I shove my hands in my pockets as I walk over and slide onto a stool at the end of the bar.

"What can I get for you, man?" the bartender asks and I order a beer. He grabs a bottle from the fridge and pops the cap off before setting it in front of me. "You want to start a tab?"

I throw a ten dollar bill down and shake my head. "No. I'm not staying long."

He nods and leaves me in peace as I take a sip of my beer and settle into my seat. I pick at the label on my bottle of beer and sigh as I close my eyes, unable to get the look on Juliette's face as she climbed into Mercedes' car out of my mind.

Fuck.

A.M. Myers

It broke my heart and it took all the strength I had to not go out there and tell her to stay and now that I'm alone, I can't decide if I made the right decision. I needed time to think and figure out how to feel after everything she revealed to me this afternoon but I just keep going in circles and kicking myself for making her leave when I'm pretty damn sure someone is after her.

Shit.

What was I thinking?

"Thanks for coming," someone says and I turn as Mercedes sidles up to the bar next to me. I nod. "You haven't been waiting long, have you?"

"No. I just got here." I look behind her. "Where's Juliette?"

She sighs. "Asleep upstairs."

"How is she?" I ask, focusing on my beer and refusing to meet her gaze. She sighs again.

"She's heartbroken… but oddly determined to earn your forgiveness."

I turn and we lock eyes. "Is that why I'm here? So you can butter me up for her?"

"No. You're here because… two weeks ago, my best friend was in more pain than I've ever seen her go through… until tonight. And you're also here because I've never seen her smile the way she does when she talks about you…"

"So you *are* here to butter me up," I scoff, interrupting her and her eyes narrow into slits as she almost shoves me off my stool.

"Stop being a bitch and listen to what I'm really

288

saying to you. You don't have to forgive her. You don't have to be with her again but don't you think you should hear all sides of the story before you make your decision?"

Sighing, I nod. "Fine."

"When she called me and told me that she couldn't remember anything for the last five years, I didn't know what to think. I mean, it's crazy but then I thought about what it would feel like to not know anything from your life. She moved to Miami five years ago to be closer to her dad and her last memory before she woke up in the hospital was the last night we went out to celebrate her move here in Baton Rouge. She literally didn't know a single thing about her life in Miami. Can you imagine that? Waking up and not recognizing a single part of your life and being told that the only person you remember is dead?"

I stare at the bottle in front of me as I try to imagine exactly what she's describing. What if I woke up and my mom and dad were gone and I was in a city I didn't know with people I didn't recognize? It sounds terrifying.

"Exactly," she says, studying my face. "But she still put on a brave face and tried to go back to her apartment with a man who said he was her fiancé but she didn't know that, not for sure, at least. She tried to get back to her daily life but she might as well have been on a different planet so she finally broke down and called me for help."

"I understand…"

She shakes her head. "No, I don't know that you truly do. When she called me, she didn't even know if we were still friends but she was so desperate for anything familiar that she took the chance."

"I understand all that, Mercedes, but why didn't she tell me about it at any point before now?"

She rolls her eyes. "God, men are so clueless... She wanted to tell you, so badly, but she was afraid that it would change the way you looked at her. She didn't want to be another project for you to fix."

The jab hits its mark and I suck in a breath as I lean forward and set my elbows on the bar. "Why are you telling me all this and not her?"

"Because I don't have any skin in the game and I can lay everything out for you without getting scared or too emotional."

I nod as I think over everything Juliette told me earlier. "This fiancé of hers... Do I need to be worried?"

"Ugh," she groans as she rolls her eyes. "No. She fucking loves you and that's exactly what she told him when he called her earlier and begged her to meet up with him."

I glance up. "He's in town?"

"Jesus Christ, not the point, dude. Did you hear what I said? She loves you."

"She does?"

She shakes her head. "Finally, he listens to me."

"What room number did you say she was in?" I ask, my heart pounding in my chest. She loves me? I mean,

I knew there was something there but hearing the words out loud makes everything fall into focus and I have no clue why the fuck I'm still down in this bar. Mercedes laughs.

"Three-oh-nine."

Nodding, I jump off the stool before turning back to her. "One more question… she mentioned her net worth earlier… how much money are we talking?"

"Does it matter?" she asks, arching a brow. I nod.

"Is it enough that someone might want to hurt her?"

Her eyes widen. "Yes."

Shit.

I turn, determined to get to my girl.

"Wait," Mercedes calls after me. "You really think she's in trouble?"

"Yes. I'll fill you in later," I call over my shoulder as I march out of the bar to the elevators. As I smash my thumb into the up button, I sigh and turn to look up at which floor it's currently on before shaking my head. "Come on…"

Time seems to slow and the numbers barely move as I cross my arms over my chest and tilt my head back, sighing. Another second passes by, feeling like a whole damn minute, and I turn away from the elevator. The door for the stairs catches my attention and I consider just running up three flights of stairs when the elevator dings. The door slides open as I whirl back toward them and I rush into the car, ignoring the annoyed looks of the two men getting off, and smash the button to make the doors close. As it starts rising, I pray that no one else stops it as I stare up at the numbers ticking off each floor we pass. When we finally get to the third floor, I breathe a sigh of relief and march down the hallway toward the room number Mercedes gave me.

Three-oh-six.

Three-oh-seven

Three-oh-eight.

"Finally," I breathe as I stop in front of her door and lift my hand to knock. My heart races and I suck in a breath as I tap my knuckles against the wood. Silence greets me on the other side of the door and I knock again, harder this time.

Open the door, baby...

I'm just about to knock again when the door swings open and she squints up at me with a confused look.

"Sawyer?"

"Can we talk?" I ask and she nods as she yawns and takes a step back. "Sorry for interrupting your nap."

She shakes her head as she closes the door behind me. "It's okay. Where is Mercedes?"

"Down in the bar." I scrub my hand over the back of my head. "She kind of ripped me a new one."

"Of course she did," she whispers, shaking her head as she sits on the couch and hugs her legs to her chest. "Are you here to break up with me?"

I shake my head. "No."

"Then why are you here?" she asks. I can see her fighting back the hope that maybe I'm here for her and it breaks my heart that she thinks so little of my feelings for her. From the moment I met this girl, she threw me off balance and challenged me but I don't know how I would go on without her. Even though we haven't even known each other for two weeks, she fucking owns me. I open my mouth to tell her just that but it doesn't feel like enough. My words pale in comparison to the things she makes me feel. Dropping my gaze to her lips, I do the only thing I can - pull her into my lap and kiss her senseless.

She gasps as she settles on my lap and grips my t-shirt in her fists like she never wants to let me go again. That's good because someone will have to kill me and pry my cold dead hands off her before I'll ever let her walk out of my life. She gasps as she tears her lips from mine and shakes her head, staring at me with tears in her eyes.

"What does this mean?"

I smile and reach up, cupping her cheek in my hand. "It means I'm an idiot and I love you."

"You love me?" she whispers, her voice barely audible as her eyes widen and I nod.

"I do."

A side smile stretches across her face and a tear streaks down her cheek. "I love you, too."

"I know." I laugh. "Mercedes told me down in that bar."

Her jaw drops and she playfully glares at the door. "That bitch."

"Don't be too mad at her, angel. It's what I needed to hear to stop being such a baby about everything you told me earlier today."

"Oh, God," she says as she turns back to me. "I hope you know I never meant to hurt you. I was just so lost and trying to protect myself…"

I lean in and steal a kiss. "I know, sweetheart. Honestly, after Mercedes explained what you've gone through, I'm in awe of you. You're so strong and if it had happened to me, I would have just fallen apart but you didn't. You took control of your life and I can't even tell you how happy I am that you did because it brought you to me."

"Sawyer," she whispers, closing her eyes and taking a deep breath like she's washing all the pain away. I can't take my eyes off her.

"My angel…"

Opening her eyes, she smiles. "I love it when you call me that."

"It's what you are. Before I met you, I was beginning to think I was going to spend the rest of my life alone… and I thought it was what I deserved."

"Why?" she asks, her brows knitted together in concern. I sigh.

"I already told you about Molly," I answer and she nods. "But there was someone else before her…"

"Someone you loved?"

I shake my head, pain piercing through me as memories flood my mind. "Not like that. Her name was Lydia and I met her when we were six. She was my best friend and we never went anywhere without each other."

"I get the sense that this story doesn't have a happy

ending."

"It doesn't," I whisper, fighting through waves of pain and guilt. "We were juniors in high school when she met Tony, this guy that worked at the coffee shop by our school. He was a little bit older than us and had a bit of an edge that only made Lydia like him more and no one could tell her anything about him."

She sucks in a breath.

"Anyway, they started dating and things seemed okay at first and then I noticed that Lydia was wearing long sleeved t-shirts in the middle of the summer and if I startled her or touched her when she wasn't expecting it, she'd jump sky high."

"Oh, Sawyer," she whispers and my eyes burn with unshed tears as I shake my head. I hate telling this fucking story - it wrecks me every time - but she needs to hear it.

"I tried talking to her and I told her over and over again how she could tell me anything and I'd always be there for her but she wouldn't open up to me. One day in art class, we were making stuff out of clay so she had to push her sleeves up and that's when I saw the handprint around her wrist. She finally broke down and told me that he had been beating her for months."

Juliette lays her head on my shoulder and I shudder as I wrap my arms around her back, holding her close as I continue.

"After talking for a long time, I finally convinced her that she had to end things and I sat next to her as she called him and told him they were done. He was pissed and he swore that he was going to make her pay. She started to panic but I told her I'd keep her safe and I went into full on protective mode. I walked her to and from school everyday, I sat outside her house until after her parents got home from work, and she stayed over at my house when she couldn't take anymore and needed to disappear."

"This is why you work with the Devils?" she asks and I nod. "Is Lydia okay?"

"No, she's not." My voice cracks and I clear my throat as I pull Juliette in tighter. "I had a dentist appointment one morning and I wasn't able to walk with Lydia to school but she promised me she was getting a ride from her mom so I thought everything would be okay… When I got to school, I couldn't find her anywhere and she wasn't answering her phone… I called her parents and her mom said that Lydia walked to school by herself that morning."

She sits up and meets my eyes. "They didn't know?"

"No," I answer, shaking my head. "She didn't want them to know and she was my best friend so I kept her secret… and then they found her body in the woods by her house the next day."

"Oh, baby," she breathes, pressing her hand to my cheek as my chest aches and my stomach rolls.

"She'd been beaten to death and it was all my fault." I close my eyes as a tear slips down my cheek and she wipes it away as she cuddles back into me.

"No, it wasn't your fault. You were just a kid…"

I shake my head. "I should have done more. I should have done better... she was counting on me to keep her safe and I couldn't do that."

"Sawyer," she whispers, sitting up and forcing me to open my eyes and look up at her. "I love your sweet, tender heart and your fierce protectiveness but some things are just out of your control. You did everything you could and then Lydia made the decision to walk to school knowing she was in danger. That was *her* choice and you can't carry it around on your back like it's yours. I can see the way it eats away at you..."

Shaking my head, I slip my hand into her hair and push her down until her lips meet mine. I can't listen to her tell me it wasn't my fault anymore when I know damn well it was but maybe, with her help and her love, I can finally put it in my past. Her body melts into mine as she grips my shoulders, kissing me back with just as much need. I grip a chunk of her hair and push her down onto my lap as I thrust up and she gasps.

"I need you, angel," I murmur and she nods, raking her teeth down my neck. My cock jumps and desire floods my body as I dig my fingers into her skin. Groaning, I grab her ass and stand up with her in my arms before turning and carrying her into the bedroom. I sit on the edge of the bed and she moans as she rocks her hips against me. I release a breath. "Baby..."

"Yes, Sawyer?" she whispers into my ear and I shiver as she does it again. Fuck. It feels so damn good and all I want to do is disappear into the sheets with her and never come out again. All my pain, all my guilt, all my fear - it's all gone the moment she touches me and it hits me out of nowhere that I'll never be able to get enough of her. There will never come a point in my life where I will feel like I've had my fill of the gorgeous, amazing woman in my arms.

Holy shit...

I'm going to marry this girl.

And unlike the last time I thought about forever with someone, I don't feel nervous, only excited to start building a life with my angel.

Never Let Me Go
Chapter Twenty-Two
Juliette

"Sawyer," I breathe as he drags the bitten end of the strawberry over my skin, starting at my hip and ending on my chest. As soon as he's done, his tongue follows. Goose bumps race across my flesh and a shiver works its way down my spine. "Is this the only reason you wanted to order room service?"

His chest rumbles with laughter. "It's one of them."

"Do I get a turn?"

"Maybe later," he answers with a shrug as he sucks my tit into his mouth and my hips shoot off the bed. As he flicks his tongue over my nipple and grips my hips, he nudges my legs open and slips in between them. Reaching across the bed, he grabs a spoon and scoops the whipped cream off of the waffles before turning back to me with a grin. I shake my head.

"Oh, no. That stuff is sticky."

He nods as he lowers the spoon to my belly.

"Mmhmm."

"Did you hear me?"

"Yeah," he answers, swirling the spoon across my skin and spreading the cream around. "You said I have to lick this off of you, then I have to take you in the shower and clean you up."

I snort. "Sounds terrible for you."

"It really does," he murmurs as he leans down and drags his tongue across my belly. I suck in a breath as my eyes roll back in my head.

"At what point in there do I get an orgasm?"

He shrugs as he continues licking the cream off of my skin. "Maybe after the shower."

"You're so mean to me," I whine and he laughs as he moves up my body and flashes me a wicked smile.

"I know."

He presses his lips to mine as I lift my hips off the bed and his deep groan settles between my legs, making me ache for more as his tongue traces the seam of my lips. My lips part and the taste of strawberries, cream, and Sawyer swarm my tastebuds and I moan. He pulls away from my lips, breathing heavily as he slips his hand between my legs and my body tenses in anticipation.

"What about now?" he asks, as his fingers brush over the sensitive nub before disappearing again. I nod and lift my hips but he pulls his hand away. He laughs. "I'll make you a deal…"

"What?"

"I'm going to ask you a question and if I like your

answer, I'll give you what you want. Sound fun?"

I frown up at him. "I don't know."

"First question," he says with a grin. "Do you love me?"

"Yes."

"Very good." His grin widens and my eyes roll back as he rubs his fingers over my clit in little circles. "Now, if you keep giving me answers I like, I won't stop."

I nod, only able to focus on his words for a second. "Okay."

"Are you mine?"

I smile. "Yes."

He hums his approval and bends down to flick his tongue over my nipple. I gasp, threading my fingers through his hair as he increases the pressure of his fingers.

"Do you ever want to be without me?" he asks, his breath warming my skin and I shudder as I shake my head.

"No."

Two fingers slip inside me while his thumb presses against my clit and I gasp, squeezing my eyes shut and clinging to him as an orgasm builds inside me.

"Will you move in with me?"

My eyes snap open. "What?"

Pulling away, his fingers slip out of me and my body screams for release as I stare up at him and try to wrap my mind around what he just asked me. He frames my shoulders between his arms and leans down to press his lips to mine.

"Move in with me."

It's more of a demand than a question and I tilt my head to the side as I study him. "We haven't known each other for that long…"

"So? I want you in my life, every single day and besides, tell me it makes sense for you to sign a lease or buy an apartment when you're just going to be living with me in a month or three or whatever is an acceptable timeline for the world."

I purse my lips. "I suppose you have a point."

"I do have a point," he agrees, his smile bright as he sits back and drags his fingers down my thigh. "Now, tell me you'll move in with me."

"You're very demanding."

"I know." He nods and I sigh as I study him for a moment before giving in.

"Okay. I'll move in with you."

His eyes light up as he leans over me again and slips his hand between my thighs, teasing my clit for a second before driving two fingers into me and pressing his thumb to my clit.

"Sawyer," I cry out as my body comes alive with pleasure and I whine, begging whatever God can hear me that he doesn't stop again.

"You want to come, baby?"

I nod. "Yes… please!"

He groans and shoves his hand behind my neck, gripping it as he begins fucking me with his fingers, hard and fast. Pressure builds in my belly, begging for release as I writhe beneath him, unable to control myself. He curls his fingers, hitting my g-spot and I cry out.

"Shh," he whispers, a proud grin on his face as he slams his lips to mine and mimics the motion of his fingers with his tongue. He curls his fingers again and my body explodes, my internal muscles clamping down on his fingers as waves of pleasure rack my body and I scream into his kiss. As he pulls away from my lips, he releases my neck and slowly massages my core as shudders, almost like the aftershocks of an earthquake, tear through my body.

"Oh... my... God," I whisper, shaking my head back and forth with my eyes closed. He laughs.

"Fuck. Watching you come apart for me is almost better than getting off myself... almost!"

Sighing, I open my eyes, still shaking my head. "I have never felt anything like that."

"That you can remember."

"No," I shoot back. "If I had experienced anything like that before, I would remember it."

He smiles and lays down beside me, dragging his fingertips lightly across my stomach. I'm relieved to see that my lack of memories isn't bothering him anymore and that it's something we can joke about.

"Are you worried about the stuff you don't remember?" he asks, avoiding my gaze as I stare down at him and I sigh.

"No. When I came to Baton Rouge, I knew I needed to focus more on the life I was building and not the one I left behind."

"I'm still worried about your fiancé."

I sigh. "*Ex*-fiance and don't be too hard on him."

"Why not?"

"Can you imagine if one morning you woke up and

I didn't remember who you were, then I left you to start a new life somewhere else with another man? He's already been through hell."

He pulls me closer and brushes his thumb over my cheek. "And what if he's the one trying to hurt you?"

"I don't see it," I answer, shaking my head. "Besides, it's still possible that no one is actually trying to hurt me."

"You were shot at… and run off the road!"

"Those could both still be coincidences. Car accidents happen all the time and it's possible someone was trespassing on your property and just target shooting or hunting. Besides, don't you think if someone wanted to kill me out in the woods, they wouldn't have missed?"

His brow knits together. "I didn't say they had good aim."

"I love how protective you are, baby," I tell him, pressing my hand to his cheek and he meets my eyes. "I just don't want you to be so busy looking for the danger that you miss the rest of your life… the rest of our lives."

Emotions flick through his eyes as he stares down at me and I can see him thinking it through before he leans down and seals his lips over mine. His kiss is tender this time and I can feel every ounce of love he feels for me being poured into his touch. It's so potent, so pure that tears sting my eyes. He pulls away and a soft smile stretches across his face.

"You ready for that shower now?"

I nod and he jumps out of bed, laughing as he scoops me up despite my squeals of protest. As we turn toward the bathroom, someone knocks on the door and he looks down at me with a scowl. I shrug and he sets me on my feet before kissing my forehead and grabbing his jeans from the floor.

"Stay here," he orders as he pulls them on and I nod as I grab my robe off of the chair and slip into it, tying it off at the waist. Sawyer runs his hand through his hair as he walks into the living room, leaving the door to the bedroom wide open so I can see everything. As I sit on the edge of the bed, I scan through all the options as whoever it is starts pounding on the door. If it was hotel staff, they certainly wouldn't knock like that and Mercedes would have called before coming over. The only other option that makes any sense is Gavin but he wouldn't come here, would he? Not after I made my feelings perfectly clear yesterday.

He opens the door and starts talking to someone but they're too far away for me to hear so I stand up and sneak into the living room.

"I'm sorry to do this, Moose, but I've got to bring you down for questioning," someone says and a feeling of protectiveness wells up inside me. I march to the door and yank it open further so I can see who is on the other side.

"Who are you?"

The man on the other side of the door turns to me with wide eyes. "Detective Rodriguez. Who…"

"Why are you here?" I ask, my heart racing as I try to think of a reason why he would need to take Sawyer down to the station for questioning. Whatever it is, it doesn't matter. He didn't do anything wrong and I will hire the very best attorney money can buy to fight whatever charges they want to throw at him. The detective glances over at Sawyer.

"As I was just telling him, there's been a report filed against him and I need to ask him some questions."

I nod. "Is he under arrest?"

"Not at this time."

"Then you can ask your questions here," I tell him, stepping back so he can come into the room. He glances over at Sawyer, who just shrugs and turns to grab his shirt off the floor where it ended up when I threw it last night. As he slips it over his head and sits down on the couch, I sit next to him and carefully watch Detective Rodriguez as he sits in a chair across from us. When he looks up at us, I give him an expectant look.

"Right," he sighs. "Do you know a Tawny Mullan?"

Sawyer rolls his eyes. "You know I do, Diego. Just tell me what the hell is going on."

"Wait. You two know each other?" I ask and Sawyer nods as he wraps his arm around my shoulders and pulls me closer.

"Rodriguez helps the club from time to time and we help him when we can."

"Look," Rodriguez says, scrubbing his hand over his face. "The department knows I'm friends with you guys so when this hit my desk, my captain said it has to be official."

Sawyer releases a breath and nods. "Okay. Yes, I know Tawny Mullan. We dated for a few months."

"And when did things end?"

"A little over two weeks ago."

He nods, writing some things down in a mini notebook. "When was the last time you saw Miss Mullan?"

"When she showed up at the club three days ago,"

he says. Rodriguez writes some more things down, nodding the whole time.

"You haven't seen or heard from her since then?"

He shakes his head. "No."

"Do you have an alibi for last night?"

"Um, yeah," I snap. "He does."

Rodriguez looks up and meets my eyes. "He was with you all night?"

"He got here around six and he never left."

"Can anyone else confirm this?" he asks and Sawyer's muscles tense up.

"What the fuck, dude?"

I nod. "Yes, I'm certain this hotel has cameras. You could also ask whoever brought our food up last night and this morning... oh, and the bartender downstairs."

"Okay," he breathes as he finishes jotting down notes and slips his notebook back into his suit jacket.

"You want to tell me what the fuck is going on now?" Sawyer growls and I lay my hand on his leg to calm him. I've never met this bitch but there's something about her that gets Sawyer's hackles up and that's enough for me. Plus, she clearly can't take a hint where my man is concerned... not that I can blame her.

"Tawny came into the station this morning to report an assault. She's got a pretty nasty black eye and she says you did it."

He surges forward. "Are you fucking kidding me? I would never..."

"Chill, okay?" Rodrigues says, holding his hand up. "I could tell pretty quickly that she was full of shit and layin' it on a little thick but I can't look like I'm giving y'all special treatment. I had to come ask you these questions, no matter how ridiculous they are."

"Yeah," Sawyer sighs, relaxing back into the couch. "Okay."

"I'll talk to the staff here and get the videotapes. That will be more than enough to convince anyone that you had nothing to do with this," he says as they both stand. As they walk over to the door, I sigh and turn to look out of the windows, wondering what this girl hoped to gain by framing Sawyer for assaulting her. It's not like it would win him back...

"What are you thinking so hard about over there?" Sawyer asks as he leans down and scoops me up into his arms. I lay my head on his shoulder and sigh.

"Just wondering what Tawny was trying to do by framing you."

He shakes his head. "You shouldn't worry about it, baby. Knowing Tawny, she was just trying to get back at me and it didn't work so we should focus on more important things."

"Oh, yeah?" I ask, smiling up at him as he carries me back into the bedroom. "Like what?"

My phone rings before he can answer and he scowls as he sits down on the edge of the bed with me in his lap. Nico's name pops onto the screen and I smile as I answer it.

"Hey, girl. What time are you getting in?"

"I actually got in last night but I thought I'd get a good night's sleep before meeting up with you to go over business," she says and I look up at Sawyer and scrunch up my nose.

"I wasn't actually planning on going into work today so you can take another day. Maybe explore the city or look for an apartment."

There is a pause on the line and my stomach flips as

I wait for her response. She sighs. "So you've decided to stay then?"

"I have and I would really love to have you here with me. It's up to you, though."

"Can I have a few days to think about it?"

I nod, smiling up at Sawyer who returns it. "Of course. In fact, take that time off as well. There really isn't much we can do right now since the contractor is still making changes to the office."

She agrees before promising to let me know her decision soon and I grin as I hang up and turn back to Sawyer.

"Now, what were those important things you mentioned earlier?"

"Well, for starters," he murmurs, hooking his fingers into the edge of my robe. "The shower I promised you and then I figure we need to go home and move you into your new bedroom."

I grin. "How do you feel about new curtains?"

"Oh, God," he groans. "It's starting already."

"Get used to it, baby," I reply and he rolls his eyes as he carries me into the shower and flips it on without stopping to let us get undressed first and I squeal as the robe molds itself to my skin. Sawyer looks down at me, fighting back laughter and I can't help but smile. Life with this man is going to be so good and I'm more than ready to get started.

A.M. Myers

Never Let Me Go
Chapter Twenty-Three
Sawyer

The blare of an alarm rips me from sleep and I open
my eyes, blinking into the haze in front of me as my
mind slowly returns to consciousness. I struggle to suck
in a breath and my brows draw together and I sit up and
scan the room. My eyes burn and sweat drips down the
side of my face. I can't see more than a foot in front of
me and it takes my mind a second to register the thick
black smoke rolling into the bedroom under the closed
door.

Fire!

Turning, I reach over to wake up Juliette but the
only thing I find is cold sheets and my heart jumps into
my throat, hammering so hard I think it might explode.
Where is she? I roll to her side and check the floor next
to the bed but she's not there. Rolling to my back, I sit
up and scan the room again, squinting into the smoke as
it gets harder and harder to see.

No.

No.

No.

Where is she?

I try to scan the room but visibility continues to decline with each second that passes as more smoke rolls into the room. Stumbling out of bed, I find my jeans and slip them on before grabbing my phone and slipping it into my pocket. Crouching down, I move toward the door. Every fire drill I ever participated in as a kid flashes through my head, telling me to get myself to safety first but there's no way in hell I'm leaving without Juliette. The heat and smoke intensify as I move closer to the door and I grab one of my t-shirts off the floor, covering my face with it before continuing toward the door. Reaching out, I press my hand to the back of the door and jerk back when the heat seeps into my skin, sucking in a breath as my mind stalls.

I try to picture the layout of my house, ticking through all the exits in my mind but it's impossible to focus as the heat surrounds me, suffocating me just as much as the smoke rolling into the room. Juliette's face pops into my mind and my chest aches.

Fuck it.

Jumping into action, I grab the door handle, yelling as it burns my skin, and yank it open. Black smoke pours into the room and orange flames lick up the wall of the guest bedroom as I run past it, looking frantically for my girl and my hand throbs.

"Juliette!" I scream over the roar of the flames, tears

stinging my eyes as I start to cough. "Juliette!"

I don't see her anywhere in the kitchen and I'm trying hard to ignore the idea that she could have been in the guest bedroom for any reason. After we got back from the hotel this afternoon, we moved everything into my room, our room now, so she would have no reason to go in there, right? My stomach rolls as I think about her stuck in that room, the fire raging all around her and shake my head.

No, she's not in there.

A faint cry pulls my attention to the living room but I can't see through the smoke.

"Juliette!"

Another cry greets me and I surge forward, crashing into one of my dining room chairs and stumbling to the floor as pain rockets through my body.

"Fuck!"

My eyes burn and it hurts to open them but I can't stop, not until me and my angel are safe. I blink against the smoke and force them open again, letting out a sigh of relief when I see Juliette's foot a few feet in front of me. Pushing through the smoke and heat, I crawl across the floor to her on my stomach, praying that she's okay. She moans when I reach her side and I roll her to her back as I glance up at the front door. It's a straight shot and I can feel the heat of the fire creeping up behind me so we don't have time to wait.

Standing, I pick her up and try to cover as much of her with my own body as I run toward the front door and kick it open. Clean air smacks me in the face and I take a full breath for the first time since I woke up and started coughing. Red lights flash and bounce around the neighborhood as two fire trucks pull up to the house and people start jumping out. Two paramedics grab a stretcher and run up to me.

"Lay her down," one of them orders and I shake my head. "Sir, we need to check the both of you over."

"I'm not letting her go."

One of them lays her hand on my arm and I jerk back. "Sir, we need to make sure she's okay. She could have inhaled a lot of smoke and we need to work quickly."

Sighing, I give in and lay her on the stretcher as her eyes flutter open and she coughs, looking up at me. "Sawyer?"

"Hey," I whisper, forcing a smile to my face as I cup her cheek in my hand. Pain sears through me from the burn on my hand but I clench my teeth to hold my reaction in. "How are you feeling?"

"What happened?"

I glance up as the fire begins to envelop my house and shake my head. "It doesn't matter. All that matters is that you are okay."

"Sir," the other paramedic snaps but I flick her an annoyed glance before turning back to my girl. Juliette turns in the stretcher to glance back at the house and gasps.

"Oh my God…"

"It's okay, baby," I whisper, my hand throbbing and my chest aching. She shakes her head and looks up at me with tears in her eyes.

"Your house."

I shake my head. "It's just a house, sweetheart. You and I are okay and that's all that matters."

"Sir, we need to look you both over," the paramedic says again, more forcefully this time and I nod as I glance over at her.

"I'm not leaving her side."

She sighs. "Fine."

I hold Juliette's hand, ignoring the unbelievable pain that radiates up my arm, as they direct us over to the back of the ambulance. As I sit on the tailgate, I watch two teams of two firefighters each run out of the house before they start blasting it with water. It's funny, I've lived in this house for five years but when I think about what I'm going to miss about the place, it's only my memories of being with Juliette in there that make me feel sad. I peek over at her as they listen to her heart and ask her what she remembers.

"Not much," she answers, shaking her head, as a bewildered look crosses her face.

"Let's see that burn," one of the paramedics says, arching a brow as she stares down at me and I sigh as I pull my hand from Juliette's and show her my palm.

"Are you hurt?" Juliette asks, turning to me and her eyes widen with concern. I shake my head, flashing her a smile that I don't quite feel.

"Just a flesh wound, baby."

The paramedic sighs. "It's a second-degree burn but it's not too bad so I suppose you're right."

A.M. Myers

"See?" I say, turning back to Juliette as the paramedic begins applying some cream to my hand and wrapping it. She sighs and sinks back into the gurney, looking a little pale. "Are you okay, Juliette?"

She nods. "My head just hurts."

"Did you fall and hit your head?" the paramedic working on her asks as she examines her head. Juliette scowls.

"I don't think so."

I shake my head. "I found her in the middle of the floor."

"You've got a pretty good lump on the back of your head."

I scowl. The back of her head? Almost like someone hit her with something and knocked her out. Holy shit… was there someone else in the house?

She meets my gaze, fear filling her eyes, and I nod. This is the third time she's come close to death recently and I'm less inclined to believe it's a coincidence at this point. A firefighter and a police officer walk up to the back of the ambulance and the firefighter holds up a plastic bag with a charred mess inside of it.

"Am I supposed to know what that is?"

He shakes his head. "This is what started the fire in your home."

"That still doesn't tell me what that is," I tell them, looking up at the house as the rest of his team continue to battle the blaze, which has now moved to the front of the house.

Glancing at the police officer, he sighs and runs a

hand through his hair. "It's a timer. It was located in the back bedroom and we also smelled gasoline all over that room."

"Are you saying this fire was set intentionally?" I ask, like I didn't already know that, and he nods. I turn to Juliette and she stares back at me with wide eyes. If she had any lingering doubts about her safety, they're all gone now.

"Do you know of anyone that would want to hurt either one of you? Does anyone have a grudge against you?"

I shake my head. "No."

"And you, ma'am?" the officer asks, turning to look at Juliette. She meets my gaze for just a moment before shaking her head.

"No."

He nods. "Sometimes these things are just random but I assure you, we will do everything we can to find whoever did this." I nod and after we shake hands, they leave us in the care of the paramedics.

"There," the one working on my hand says as she finishes wrapping my burn. "Try to rest that hand."

"You got it," I say, standing up. "Now, if you'll excuse me."

She nods and takes a step back, turning to help her partner look over Juliette. I walk across the street and pull my phone out of my pocket, dialing Streak's number.

"Yo," he answers. "What's up?"

I suck in a breath and run my hand through my hair.

"I'm watching my house burn down right now."

"Fuck! Are you serious?"

"You think I'd joke about this?" I growl.

"No, of course not."

"This is the third time Juliette has almost died in a month. Have you found anything?"

He sighs. "How about we meet up tomorrow and I'll fill y'all in but I gotta warn you, it's not much."

"Yeah, okay. We'll talk tomorrow," I tell him and after we hang up, I run my hand through my hair again, staring up at the dying flames and the charred rubble that I used to call a home. I just hope I can end this before whoever is trying to hurt my girl actually succeeds.

Never Let Me Go
Chapter Twenty-Four
Juliette

"What is that frown for, sweetheart?" Sawyer asks,
smoothing his thumb over my eyebrows as we lay on
the bed in his room at the clubhouse. I sigh as I turn to
him. My teeth sink into my bottom lip and my stomach
rolls.

"Sawyer... I'm so sorry about your house."

The guilt has been eating away at me since I saw
the flames consuming his house last night but he hasn't
once blamed me even though we both know I'm the one
that brought all this drama into his life. He's just
amazing and he deserves a whole lot better than I'm
giving him. Sighing, he pulls me into his arms.

"Baby, I've told you *multiple* times that it doesn't
matter. It's just a house."

"I'm going to buy you a new one," I promise and he
shakes his head. It's the least I can do. I mean, the man
literally carried me out of a house as it burned down

around us and sat with me all night in the emergency room as they treated both of us for smoke inhalation. They tried to put us in different rooms but Sawyer wasn't having any of that and after arguing with him for ten minutes, they just gave in and cleared a space for him in my room.

"Us. *We're* going to buy *us* a new house."

I peek up at him with a pleading look. "Please let me make this up to you. It would be nothing for me to buy any house you want."

"Baby girl," he breathes. "The only damn house I want is the one you're in so how about we take this shitty situation and use it as an opportunity to start over and build our home, *together*."

"You're amazing."

He grins. "I know."

"Oh my God. You just ruined the moment," I say, rolling my eyes as I push him away from me and he laughs as he pulls me back into his body and presses his lips to mine. Moaning, I melt against him as my eyes close but he pulls away too soon.

"Are you ready to get out of bed and go talk to Streak?"

My heart skips a beat. "Has he found anything?"

"Only one way to find out, angel. And we should do it soon since I need to go soon."

"Okay," I sigh, nodding. I'm not sure that I'm ready to find out any information that Streak may have uncovered but it's time to face this thing head on. After the car accident, I assumed it was just that - an accident

- but after being shot at and almost burning to death in a fire, I have to admit that something more is going on here.

After we get dressed, Sawyer takes my hand and leads me down the hallway to Streak's room, or as Sawyer called it, his lair before he knocks.

"What?" a voice yells from behind the door and Sawyer rolls his eyes.

"Get your ass up and come talk to us."

Something slams against the door and I jump. "Fucking make me."

"He's not a morning person," Sawyer says with a grin as he opens the door. Marching into the room, he grabs a cup full of water off the desk and holds it over the half naked body on the bed. "Last chance before I dump this on you, fucker."

"Asshole," he growls, peeking open his eye before turning to me and sighing. "Fine. I'm getting up."

I stare at the floor as he stands up in a pair of boxer briefs and nothing else. He scoops a pair of jeans off of the floor and pulls them on before walking across the room and plopping down in the chair in front of his desk.

"You can't put a shirt on in front of my lady?" Sawyer snaps and Streak's eyes flick to me.

"Why? She been living in a cult and never seen a man's chest before?"

Sawyer shakes his head. "I'm gonna kick your ass once you're fully awake."

"Bring it, pussy," he snaps, wiggling his mouse to

wake his computer up. "Now, you want to hear what I found or not?"

I nod. "Please."

"Ooh, manners… I like it," he says, flashing me a cocky grin and I can't help but giggle. "But unfortunately, I haven't found much of anything yet. Gavin is broke as shit but it's not like he benefits from your death so I can't see why he would hurt you."

Something nags at me and I scowl, trying to pin it down but it's like each time I get close, the wind picks up and blows it away from me again. Why? Why did that statement impact me?

"Something wrong?" Streak asks and Sawyer turns to me.

"Baby?"

I shake my head. "Something about what you said… It triggered… something but I don't know what it is…"

"Okay," Streak says, nodding as he studies my face. "I'll keep digging then and get back to y'all."

Sawyer nods and takes my hand before leading me out of Streak's room. We walk back to his room and he sighs as he pulls me into his arms.

"It's about time for me to go. Are you going to be okay?"

I nod. "I'm good, baby. Go run your errand and don't worry about me. I'm safe here."

"Okay," he sighs but he doesn't release me. I laugh and swat at his chest.

"Sawyer, I'm fine," I assure him, pushing up on my

tiptoes and kissing his cheek before dragging my lips to his ear. "Go and get this done and when you get back, I'll be waiting in bed. Naked."

He groans and nods before pulling back to meet my gaze. "No leaving the clubhouse without one of the guys, okay?"

"I won't even leave the clubhouse at all," I promise him and he nods as he leans down and presses his lips to mine.

"Let's get a move on, Moosie-Poo," someone calls and Sawyer rips himself away from me with a growl. I scrunch up my nose.

"I really hate your name."

He rolls his eyes. "Join the club, angel."

"Moose!" someone else yells and he sighs as he takes a step back.

"I gotta go. I love you."

I smile. "I love you, too."

Standing in the doorway to his room, I watch him disappear downstairs before turning to look at his bed. It was a rough night but as much as I would like more sleep, I feel like I should go downstairs and make an effort to get to know some of these guys that are such a big part of Sawyer's life. Ducking into the room, I grab my phone before going downstairs. A few of the guys are playing pool at the far end of the room while another is sitting at one of the tables, looking over paperwork. He looks up and kicks the chair next to him out for me to sit in.

"Hi," I say as I sit down and he offers me a warm

smile as he extends his hand.

"I'm Fuzz."

I shake his hand and nod. "It's nice to meet you."

"You look a little overwhelmed," he replies with a laugh that puts me at ease and I smile as I nod.

"Just a little bit."

He nods, closing the file in front of him. "Sounds like you've had a crazy few weeks."

"Yeah," I scoff. "That's one way of putting it but I suppose this is just every day for you guys, huh?"

"Naw, not really. Most of the time, things are pretty chill… it's just been a bad year."

I nod, studying him. "Sawyer said something about that. I'm sorry."

"Thank you."

"Is that what all this is?" I ask, pointing to the folders and he nods. "Did you find anything?"

"Nope. It's frustrating as hell but it's kind of nice to get back to my roots."

I scowl. "What do you mean?"

"I was a cop before I joined the club." He laughs. "That's why they call me Fuzz."

"Oh."

"Actually, I learned something from my cop days that I was thinking might help you if you want to give it a try."

Pursing my lips, I consider his words. A part of me is terrified of what I might uncover in my forgotten memories after everything that's happened since I woke up in the hospital but my desire to know the truth overpowers that.

"Okay. What do I need to do?"

"I had this case one time," he says, leaning his elbows on the table. "Where a woman lost her memory like you and the department sent her to this doctor who walked her through unlocking her memories and I could try doing the same thing with you."

I suck in a breath and nod my head. "Let's do it."

"Close your eyes," he commands and I comply. "Now, I want you to lock onto a memory from your past and it doesn't matter how small or foggy it is, just pick one."

I nod, choosing to think about the feeling I got up in Streak's room when he said Gavin didn't benefit from my death.

"You got it locked in?"

"Yes."

"Good. Now, I want you to immerse yourself in the memory. Don't just let it play in your head. Imagine you're really living it again."

My brows draw together as I focus on the emotion I felt upstairs and a picture pops into my mind and I gasp, my eyes snapping open. Fuzz's eyes widen.

"What did you see?"

I shake my head. "I didn't have an exact memory, just a nagging feeling that I felt upstairs and when I focused on it, I saw myself in my apartment in Miami. It was raining and I was staring out of the window, crying."

The guys across the room start laughing and Fuzz

glances over his shoulder before standing up and gathering his folders.

"We should do this somewhere quiet."

I nod and follow him as he leads me into a room with a long wooden table in the middle and chairs positioned all around it.

"This is the war room."

I arch a brow. "War room?"

"It's where we meet to talk about... well, anything important."

Nodding, I sit in one of the seats and he slides into the one next to me. "Okay, ready to do this?"

"Yes."

"Close your eyes again and focus on that image that popped into your mind."

Sucking in a breath, I bring the image to the front of my mind and focus on it as I nod.

"Now immerse yourself in it. What can you see?"

"The rain... my reflection in the window... I have tears running down my face... there's a fire in the fireplace behind me..."

"Good. Now, what can you smell?"

I shake my head. "The fire... cleaning products... perfume..."

"You're doing great, Juliette. Can you hear anything?"

My hands tremble and my stomach flips as I lose myself deeper in the memory, the fog surrounding it dissipating with each second that ticks by. "The rain... the cracking of the fire..."

"Anything else?"

"There's something…" I say with a nod, focusing on what the other sound is. "It sounds like voices and music but it's muffled… maybe a TV playing in another room…"

"Good. Now, this is the most important part. What do you feel?"

I gasp as a wave of despair washes over me. "Oh, God."

"What is it, Juliette?"

"I'm so sad and scared…" I whisper, tears stinging my eyes as my heart hammers in my chest. "I want something… I'm desperate for it… and angry… so, so angry…"

"Okay. I want you to just focus on these feelings. Let them fill you up and see if you unlock anything else."

Breathing deeply, I do as he says, letting the emotions pour in and tears begin pouring down my face as another image flickers across my vision. This time, I explore it myself, immersing myself in what I can see, what I can smell, and what I feel.

"Oh my God," I whisper, gasping for breath and Fuzz grabs my hand, jerking me out of my memories. I open my eyes and meet his.

"What did you see, Juliette?"

I press my hand to my chest, shaking my head as I try to rein the emotions back in. "Gavin… he was holding me captive in the apartment. I found out something I wasn't supposed to and when he realized I knew, he lost it…."

"Can you remember what you found out?"

"No," I whisper, shaking my head, and he nods as the door to the war room bursts open. Sawyer charges in and sighs when he sees me.

"There you are." His gaze drops to my hand in Fuzz's grasp and his eyes narrow as he takes a menacing step forward. "What the fuck is going on in here?"

"Sawyer," I whisper, more tears filling my eyes as I drop Fuzz's hand. "Why are you back? I thought you had to go run an errand?"

He shakes his head. "Chance and Storm said they could handle it on their own. They thought I should be with my girl. Now, I'm going to ask again… What the *fuck* is going on here?"

"He was helping me remember."

"Is it working?"

I nod and his eyes widen as he steps into the room and closes the door behind him. He rounds the table and sits on my other side, running his hand through his hair as he grabs my hand. "What do you remember?"

I relay everything I just discovered to him and he studies me before turning to Fuzz. "Sorry I almost killed you, brother."

"It looked bad out of context," Fuzz answers with a shrug.

"Can we keep going?" Sawyer asks, his gaze flicking between Fuzz and me. Fuzz nods.

"As long as Juliette can handle it."

I suck in a breath and nod as my stomach rolls. "Let's do it."

"All right, Juliette," Fuzz says. "Same thing as last time. Close your eyes and focus on the memory, then feel it, relive it."

I nod and do as instructed, closing my eyes and letting the memory flood back in. I'm standing in my bedroom, staring at something but the words on the page are still blurry. Gavin walks in and our eyes meet...

"What the fuck is this?" I hiss, holding the paper up and he pales, taking a step toward me as he shakes his head.

"Please, baby. I can explain."

My eyes widen. "You can explain? There's no fucking reason you should have this information unless you were planning to use it against me!"

"I know it looks bad," he replies, desperation flashing across his face. "But you have to let me..."

"I don't have to let you do a damn thing!" I crumple the paper up in my hand and reach down to grab a file off the bed before charging past him into the living room. He follows me as I march over to the fireplace and toss everything inside, watching as the flames consume it.

"Jules, baby... please," he pleads behind me. "I've made some mistakes and I'll tell you everything but you have to know that I love you more than anything."

I shake my head and turn back to him. "I don't know that. I don't know anything anymore."

Staring at him across the room, I know there's no way I could trust him again, not after what I just found and there's too much at stake to take the chance that he won't use the information he has against me. I shake my head and walk past him into the bedroom before grabbing my suitcase out of the closet and tossing it on the bed.

"Where are you going?" he asks as he walks into the room and I barely glance in his direction as I start pulling clothes off of the racks.

"My dad's house."

He shakes his head. "We can fix this."

"No, there is no fixing this." The only thing left to do is go to my dad and figure out how to clean up this mess. God, how did I allow this to happen? How did I not see the signs?

"I can't let you leave me. Don't you understand how much I love you? How much I've risked for you?"

"It doesn't matter anymore. This," I gesture between the two of us before gesturing around the room. "All of this doesn't matter anymore because it's been a lie all from the start."

I toss some clothes in my bag before brushing past him and walking into the bathroom to retrieve my toiletries.

"I'm going to make you see," he murmurs and I glance over at him as he stands in the doorway to the bathroom. "You're not leaving until I can make you understand."

He takes a step back and as it registers what he's

planning to do, I jerk forward to stop him, but it's too late. The bathroom door slams shut and when I try the handle it doesn't move. My heart races as I pound on the door.

"Gavin!"

"I'm not the one you need to be worried about," he says. "But don't worry. I promise you I'm going to fix this."

I open my eyes with a shudder and Sawyer squeezes my hand.

"What did you see, baby?"

"Gavin betrayed me. He has this file full of information on me and who knows what else… and when I tried to leave, he made me his prisoner."

A.M. Myers

Never Let Me Go
Chapter Twenty-Five
Juliette

"And the last thing I remember is that he was holding me as his prisoner," I say, my stomach rolling as the nine pairs of eyes stare at me with shocked expressions. We have been in the war room for the past twenty minutes going over everything we know about my case so far which isn't much when you see it all pinned up on a cork board like Streak did. I swear, the more we dig into this, the more hopeless it feels and more than once I've found myself wondering if we're seeing things that aren't really there.

"For how long?" Chance asks and I shake my head. No matter how much Fuzz, Sawyer, and I worked this morning, we couldn't break past the memory of Gavin locking me in the bathroom and no matter how much they both assured me that it was okay, I can't help but feel like I failed.

"I don't know."

"How did you make it out?"

I shake my head again as my chest feels tight. "I don't know."

"But somehow, you ended up with your dad and y'all got into the accident?" Kodiak asks, his face drawn together in concentration and I nod.

"Correct."

Blaze sighs. "Do you have any idea what was in the folder?"

"I remember saying that the only reason he would have the information is if he was going to use it against me but when I try to focus on the paper itself, it's just blurry."

Storm turns to Streak. "Did you find anything that can help us?"

"Oh, yeah," he answers, rubbing his hands together. "Juliette gave me permission to speak to her father's lawyer and he was very helpful. Up until two days before the accident, one Gavin Alexander Hale was listed as the beneficiary on Juliette's will."

"And how much money was he going to get in the event of your death?" Fuzz asks and I suck in a breath.

"Before my father's death, between what was left of my trust fund and what I had made through my business, somewhere around three million."

He nods. "And after your father's death?"

"Three hundred and fifty million," I whisper and a wave of shock ripples through the room.

"Holy fuck," Chance breathes, eyes wide as he falls back in his chair and scrubs his hand over his short hair.

"Sounds like a motive to kill someone if you ask me," Henn growls, shaking his head. Sawyer sucks in a breath, his shoulders tensing. I grab his hand and give it a squeeze.

"Except he doesn't get that now."

"Vengeance is always a sound motive to kill someone," Streak points out and a few of them nod in agreement.

"Are we sure that he knows he was taken off the will?" Smith asks.

I shake my head. "Clearly things weren't good between us right before the accident but I don't see how he could know."

"So," Sawyer continues, leaning back in his chair as he pulls my chair closer. "As far as he's concerned, as soon as he kills you, he's in for the biggest payday of his life."

"Hey, speaking of payday," Streak says, flashing me a wide smile. "I would *love* a new bike."

"Absolutely fucking not," Sawyer snaps, reaching around me to shove him. Laughing, he holds his hands up.

"Chill, man. It was just a joke."

Sawyer sends a cold look around the room. "And it will be the last fucking one I hear. She trusted us with this information and if y'all are assholes about it, I'm out."

"It won't happen again," Blaze agrees, sending a glare at Streak and he nods.

"Okay, boss. Sorry, Juliette."

"Now," Blaze snaps, smacking his gavel on the table. "Back to the matter at hand. How do we deal with Gavin?"

Streak shakes his head. "There is no proof. The car accident and the shooting in the woods look like accidents or coincidences. As for the fire, I've reached out to Rodriguez and fire investigation has nothing yet."

"And you can't find anything on this guy?"

"There's literally nothing to find because eighteen months ago, Gavin Hale didn't even exist."

I release a breath as my heart stalls and the information seeps into my mind.

"And let me tell you, whoever faked his paperwork is damn good because I had to mine that shit out of the deepest corner of the dark fucking web. For nine months, he lived a seemingly normal life and then he met Juliette. He's spent every cent he had trying to pretend that their lifestyles were similar and now, he's broke as a joke."

"Another option for his motive," Storm muses and Streak nods.

"But it doesn't matter 'cause we still don't have proof."

"What if I wear a wire?" I suggest, sucking in a breath as my mouth goes dry. "And confront him."

Sawyer shakes his head as he glares over at me. "Absolutely not."

"Actually…"

"No," Sawyer barks, turning his rage to Streak, who

sighs and rolls his eyes.

"Look, I get it, okay? You love her and you can't stand it if anything happens to her but if we don't do something, I have a feeling this won't end well for her. You guys barely made it out of that house unharmed and each time he attempts something, he gets a little bit closer to succeeding."

I lay my hand on Sawyer's and he meets my eyes. "He's right. We have to end this."

"I am not risking your life for this," he growls, begging me with his gaze to side with him but as I think about the fire, I can't do it. Streak is right. We've been incredibly lucky up until now and I can't take the risk that next time, we won't be.

"I'm sorry, baby, but I'm doing this."

Blaze hits his gavel against the table and stands up. "I'll call Rodriguez."

We stare at each other as the rest of the guys get up and file out of the room and when we're alone, he pulls me out of his chair and into his lap as he shakes his head.

"Angel..."

"I know you're scared, Sawyer... I'm scared, too, but we can't keep doing this. We've only been together for a few weeks and it's been a roller coaster. I want to have a regular, happy life with you, not more of this."

He sighs, his fingers kneading my hip. "There has to be another way."

"You know there's not."

"I can't lose you," he whispers, his voice thick with

emotion and I remember the story about Lydia that he told me in the hotel as I press my hand to his cheek and press my forehead to his.

"I love you way too much to leave you, Sawyer."

He shudders and his arms wrap around my waist. "I still don't like this."

"I know," I answer with a nod. "But once we make it through this, I'll spend the rest of my life making it up to you."

"You mean that?"

I nod. "I do. I want to marry you and have babies with you and build a life with you."

His hand slips into my hair and he pulls me down onto his lips in a bruising kiss that leaves me breathless as he nods.

"I'm fucking holding you to that."

I smile. "Good."

"Juliette," Blaze says, walking back into the room with Storm and Chance. "I've got Rodriguez on the phone. He wants to see if we can call Gavin and set up a time to meet and record the call."

"Does this mean she won't have to meet with him?" Sawyer asks, his eyes lighting up and Blaze shakes his head.

"Not exactly," Rodriguez answers as Blaze sets the phone down on the table in front of us. "If we're going to charge him and get him out of your lives for good, we need him to either admit to everything on tape or demand a certain amount of money and then take that money from Juliette."

I release a breath. "Okay."

"Your main objective here, Juliette, is to get him to admit to trying to hurt you but if he won't do that, steer the conversation toward the money and see if he'll take the bait."

I nod. "Got it."

"Okay. Make the call and hit me up when you're done so we can figure out a plan going forward."

We all agree and once we end the call with Rodriguez, I pull my phone out and bring up Gavin's number. Blaze sets his phone in the middle of the table and presses record before nodding at me. As I suck in a breath, I dial his number and put the call on speaker.

"Jules?" he answers on the third ring.

"Hi, Gavin. I need to talk to you."

He releases a breath. "Of course. I'll meet you anywhere."

"No," I reply, shaking my head. "Just over the phone for now."

"Okay... what's up?"

Sawyer rubs my back and my stomach rolls.

"Do you have anything to do with the fire at Sawyer's house? Or me almost getting shot in the woods? Or the accident?"

He's silent for a moment and my gaze flicks around the room as my heart races.

"It's complicated, baby. Maybe if we meet up, I could explain it to you."

I shake my head. "That's not going to happen. I remember you locking me in that bathroom."

"Oh, God…. No, you don't understand…"

"I understand perfectly, you played me and now you're trying to kill me."

"No, no, no… I would never hurt you, Jules. Never."

I glance over at Blaze who motions for me to move on and I nod.

"Was this always about the money?"

He releases a breath. "No… I mean, it was… but…"

"Look, this is over. You know that so why don't you just go. Leave me alone and I won't press this further. You can have a second chance."

"I… can't do that."

Sawyer pulls me down into his lap.

"Why not?"

He doesn't respond right away and the silence stretches between us before he hisses a curse. "I need the money, Jules. It's the only way."

"I knew it," I scoff. "How much?"

"Give me thirty million and you'll never see me again."

Rage boils in my blood as I stare at the wood grain of the table and nod. "I'll get back to you."

I hang up before he can say anything else and Blaze stops the recording as Sawyer turns to me with a smile but I shake my head and push off his lap. All of this pain, all of this suffering because of money and it makes me hate the life I've lived up until now.

It's time to end this for good and then it's time to

Never Let Me Go

make some changes because no amount of money is
worth the people I love.

*   *   *   *

"Are you nervous?" Sawyer asks, stepping up
behind me as I inspect my reflection in the downstairs
bathroom mirror. I twist to the side, trying to determine
if there is any way to see the wire Rodriguez taped to
my body before he left the clubhouse an hour ago. I
sigh and turn around to face him as I lean back against
the sink. "You don't have to do this, you know."

"Sawyer," I whisper, gripping his upper arms as I
close my eyes. Last night, after I had calmed down
from my call with Gavin and in between rounds of earth
shattering sex, Sawyer tried every way he could to
convince me not to do this and as much as I love his
protectiveness, there is no way in hell I am backing out
now. Each time I think about my dad dying over his
money or almost losing Sawyer over some damn
money, I get so mad I see red. But it doesn't matter how
much I remind him that his life is in just as much
danger as mine because his only concern is me.

I can't keep going like this.

We can't keep going like this.

Sighing, he holds his hand up. "Okay. I'm done."

341

A.M. Myers

"Thank you." I push up on my toes and press a kiss to his lips. He hums in approval as he wraps his arms around my waist and lifts me off the floor briefly before setting me back down. I smile as I pull back and look up at him. "I have an important question for you."

"What?"

"Can you see the wire under my shirt?"

He glances down and shakes his head. "No. Maybe you should open it up a little bit more and I'll check if I can see it, then."

"And why would I do that?" I ask with a laugh. He grins.

"Because you love me."

I shake my head as I playfully narrow my eyes at him. "Maybe later."

"You ready to do this?" he asks, holding his hand out to me and I nod as I take it and grab the strap of the duffle bag full of money. His fingers intertwine with mine and I take a deep breath, feeling peace flow through me. It's crazy to think about just how much has happened since I met Sawyer down in Miami and if you had asked me five years ago, I would have told you there's no way you could fall in love with someone so quickly and so completely but I was wrong. A part of me feels like my mom is hanging out in heaven, watching over me and laughing as she sent Sawyer in my direction because she always believed in love at first sight. I smile as we walk out into the bar. It's nice to think that she's been with me this whole time, though.

Never Let Me Go

"Jules!" The voice pierces through my thoughts and my eyes snap open. Blaze, Storm, and Kodiak are fanned out in front of us, their postures rigid and guns aimed at Gavin as he stands just inside the door of the clubhouse with a gun pointed at me. I suck in a breath and Sawyer's hand tightens.

"Gavin… what are you doing here? We were supposed to meet downtown."

He nods. "Yeah, that was the plan until your new little boy toy called me and told me to come here."

"What?" I turn to Sawyer but he refuses to meet my gaze and I rip my hand free. He reaches behind me and I'm just about to jerk away from him when I feel him flip the mic on. He planned all of this? Was everyone else in on it? When Rodriguez left earlier, I assumed he was going to scope out the place we planned to meet but maybe he didn't. Maybe he never left at all. I glance up at Sawyer and he nods, almost like he can read my thoughts. Sucking in a breath, I turn back to Gavin and hold up the bag of money Rodriguez supplied us with. It seemed a little ridiculous to accept money from the cops when I had plenty of my own to use but he assured me this was the better way to do it since the bills were marked and all the money would go into evidence while Gavin was tried.

I toss the bag past the guys and narrow my eyes at Gavin as his gaze flicks down to it. "There you go. It's what you always wanted."

His face crumples as he takes a step forward.

"Not another step," Storm snaps and Gavin freezes.

"I want you, Jules. I love you."

Sawyer shakes his head. "Bastard."

"It's okay, baby," I whisper, laying my hand on his arm. I'm more than capable of handling this asshole.

"How about you just take your money and flee like the cockroach that you are, Gavin? You never cared about me because if you had, you never would have been able to kill my father and make two other attempts on my life."

He sighs, the stress of this situation starting to show on his face. "This thing is more complicated than you can imagine."

"I don't care. Take your money and leave."

"Juliette, please," he pleads as he inches forward and Kodiak takes a step forward, his face etched with intensity and his gun leveled at Gavin's head.

"You heard the lady. Get your goddamn money and get out of our clubhouse," Blaze orders and defeat flashes across his face as he nods and creeps forward to scoop the bag off of the floor. As soon as his hand is on the bag, the door bursts open and police flood into the room with guns drawn. Gavin's pistol clatters to the floor and he throws his hands over his head as the guys tuck their weapons back into their holsters.

Rodriguez steps forward and begins reading Gavin his rights as he puts him in handcuffs and Gavin's eyes sweep over the room, frantic, until they land on me.

"Juliette! Wait!"

Rodriguez passes him off to another officer as Gavin struggles against his hold.

"Please! She needs to know everything!" He whips around and manages to break free of the officer's grasp, running straight for me. Sawyer steps in front of me but before Gavin reaches us, Blaze's arm goes out, clotheslining him. He falls back with a thud and two officers appear at his side, ripping him off the floor.

"Juliette!" he calls, his voice weaker this time. "I need to tell you about everything! I need to explain."

"Get him the fuck out of here!" Rodriguez bellows at the officers, who seem content to let Gavin stand around and run his mouth for their entertainment value. Sufficiently scolded, they nod and drag Gavin outside as he continues to scream about needing to tell me the truth.

"You okay, baby?" Sawyer asks, stepping up behind me and wrapping me up in his arms. I turn in his grasp and bury my head in his chest as I take a deep breath for what feels like the first time since I woke up in the hospital. Relief washes over me, so potent that I burst into tears.

"Oh, angel," he breathes as he scoops me up in his arms. I can feel everyone's eyes on me and like he can read my thoughts, he turns away from them and carries me up to his room where I completely fall apart before he puts me back together again.

A.M. Myers

Never Let Me Go
Chapter Twenty-Six
Sawyer

My stomach flips as I drive the truck onto the property and glance over at Juliette in the passenger seat, the blindfold I made her put on as we were leaving the steakhouse still firmly in place. She looks absolutely incredible in the new red dress Mercedes stopped by the clubhouse to bring her and I can't wait to get her back to my room and strip it off her but there are more important things to focus on right now - like the ring burning a hole in my pocket, the one Mercedes slipped to me when Juliette wasn't looking. Apparently, it's her dream engagement ring - one she designed and had made but never had the heart to sell because it owned such a special place in her heart. I guess I'm just lucky Gavin decided to buy her a different ring instead of proposing with this one. Or like most things when it comes to our whirlwind of a relationship, it was meant to be.

"Where are you taking me?" she asks, gazing around like she can still see as I pull the truck to a stop and she reaches up to touch the blindfold.

"You'll find out in a second. We're here."

She smiles. "Can I take it off now?"

"No. I'm coming to get you. Just hold on."

She scowls and crosses her arms over her chest, making me laugh, as I jump out and run around to her side, pulling the door open.

"Take my hands," I instruct and she places her hands in mine. I help her slip out of the truck before guiding her around the front to the perfect spot that overlooks the lake. "Are you ready?"

"I don't know," she huffs, her patience wearing thin and I laugh as I untie the blindfold, letting it fall from her eyes. She blinks as the world comes into focus and gasps. The lake stretches out in front of us, framed by trees and glistening in the moonlight as millions of stars paint the sky over our heads and it's the perfect backdrop for this night. "Oh, Sawyer. This is incredible."

"You think so?"

She glances over her shoulder. "Yes! I could stay here for hours."

"What about forever?"

"What?" she asks, glancing around like she's missing something and I smile, my heart hammering against my ribs.

"The property is for sale and we're in the market for a new place to live so I thought we could build our dream house here."

Sucking in a breath, she nods. "With big windows that look out over the water…"

"Exactly." One of the things I love the most about this woman is that, at her core, she is a dreamer. She doesn't spend too much time worrying about what she should do or what is acceptable because all that matters is how it makes me feel.

"It's perfect!" she squeals, spinning around in my arms and pulling me into a hug. I bury my face in her neck, breathing in her scent as I slowly work up the courage for the next part.

Okay, Michelson. It's now or never.

Releasing her, I step back and reach into my pocket. "There's one more thing."

"What?"

I pull the ring from my pocket and drop down on one knee, my eyes locked with hers the entire time as my hands shake like crazy. Her gaze flicks to the ring and she scowls for a second before gasping as tears spring to her eyes.

"That ring…"

I smile. "Do you remember it?"

"Yes. I designed it… but…" She scrunches up her nose in confusion and I know she's struggling to piece it all together. More memories have started coming back in the last couple of days but she is still missing huge gaps of information and the timelines don't always make sense.

"Mercedes told me you designed it but you were

never able to sell it because it was special to you and as soon as I saw it, I knew I couldn't ask you to spend the rest of your life with me without it."

She gasps, pressing her fingers to her lips as tears spill down her cheeks. "Oh, Sawyer."

"Juliette Kathleen Shaw," I start, my heart racing and my skin tingling with awareness. "I love you. In fact, I'm pretty sure I fell in love with you as soon as I saw you from across the parking lot of that diner. I love the woman you are today, so fierce, funny, kind, and generous and I love the woman you're going to be tomorrow and the woman you're going to be one hundred years from now and I love every variation of the woman you're going to be all the years in between. If you never get all of your memories back, I'll love you then and if you wake up tomorrow with those five years you're missing, I'll love you then, too. You are everything and you made me believe in myself and in love again with just a look. So, what do you say, angel? You want to marry me, have babies with me, and build our life together in this spot that was so clearly meant for us?"

Tears spill down her cheeks as she smiles down at me, so much love in her eyes that it smashes into me and almost knocks me over. I can see it all now. Our kids running through these fields, laughing and playing. Our home, filled with love and our future here together. My angel, Juliette, by my side through it all. She opens her mouth and I suck in a breath, so eager to hear her answer.

Never Let Me Go

"Well, isn't this touching," someone sneers and we both turn as a woman steps out of the woods with a gun in her hand, aimed at Juliette. My stomach drops and my heart jumps into my throat as the woman advances on us, her fury aimed at the love of my life.

"Nico?" Juliette gasps and my eyes widen as I try to piece it all together. Nico? Her friend? Why the hell is her friend pointing a gun at her? "What are you doing?"

Nico scoffs. "What am I doing? I'm getting what I'm owed."

"What you're owed?"

My eyes never leave the gun in Nico's hand as I stand up and tuck the ring back in my pocket. She turns to me, pointing the gun in my direction.

"Don't you fucking move!"

I hold my hands up, happy to have the gun off of Juliette. "Okay. I'm not moving."

"Nico… what is it you think you're owed?" Juliette asks and I bite back a curse as Nico turns back to her. The gun in my waistband feels even heavier as I slowly move my hand behind my back, careful not to move too quickly and alert Nico.

"The money, Juliette!" Nico screams. "Did you really think Gavin was working alone?"

Juliette's mouth drops open. "You? But you were my friend?"

"Yeah, and let me tell you what a torturous few years that was."

"But why?" Juliette asks.

"Jason and I were happy, you know? Before you

came along anyway."

I arch a brow. "Jason?"

"Gavin," she growls, flicking an annoyed glance at me. "See, we've been working together, running cons on people just like you for years and he was *mine* but then the idiot has to go and fall in love with you *for real*. Now, all of the sudden, he can't possibly take your money or leave you and do you know where that leaves me?"

"Screwed," Juliette answers and Nico nods.

"And heartbroken. He was the only man I ever loved and you had to take him from me," she hisses, taking a few steps toward Juliette. Sucking in a breath, I whip the gun out of my back before leveling it at her.

"Don't move!"

She turns to me, her gaze flicking down to the gun in my hand before she grins. "You're not going to shoot me."

"Yes, I will," I growl as I pull the lever back and blow out a breath. The sound of sirens fill the air and Nico starts backing up toward the trees as she looks wildly between Juliette and me. I glance over and notice the phone hidden behind Juliette's back at the same time Nico does and she surges forward, the gun stretches out in front of her as she shakes with rage but I don't give her a chance to fire, pulling the trigger.

The bullet tears through her shoulder and she screams as she collapses into the dirt, clutching the wound. Police cruisers tear into the lot but I don't take my eyes off of Nico or the gun until two policemen rush over and order her to drop it. It falls to the dirt and Juliette releases a breath as she launches herself at me. They drag Nico up off the ground and lock her in handcuffs. Holding Juliette tight with one arm, I slip the gun back into my waistband and bury my nose in her hair.

"I swear, I'm never letting you out of my sight again," I whisper and she nods, clinging to me as her tears seep into my t-shirt. Fuck, I don't know what I would have done if I had lost her. She pulls back and meets my eyes.

"Where's the ring?"

I search her eyes for a moment before grinning. I set her on the ground and pull the ring out of my pocket before slipping it on her finger. Once it's on, she launches herself at me again and presses her lips to mine as I wrap my arms around her waist and lift her off the ground.

"Is this enough of an answer?" she asks in between frantic kisses. "Or does it need to be official?"

I shake my head and kiss her again. "Naw, angel. I think I got the message."

A.M. Myers

Never Let Me Go

Epilogue
One Year Later
Juliette

Big, white fluffy clouds, the kind you only find on a perfect summer day, roll across the deep blue sky and the sun shimmers on the surface of the lake just through the trees, beckoning me to dip my toes in the water. Rubbing my hands over my expanding belly, I take a deep breath, obsessed with how peaceful I feel out here. Sawyer walks up beside me and sets the box in his hands down before slipping his arm over my shoulder and pulling me into his side.

"You did real good, angel."

I beam as I stare up at the stately southern style home we've spent the last year designing and building as pride wells up in my chest. Before Sawyer suggested that we build our dream house out here on the same land he proposed to me on, I never even thought about designing a house but looking out at our surroundings, I knew just what this place needed. It's elegant without being too flashy or over the top, homey despite its size and the kind of place that I can see all our friends and family hanging out around for years to come.

Glancing over to the spot where Sawyer dropped down on one knee and popped the question, all I can do is smile. Some people can't understand how I can still live here after being held at gunpoint by someone I thought was my friend but for me, after everything else that happened, it was a nice little piece of closure. After that night, for the first time in a month, I knew I was safe. Gavin, or Jason as we later found out, and Nico were both charged with my father's murder as well as the two attempts on my life and the attempt on Sawyer's life in addition to a slew of lesser charges they managed to rack up during their little scheme and they accepted plea deals for twenty-five years each, which means I don't have to worry about them ever again.

I suck in a breath and scowl, pressing my hand into the side of my belly as our son delivers a swift kick to my ribs and Sawyer glances down at me.

"You need to go sit down, baby. I'll take care of the last of these boxes."

I nod and release a breath. As much as I want to yell at him for trying to tell me what to do, my feet are killing me right now and it's a billion degrees out here. "Okay."

I turn to him and he gives me a quick kiss before picking the box up off of the ground and carrying it into the house as I waddle behind him. As I turn to the water, I smile. The lake is one of my favorite things about this property and I can't wait to sit out on the back porch with a big glass of sweet tea to watch the sun set over the water.

"Woman," Sawyer calls, stepping out onto the porch. "Hurry your ass up."

I level a glare at him. "You try carrying this linebacker around, you ass."

"Fine," he says with a shrug as he jumps down the stairs and runs over to me. I scream as he picks me up like I weigh nothing at all and carries me to the house. "Doesn't seem that bad to me."

"Let's trade, then. You can be pregnant and I'll just run around, drink beer, and make jokes."

He grins. "Have I mentioned today that you're absolutely stunning, Mrs. Michelson?"

"Don't you try to butter me up!" I yell, twisting my lips to try and hide my smile. He laughs.

"What if I tell you that I love you?"

I nod. "You damn well better. Your son is boxing my bladder."

"Is he now?" he asks as he carries me into the living room and sets me down on the couch. Kneeling in front of me, he presses his hands against my belly.

"Franklin," he says, his face serious and I smile. As soon as we found out we were having a little boy, Sawyer suggested we name him after my father and I fell in love with the man just a little bit more. He said he owed his whole life to my dad's sacrifice so it only seemed right that his grandson carry on his name. "I know you haven't seen your mother yet but just take it from me, son, she's an angel which is why I can't have you being so mean to her, you hear?"

I run my fingers through his hair and shake my head. "I love you."

"I love you," he answers, smiling up at me and I lean down as I cup his face in between my hands and press a couple of quick kisses to his lips. As he pulls away, his arms wrap around my waist and he pulls me to the edge of the couch. "I've got two more boxes out there and then what do you say we go grab some pizza?"

I moan and my eyes roll back as I nod. One of the things I've been craving the most during this pregnancy is this bacon cheeseburger pizza at this little place downtown - honestly I could eat it all day, every day. "Yes, yes, yes."

"'Kay. You rest until I get back," he instructs and I nod, giving him a mock salute and he shakes his head as he stands up and walks back outside to get the last of our boxes. We really didn't have much to move in since we moved into a furnished apartment while this one was being built but I did have fun dropping some cash on all new wardrobes for both of us and the baby. Plus, we got a lot of stuff at the wedding that needed to be packed and moved over here. Turning my head to the side, I smile at the photo from our wedding that Sawyer already set up on the end table. We got married in the little park where Sawyer first dropped down on one knee in front of me, the same park where we had our first date, three weeks after we proposed. Neither one of us wanted to wait and I didn't want to have a big flashy event so it just made sense to choose the place that was so special to both of us.

Sighing, I lie back on the couch and rest my hand on the top of my belly as I gaze around the house, noticing all the little details that I painstakingly picked out to bring everything together. It's everything I ever imagined my home being and I can't wait to see kids playing and running through the hallway or my family gathered around the table for dinner. Franklin kicks me again and I rub my hand over the spot as I realize I haven't seen his room yet and try to get up.

Sawyer walks back into the house with the last two boxes as I collapse back onto the couch with a huff and he narrows his eyes at me. "What were you doing?"

"I was going to look at Franklin's room," I say and he shakes his head as he sets the boxes down and comes over to me, holding out his hands.

"No, no, little lady. We're going to get dinner."

I take his hands and groan as he pulls me to my feet. "Well, I'll just go look at it real quick."

"No can do," he shoots back, wrapping his arm around my shoulders and steering me toward the front door. I scowl.

"Why don't you want me to see his room?"

He shakes his head. "No reason."

"Liar."

Stopping right in front of the door, he sighs. "It's a

surprise, okay?"

"I don't like surprises," I answer, remembering how stressed I was as I rode in the truck, blindfolded, on the night he proposed and he laughs.

"Yes, I know but I've got like a whole thing planned so maybe you could just go with me on this."

I turn to look down the hallway before turning back to him with pursed lips. He studies me for a second before rolling his eyes.

"You're not going to be able to go with it, huh?"

I shake my head. "Nope."

"Okay... I'll show you now but I get husband points for the romantic plan I had for later."

"Deal," I say with a nod. "You get all the husband points, now show me."

Nodding, he leads me down the hallway to our son's room and makes me face toward the slightly open door before covering my eyes. His breath brushes along my skin and I suck in a breath as my nipples pebble.

"You ready?"

I nod and I hear the door open. "Okay, open your eyes."

My eyes blink open and I take it all in, the navy blue wall behind the white crib, the paintings of baby animals up on the wall, the plush rocking chair in the corner and Franklin's name spelled out in gray letters, as I gasp.

"Sawyer," I whisper, tears welling up in my eyes. It's absolutely perfect and I can't wait to bring our son home to this room. Turning to face my husband, I slip my arms over his shoulders and press a kiss to his lips. He hums as his arms wrap around my waist and he pulls me as close as he can with my belly in the way. Pulling back, I look up at him and smile.

"I'm the luckiest girl in the whole world and I love you."

He smiles. "I love you more."

I scrunch my nose up and tilt my head to the side in protest and he laughs but I have to admit to myself that he just might be right. My man is all heart and I wouldn't have him any other way.

A.M. Myers

Want to make sure you never miss a new release from me again *and* get access to never before seen scenes and exclusive content?

Sign up for my newsletter now!

http://eepurl.com/cANpav

A.M. Myers

Other Books by A.M. Myers

The Hidden Scars Series

Hidden Scars:
https://www.amazon.com/dp/B014B6KFJE

Collateral Damage:
https://www.amazon.com/gp/product/B01G9FOS20

Evading Fate:
https://www.amazon.com/gp/product/B01L0GKMU0

Bayou Devils MC Series

Hopelessly Devoted:
https://www.amazon.com/dp/B01MY5XQFW

Addicted To Love:
https://www.amazon.com/dp/B07B6RPPPV

Every Breath You Take:
https://www.amazon.com/dp/B07DPNTV2G

It Ends Tonight:
https://www.amazon.com/dp/B07JL4FJ18

A.M. Myers

Little Do You Know:
https://www.amazon.com/dp/B07M812N1T

Every Little Thing:
Releasing August 2019

Wicked Games:
Releasing February 2020

The Worst in Me:
Releasing May 2020

Blurred Lines:
Releasing August 2020

About the Author

A.M. Myers currently lives in beautiful Charleston, South Carolina with her husband and their two children. She has been writing since the moment she learned how to and even had a poem published in the sixth grade but the idea of writing an entire book always seemed like a daunting task until a certain story got stuck in her head and just wouldn't leave her alone. And now, she can't imagine ever stopping. A.M. writes gripping romantic suspense novels that will have you on the edge of your seat until the end.

When she's not writing, you can find her hanging out with her kids or pursuing other artistic ventures, such as photography or painting.

Made in United States
Orlando, FL
17 June 2023

34235115R10202